Sinner

Volume One

By Zafeer Alam

Author: zafeeralam99@gmail.com

Design: Asura Hunter / hunterasura303@gmail.com

Special thanks:

Derek Ehiorobo
Kibikino Akatsuki
Kyron Elam
Melikai Grant
Mya
Ramsey Livingston
Ryan Rajakulam

Zayden Fareno woke up from his sleep as morning arose. He quickly got out of bed, *"—I hope it's in the mail today!"* he thought as he rushed down the stairs of his home and out the front door.

He burst to the mailbox and took out the mail. His mouth dropped as he read the envelope: *"From: Sinara Academy."*

"—Finally!" cheered Zayden out loud. He opened the letter and read it.

"Congratulations Zayden Fareno! After careful evaluation, we have decided that you have the potential of what it takes to be a remarkable Sinner. This is the first Sinning competition held at the Sinara Academy since the annual events that took place 3 years ago, we are looking forward to seeing you at the competition. Full details on the events will be announced upon arrival."

Zayden tensed, "After all this time," he spoke, "I actually got my chance to go into the competition!"
He looked up to the sky and felt the heat, *"I should make use of the good weather,"* he thought as he went to the middle of his front yard.
Zayden's neighbour, Reno, sprinted to him.
        "—Zayden! Look what came in the mail for me!" yelled Reno as he waved his Sinara Academy letter, "Can you believe they actually took me in?!"
Reno Rossard was a close friend of Zayden's for the past few years, he wore a thick brown shirt along with shorts and brown boots.
        "Yeah, why wouldn't they?" spoke Zayden, "Now we both have the chance to learn from the best."
"—You're right!" nodded Reno, "Because we both got accepted into one of the best Sinning Academies in the world!"
        Zayden then went down to do push ups, "You can't really say we got accepted yet," he tensed, "We still need to pass the whole competition."
"—I know that too," blurted Reno, "But now we have the opportunity!"
        Zayden went down as he put more effort into his routine.
"—Anyways," went on Reno, "Why are you training right now?"
Zayden paused, "I don't want to disappoint the Sinegious once I win the competition," he answered.
        Sinegious is the official name that is given to the ultimate authority of a Sinning Academy.
"Oh, now you sound cocky thinking you already won the competition," remarked Reno.
        "I'm not cocky, I'm just confident. That's all," corrected Zayden as he went down for a push-up, "I know I have long ways to go before I achieve my dream of becoming a Full-Fledged Sinner," he stood up and looked to Reno, "And this competition is just one step towards that!"

"A Full-Fledged Sinner..." repeated Reno, "You're still on that?"

Zayden was quiet.

"...Zayden?" Reno called out again, "Hey—"

"—Yeah I'm still on that what do you think?!" broke in Zayden, "I'm going to become a Full-Fledged Sinner!"

"Well..." went on Reno, "If you say so, I mean—we've heard it countless times that no one else could become Full-Fledged...it's impossible."

"Yeah yeah," Zayden brushed it off, "And you also told me that one day you're going to beat me, and that seems a lot harder than what I'm trying to do."

"Hey well—I said one day and that can even be tomorrow!" uttered Reno.

Zayden snickered, "Wait—why do you have your bag with you?" he asked.

"I'm taking this to Wavern City of course!" remarked Reno.

"Why there?"

"—That's where the Sinara Academy is! It says it on the back!" he told Zayden, "The ship to Wavern is almost here and I need to get to the dock, see you there!" Reno waved as he burst down the passageway.

"—What does it say on the back?!" Zayden thought to himself. He quickly ran over to the letter he left on the ground and flipped it over.

"All participants must be at the Sinara Academy in Wavern city by midnight," he read the letter, "Or else you will be disqualified."

Zayden worried, "—I need to pack!" he realized as he burst back inside his home.

Zayden rushed up the stairs and headed to his bedroom. He stuffed all his clothes in his back pack and changed into a white, high collar jacket over a tan sweater vest, along with black pants and boots. He combed his medium length brown hair.

He then slowly walked over to the table where a red wristband was placed beside a picture of him and his parents, "Every day I'm getting closer to reaching my goal," he thought as he put on the wristband.

3

Zayden finally went down the stairs and burst out the front door.

After a few moments, Zayden reached the dock and walked up to the boat, *"This is it,"* he thought.

"Hello sir," greeted one of the staff, "Are you here for the ship heading to Wavern City for the Sinara Academy?"

"Yes I am!" smirked Zayden.

"Alright then," nodded the man, "Make your way to the line at the left side where you will be taken to your room for the trip," he pointed.

Zayden made his way and stood at the back of the line, *"There has to be at least 20 people here!"* he saw, *"All of them look so different from one another... what's this weird stomach feeling I have?!"* he worried, *"Is Reno already on the ship?"*

After a few moments, the line began moving onto the ship. The attendant instructed the other participants to their rooms to stay for the ride. Two people were to share a room.

"—Reno, Reno, where are you?!" Zayden whispered to himself, *"Everyone looks serious,"* he thought, *"Well...almost everyone,"* he saw Reno in the back leaning on the wall.

Reno was fast asleep.

Zayden quickly ran over to him, "Reno let's—"

"—Hello Participant Zayden," broke in the ship attendant, "I'll take care of participant Reno and make sure he gets into his assigned room along with participant Soro," she assured, "Can you please go to your reserved room near the back of the ship?"

Zayden saw her, "Oh, sorry," he spoke, "I never knew."

Zayden turned around and walked to the back, *"Reno really is something else,"* he thought, *"How can he be sleeping in such a tense environment!"*

At the back of the ship, Zayden found his name on his assigned room, and listed under was another participant, *"Kaesar Kinnuan,"* he read.
Zayden opened the door as he saw him.

Kaesar was a boy with spiky white hair, very light skin and blue eyes. He was lean, and wore a baggy blue-gray shirt underneath with a white full-sleeved on top. He was also wearing long baggy pants.

"I'm Kaesar," he spoke, "I assume your Zayden...let me move my things from your side of the room."
"Yeah, I'm Zayden," he quickly spoke as he took off his bag and looked around the room.

Kaesar laid on his bed with his hands behind his head, "Are you good?" he asked, "Not that it really matters to me..."
"—No I'm fine," uttered Zayden, "Trust me..."

"Alright," murmured Kaesar, "If you say so."
"—There are just 5 minutes before we depart!" the ship attendant announced through the speakers.

"—What's that?!" panicked Zayden.
"And just a reminder," the attendant continued, "You are not permitted to leave your room until we arrive, thank you!"

"Relax, it's just the attendant," assured Kaesar, "I thought you weren't worried?"
Zayden uncomfortably laid down on his bed.
"Just calm down and kick back," advised Kaesar, "It's going to be a long ride."

"I need to get a hold of myself," thought Zayden, *"I look like a fool! I know I'm better than this!"*
"It looks like we have everyone boarded aside from one person!" announced the Attendant, "Nonetheless, we will now be on our way to Wavern city looking to arrive by approximately 8:00 pm!"

Zayden listened, *"Maybe some sleep will calm me down..."* he thought.

With hours passing by, the destination was nearing. Most of the participants were asleep in their rooms while a few others were awake.

Zayden laid on his bed, "Hey…Kaesar, right?" he spoke.

There was a moment of silence.

"Are you awake?" asked Zayden as he sat up.

"Hm, yeah…" murmured Kaesar.

"Can I ask you something?"

Kaesar titled his head up as his eyes were closed.

"You seem so relaxed," remarked Zayden, "And I don't know if you noticed, but I'm nervous. This never happened to me before…"

"How could I not notice, you're shaking," thought Kaesar, "Honestly, it's understandable that you feel this way," he spoke up, "We're headed to the Sinara Academy in Wavern, a highly respected Sinning Academy in the most attracted city, I don't blame you for being nervous."

"Really?" uttered Zayden, "My body just became shook when I saw the other participants."

"Yeah, I'm a bit nervous too, but I don't let it show," explained Kaesar, "The way you carry yourself is important when it comes to your mentality. People on this ship are skilled and experienced in Sinning, I'm sure they'll quickly smell fear."

"That makes me even more nervous," thought Zayden, "Between you and I," he spoke, "I don't have any experience in actual fighting, aside from a few spars with a friend."

"That sucks, I hope we're put up against each other during the competition," spoke Kaesar, "I'll look good."

"—No seriously," blurted Zayden, "I never really learned from anyone…".

"We may be similar there…" thought Kaesar, "So nobody helped you control your Sinning ability?" he asked as he sat up on his bed.

"Nope," remarked Zayden, "Nobody could have."

6

"How about your parents?" went on Kaesar, "You should've asked them for help. They must have some knowledge."

"Of course I did—I begged," remarked Zayden, "But my Mom was never around for the past five years or so, she's been really sick."

"Oh, how about your Father?"

Zayden paused, "That would be impossible..." his voice became soft, but then his expression changed, "I heard when he was younger though he was an amazing Sinner!" smiled Zayden, "People told me his Ability to Sin was like no other!"

"Oh okay," murmured Kaesar, "So then—"

"You wouldn't believe it!" smirked Zayden, "I heard stories where Fire would be coming out of his body as a weapon and as a shield! Attacking others in battles, saving people, he was untouchable!"

Kaesar carefully looked to Zayden, *"It's the first time he doesn't look too worried,"* he saw, *"Before his eyes looked unsettled, but now it's filled with excitement."*

"Oh, so you Sin Fire I assume?" he asked

"Yeah but—sometimes I hate it," remarked Zayden. Zayden's Sinning Ability was Fire, so when he Sinned, Fire would naturally surround his body. When one Sins, he/she is triggering his/her Sinning ability, hence being called a Sinner.

"I can't control it and it hurts," continued Zayden, "There's a reason I always wear full sleeved clothing," he rolled up his sleeve, "I got so many burns on my arms, it's kind of embarrassing," he snickered.

"That does look bad," saw Kaesar after a detailed look, "Do you notice how most of them are on your right arm?"

Zayden looked to his right arm.

"Practice Sinning with your left more often," suggested Kaesar, "Your overall Sin will improve."

"...Yeah, you're right," realized Zayden and paused, "Hey Kaesar, you want to go one on one when we're land at Wavern? I need practice, and I can work on

7

my left arm too! You'll be my first opponent aside from Reno!"

There was a pause, "…Are you sure?" asked Kaesar.

Zayden clenched his fists, "—Why not?!" he smirked.

Kaesar took a moment, "Well, a 5-minute fight wouldn't hurt," he muttered, "I don't need to be worried."

"Why do you assume that?" spoke Zayden, "Y-You haven't seen anything I've done!"

Kaesar exhaled, "You're still nervous," he remarked, "The stuttering makes it obvious."

There was a pause, "Yeah…I have a lot of things going through my mind," muttered Zayden, he looked down to his wristband.

"…Like what?" asked Kaesar.

"No, it's in the past," murmured Zayden, "Leave it there."

"Just talk," spoke Kaesar, "You'll be a lot calmer once you do."

After a moment, Zayden began to tell his story.

"Like I said before, my Father was an amazing Fire Sinner, my mother told me many things about him," recalled Zayden, "He used to Sin in combat and for enjoyment, we all do…"

Kaesar listened.

But then Zayden tensed, "Until one day, he got careless and severely burned my Mother, which left her in coma for three weeks," he remarked, "After that incident, I was told by my family that my Father was depressed and completely stopped Sinning. But my Mother didn't care about her own wounds, instead she saw even greater potential in my Father to become a Full—"

"—Attention all participants!" announced the attendant, "We are just 10 minutes away from arriving at Wavern!"

There was a moment as the two heard her. Kaesar then turned back to Zayden.

"So, my Mother kept telling my Father to become stronger with his Sinning Power…"

Kaesar continued to listen.

8

Zayden then smirked, "—My Mother wanted my Father to be a Full-Fledged Sinner!" he recalled.

Kaesar's attention was caught, *"A Full-Fledged Sinner..."* he thought, *"That's a controversial issue to say the least."*

"She really wanted someone from our family to be Full-Fledged," went on Zayden, "Even after the incident with her being burned, she urged my Father again and again to continue Sinning, but he refused it. Eventually, my Mother got angry with him because my Father had promised her before that he would reach the state of a Full-Fledged Sinner, and she really hoped one day he would."

Kaesar paused, *"Everyone's got a story,"* he thought, *"I wonder how's it like..."*

"And now, my Mother looks to me to achieve this goal for her," revealed Zayden, "She made me believe that I can become a Full-Fledged Sinner. She made sure I practiced by Sinning Ability everyday," he tensed, "Her passion for Sinning rubbed off on me, so I promised her back then that I would become a Full-Fledged Sinner in place of my Father!"

There was a moment of silence, "...This is a long story," exhaled Kaesar.

"You wanted me to tell it to you!" remarked Zayden.

"I didn't say I wasn't into it," recalled Kaesar, "Continue."

"Oh so—" uttered Zayden, he pointed to the red wristband he wore, "One night after my Mother saw me Sin, she gave me this red wristband telling me that some of my Father's Sinning power is within it."

Zayden then looked back up to Kaesar, "My Mother told me that she had to stay in the hospital for a long time as the burns on her body wouldn't go away," he went on, "So she gave me this wristband saying that if I ever couldn't take care of myself, the wristband would help me..."

There was pause.

Zayden smirked, "Now I live alone with only one goal to make my Mother's dream a reality!" he stated, "I have to become a Full-Fledged Sinner."

Kaesar paused, "...I see what you mean," he spoke, "I didn't expect you to go on for that long though." "—In short, I'm here from my Mother!" smiled Zayden, "Why are you here? I want to hear your story too."

Kaesar took a moment, "...Actually I—" "We have now arrived at Wavern!" announced the Attendant, "Exit your room as we will be heading to the Sinara Academy!"

They heard her, "...Forget about my story," spoke Kaesar as he stood up and made his way to the room's door, "Let's get out of here," he murmured as he opened it and walked away.

Zayden saw Kaesar go, he then walked out of the room as he went into the hallway of the ship.

He turned his head to the right, "—Reno?!" he saw as he rushed over to him, "I thought the Attendant took care of you! Wake up!" he shook him.

Reno was hardly awake, "—Shut up!" he uttered. "...Alright then," murmured Zayden, he stood back up, "Stay here," he shrugged his shoulders.

"—Will all the participants please follow me!" announced the Attendant at the front of the hallway.

All the participants looked to her. "I will take you to the Sinara Academy!" smiled the Attendant.

The participants were lead out of the ship and onto the Academy's fields. The Sinara Academy was a huge mansion with many windows. The red front door was big with a well cleaned lawn in front. There was a lot of space filled with grass around the Academy for Sinning purposes. After a moment, the participants were lead into a red carpeted room.

"—Man it's cold in here!" yelled Reno as he walked up beside Zayden and Kaesar, "I don't feel tired anymore!" "Glad you made it," snickered Zayden, "Get use to the cold though, Kaesar just—"

"—Wait!" stopped Reno, "Who the heck is Kaesar?!"

Kaesar turned his head back to the two, "That would be me," he spoke.

"—Oh yeah, you wouldn't know Kaesar," recalled Zayden, "He and I were paired up in the same room."

"Oh," understood Reno, "Nobody was with me…at least I don't think so."

"You were sleeping the whole time so I doubt you would even notice," snickered Zayden.

"—No I think I would notice! But that's good for us," chuckled Reno, "Someone is eliminated before the competition even starts!"

Kaesar looked to him, *"This is most likely the one Zayden was talking about sparring with, Reno,"* he saw, *"He seems pretty weak."*

"I've been waiting for a long time for this tackle!" shouted someone from the back of the room.

"—What happened?!" uttered Zayden and Reno, they quickly ran to the back.

Kaesar walked behind as a crowd full of participants huddled around the two arguing.

"You don't say those things without action!" smirked a participant, his name was Dedrian, "Nobody disrespects me!"

Dedrian Bellard was one of participants competing at the Academy. He was a boy with a serious looking appearance along with messy dark brown hair.

"You know what has to be done!" smirked another participant behind Dedrian.

"—I don't need you Rajaul!" yelled Dedrian, "There's no reason for anyone else!"

"…Alright," exhaled Rajaul, "Just don't make a mess, I wouldn't want to be disqualified for a stupid reason."

Rajaul Glanni was Dedrian's friend. He had spiky maroon hair with visible eye bags. He was competing in the competition as well, but was only interested in seeing Dedrian succeed.

"You sound pretty confident," spoke the other participant across from Dedrian, his name was Toran, "You know I Sin Water, right?"

"—That doesn't mean anything!" smirked Dedrian as began Sinning, "Fire burns down everything with enough force!" Flames began flowing around his body. Zayden was shocked, *"—He Sins Fire just like me!"* he saw.

Toran started to Sin as Water overflowed around him, "Let's go," he spoke.

There was a pause.

Dedrian and Toran charged at each other and locked fists.

"—Uh," groaned Toran.

"—You sounded confident!" yelled Dedrian, "Where did all of it go?!"

"I'm not—" uttered Toran as he let go of Dedrian's hands.

Dedrian quickly put out his arms as he Sinned a wave of Fire from his palms.

Toran's eyes widened as he saw the burst of Fire coming, "—Oh," he jumped up in the air.

"—So obvious!" smirked Dedrian as he appeared in front of Toran and bashed his fist into his gut.

"—Uh," Toran's mouth dropped as he landed on the ground holding his stomach.

Dedrian landed a distance away.

"—Not finished yet!" shouted Toran as he put out his hand and clenched it.

A large wave of Water rose behind him.

"—Oh crap!" uttered someone in the crowd, "—This is already getting out of hand!"

"—Are you serious?!" Dedrian heard the voice, "This tackle is light!" he charged forward again.

Toran opened his hand as he Sinned the large wave of Water forward, "—You won't get through!" he yelled.

"—Shut up!" shouted Dedrian as he put his hand into the ground.

"—What?!" saw Toran.

A line of Fire quickly burst up from the surface. The wave of Water and Fire clashed and faded away.

"—How does he think so quick?!" saw Zayden.
Toran's eyes widened as Dedrian appeared in front of him, "When did you—" he saw.

Dedrian swung his arm, "—Fire Sinners always win!" he shouted as he bashed Toran in the face crashing him to the side.
All the participant turned their heads as Toran broke into the wall.
There was a moment of silence.

"...Don't get up," spoke Rajaul, "Dedrian won't stop."
Fire continued to surround Dedrian, "You started it," he smirked, "I just ended it."
Kaesar looked to Zayden, "You see that," he spoke, "That's how you control Fire."

Zayden was in shock, *"That fight was so short,"* he thought, *"I need to be as strong as him if I want to win this competition."*
Most of the crowd stopped huddling and walked away.

"—Yes!" cheered Reno, "Another one down! Keep it up!"
Some of the participants turned around.

"—Someone else get in!" urged Reno, "Let's have an early start to this—"
But then he was pushed inside the circle, "—Hey watch it!" shrieked Reno.

"Let's see you keep it up!" dared one participant.
"—Huh?!" uttered Reno, he turned his head across from him, "Wait I—"

"—So someone else wants to tackle?!" yelled Dedrian as he stared him down, "These early starts to the fights don't bother me!"
"—I-I don't," stuttered Reno as he stood up, "I'm kind of tired! I just woke— "

"That doesn't matter to me!" yelled Dedrian.

Zayden quickly looked to the right, *"Shouldn't the attendant stop them?!"* he saw her watching along, *"Does this always happen at the Academy?!"*

Dedrian Sinned again as Fire surrounded him, "You oppose me!" he shouted, "That means we have to tackle!" The crowd heard him as they roared in excitement.

Reno looked around, "—How did it even come to this?!" he worried, "I don't want to fight anyone!" Dedrian smirked from the other end, "—Stop talking like that!" he shouted and charged forward, "It makes you look weak in front of everyone!"

Everyone saw Dedrian rushing to Reno.

"—Wait!" yelled Reno as he shook his head, "I'm not—"

But Dedrian's fist inflamed in Fire as he swung his arm, "Well too—"

"—It doesn't have to get to this!" yelled Zayden as he burst in front of Reno and caught Dedrian's fist, "The competition hasn't even started!" Zayden had Dedrian's fist in his palm, the two locked eyes.

The crowd was stunned.

Small Fire appeared around Zayden, "I didn't mean to Sin," he murmured.

Dedrian smirked as he broke free of Zayden's hold, "—Another Fire Sinner?" he saw, "It's good to see that I'm not the only one!"

The crowd watched them as they were face to face. Reno opened his eyes, "—Zayden?!" he saw his back and yelled, "Yeah take him on! His Fire is nothing compared to yours! You're a much better Sinner!"

"—Much better Sinner?!" heard Dedrian, he took a small jump back, "—Tackle me! Fire Sinners do it the best anyways!"

Zayden paused, "I do Sin Fire," he spoke, "But I'm not interested in tackling with you...whatever that means."

Dedrian took a moment, "It's been a while since I've encountered another person who Sins the same Ability," he smirked.

14

"This is the first time I've seen another Fire Sinner in my life," remarked Zayden, "...Aside from my Father," he murmured.

There was a moment of silence.

Dedrian looked back to Toran who was unconscious on the ground, "—Alright," he turned back to Zayden, "I'll keep this tackle for later!" he declared, "Just don't expect me to be soft in the competition!"

Zayden listened to him as everyone watched on. "I'm looking forward to tackling with you," tensed Dedrian.

The two of them stopped Sinning as the Fire around their bodies went away.

After a moment, Zayden and Reno walked to Kaesar, "You got involved quick there," remarked Kaesar.

"—I had too!" tensed Zayden.

"Calm down," exhaled Kaesar, "Before you burn yourself."

So his name's Zayden..." heard Dedrian walking back, *"He and his friends think lightly of me... I'll have to make sure I change that opinion!"*

Rajaul saw Dedrian coming to him, "I'm surprised you let him go," he recalled, "Or were you scared?"

"Scared?!" yelled Dedrian, "You know I'm not like that! He and I will have our tackle soon! And when that happens, everyone will see me catch his—"

"—Hold up!" shouted one participant, "—Don't back out now! The fight isn't over!"

Zayden and Dedrian turned, but didn't move.

Some of the other participants booed as the roars got louder.

"—If they're not fighting!" yelled another as he began to Sin, "Then I'll—"

"—Do what?!" smirked another, "Start a fight yourself?!"

Other participants pushed each other into the circle, things were getting out of control as they shouted.

Kaesar eyed away, *"Pointless,"* he thought.

"I'm just saying!" yelled one of them, "Don't you think—"

15

"I believe that's enough," a man raised his voice on the other side of the room.

The participants took a quick look and quickly stopped their movement.

The man went on, "As much as I love viewing battles, now is not the time."

The room was silent as everyone listened.

"This is the first Sinning competition held at the Sinara Academy in the last three years," remarked the man as he stood a distance away from the rest, "We're expecting the winners of the competition to be the three who will carry the name of the Academy to higher reaches."

The participants nodded.

"As most of you know," remarked the man, "I am Adalo."

Adalo Shuesi is the ultimate authority of the Sinara Academy, making him the official Sinegious of the Sinning Academy. He was a tall man with brown eyes and short black hair that was combed to the back. He also had short stubble of facial hair. He wore a thick dark green full-sleeved shirt, and black pants with two white belts.

"Is that really Adalo?!" uttered someone.

"—Of course it's Adalo! Who else?!" broke in the Attendant, "That's why you came here! You all want the greatest opportunity to learn from the best in the whole District! Adalo's Sinning is widely recognized by everyone! How can you not notice him?!"

"—Okay Flare," exhaled Adalo, "You know I can speak for myself."

"...So, the Attendant's name is Flare," noted Zayden.

Flare Mariac was the attendant of the Sinara Academy. She was someone who the participants could ask for instructions and information, she also directed the participants with what they needed to do and where they needed to go. She had shoulder-length blonde hair and blue eyes wearing a yellow top.

Reno saw her as he took a moment, *"Flare..."* he began to blush, *"I wish I had a girl like her talking about me like that."*

16

"Oh," smiled Flare as she took a step back, "I might've went too far there," she chuckled.

Adalo continued, "I'm here to observe and critique your every single movement throughout this event," he addressed, "You're here to compete in competitions that will challenge your Sinning Abilities like never before," he went on, "And after the three stages, there will be three winners who will be selected and have the opportunity to train with me in becoming a stronger Sinner. They will learn anything and everything they want to know about Sinning."

The participants understood as they got excited. "You are all the future of Sinning as most of you range from 14-17 years old," remarked Adalo, "Whether you're a Combat Sinner or a Farmake Sinner, you all have distinct reasons to perfect your Sinning Abilities."

After a moment, Smoke began appearing Adalo, "And with that said," he spoke, "The competition begins tomorrow."

"Is that his—" uttered someone in awe.

Adalo's body turned into Smoke as he vanished from the room.

The participants understood and began chatting amongst each other, *"Three stages and three winners..."* recalled Zayden, *"I wonder what's in—"*

"Hey Zayden," Reno called for him.

"Hm?" he turned back.

Reno snickered as he scratched his head, "Thanks for having my back," he recalled, "Even though I kind of expected it."

"Obviously!" smirked Zayden, "You know me well enough to know that you don't have to thank me! We always have each other!

"Yeah!" nodded Reno as the two knocked knuckles.

Kaesar saw the two as he stayed quiet.

"—Attention all participants!" addressed Flare, "It is now 10:00 P.M!"

The participants turned to her.

17

"The participant forms where you state your personal information are placed in the Sinara Procedure Room!" she addressed, "Have your form filled out and handed back to me at the Sinara Service Desk by midnight. If not, you will be ineligible to compete!"

Reno listened, *"—I'm going to quickly fill out my form if I get to see her!"* he thought.

"I will now to direct you to the rooms you will reside in!" went on Flare as she began walking out of the room, "Follow me up the stairs!"

Reno burst to Flare as he walked beside her with a smile.

Zayden walked with the rest of the participants as Kaesar stayed back.

"Hm?" Zayden turned his head, "Kaesar, aren't you coming?"

Kaesar had his eye on the spot where Adalo vanished, "Yeah, I am," he spoke and turned back, "Just had to take in Adalo's actually here."

After a moment, the two walked out of the room.

The participants followed Flare up the stairs, "—Hey Flare!" beamed Reno beside her, "I'm Reno! How are you doing?"

Flare turned her head, "Hello participant Reno," she smiled.

"—I Sin Rock!" gloated Reno, "Pretty cool huh?!"

"Good for you participant Reno," remarked Flare, "Be sure to include that on the form I mentioned."

"—Uh…" uttered Reno, *"I'm getting nowhere like this…"* he worried.

After a moment, they reached the participants' rooms, "You may now choose your residence!" instructed Flare, "You will find the keys inside, and I will be at the front desk if you need me! Remember to have your forms in by midnight!"

The participants listened to her.

Zayden, Kaesar, and Reno chose their rooms beside each other. Some of the participants headed to the Sinara Procedure Room, while others headed outside to do some preparations.

Kaesar stayed in his room as he began closing the door, *"I shouldn't—"*

"—Wait!" burst in Zayden as he stopped the door, "You agreed to fight me when we landed here!"
There was a moment as the two looked to each other.

"...Alright," accepted Kaesar, "But after I fill out my form," he told Zayden as he opened the door and walked down the hallway.
"—Kaesar!" Reno quickly rushed beside him, "Wait for me! I need to fill out my form too!"

The two walked down the hallway together.
Zayden saw them go as he went back inside his room, "Uh," he groaned as felt the burns on his arm, *"That little moment with Dedrian got my arms hurting again..."*

Kaesar and Reno went down the stairs and were in the hallways on the main level.

"—Do you think Flare notices me?!" asked Reno, "I mean—More than everyone else of course!"
Kaesar paused, "That doesn't matter," he remarked, "We're here for the competition, not for her."

"—But still!" went on Reno, "She's really something to look at!"
Kaesar took a moment, "Yeah as the Attendant, she's doing well," he spoke, "But moving on, how long have you known Zayden?" he asked.

"Hm? About four years," recalled Reno, "He came into our village back then, and we became close ever since!" he smiled, "How long have you known him?"
"What? I just met him a few hours ago from the ship..." murmured Kaesar, "I thought Zayden mentioned it."

"—Oh yeah," chuckled Reno, "I forgot."
Reno laughed as Kaesar turned to him with a confused look.

They continued walking, "—Oh before I forget!" recalled Reno, "What do you Sin?!"
Kaesar had a light smirk, "I Sin Ice," he spoke.

"—I Sin Rock!" smiled Reno, "That's so cool though you Sin Ice! I've never seen someone who can do that!"

"Then you're in for a surprise," remarked Kaesar.

"—How so?"

"Watch Zayden's fight against me on the Academy's fields," insisted Kaesar, "I'll show—."

"Zayden's going to destroy you!" broke in Reno, "Oh I mean—You're going to fight Zayden?!" he changed his words.

"I heard what he said the first time," knew Kaesar.

"You should be careful," advised Reno, "You really don't want to be injured before tomorrow."

Kaesar paused, "I'm sure I'll be fine," he spoke.

He and Reno made it to the Sinara Procedure Room and began filling out their forms.

On the upper level, Zayden was in his room by himself. He was on one knee as he unpacked his bag, "—Uh," he grimaced in pain again from the burns on his arms.

After a moment, Zayden stood up, *"These burns are starting to hurt a lot,"* he thought, *"But I can't complain right now, I need to give Kaesar my best."*

He exited his room as he walked down the hallway holding his right arm.

But then Zayden tightened his hold on his arm as he fell back to the wall, *"I'm sweating so much!"* he thought, *"But why?! I hardly Sinned!"* He rolled up his sleeves for fresh air.

Another participant walked by as she passed the corner and looked to him, "…You're hurting," she spoke, "Aren't you?"

"—No, I'm fine!" denied Zayden as he let go of his arms, "Just catching my breath," he turned his back and put his sleeves down.

"I saw that!" remarked the participant from behind, "Roll up your sleeves down!"

"—What?!" uttered Zayden walking away, "I don't know—"

"—Don't play dumb!" yelled the participant as she appeared beside Zayden, "—I saw your burns!" she took Zayden's arm and rolled his sleeves up.

20

"—Oh those!" uttered Zayden, "They're nothing!" and in his thoughts, *"I can't let anyone see my burns, it'll show weakness."*

"I can heal them for you," remarked the participant, "I'm sure you've heard all about me."

Zayden stayed quiet.

There was a pause, "I'm Aviva," she stated as she rolled her eyes, "Everyone knows about me…" she murmured.

Aviva Kallent was a Farmake Sinner, she had long red hair which were tied up along with blue eyes. She wore a pink outfit with dark shades and outlines.

Zayden heard her, "That's fine and all," he spoke as he struggled to break the hold on his arm, "But I—"

"—No let me see it," demanded Aviva as she looked to the burns on his arms, "I should at least do something helpful while I'm here…"

"—This isn't my weakness!" assured Zayden, "Fire doesn't hurt me at all! It's nothing!"

"Doesn't look like nothing to me," saw Aviva, "It looks like someone who has trouble with his Sinning Ability."

Zayden shook his head.

But then Aviva put her hand on Zayden's arm as it had a Pink aura, "I'm a Kallent," she muttered as the burns went away, "Let me do what I've always been hearing about…"

Zayden felt the cold breeze on his arm, "Wait—How are you?" he uttered.

"And…we're done," finished Aviva.

"Uh—thank you! I'm Zayden by the way," he spoke, "You said you're Aviva, right?"

"Yeah, and no problem," she spoke, "It's not like I have anything else to do…"

"—What Sinning is this?" asked Zayden.

Aviva took a moment, "I'm the same as you," she remarked, "But while you're a Combat Sinner, I'm a Farmake Sinner," she stated, "So we usually don't have any abilities like Fire or Ice, our powers are a different category, it's hard to explain actually."

Zayden listened, "Oh, I guess—"

21

"—Oh look!" beamed one participant from across the hallway, "It's a Kallent! She's really there!"

Zayden and Aviva quickly turned their head.

The participant burst down the hallway pushing Zayden out of the way, "—I'm Kara!" she smiled as she held Aviva's hands, "I'm super excited! This whole competition is going to be way more fun with a Kallent!"

Kara Cherry was another participant who was a Farmake Sinner. She had long orange hair and eyes. She wore a while long sleeve shirt with a collar tied and a red ribbon under a black vest and leather boots.

Kara took out a lollipop from her pocket and put it in her mouth, "Please tell me Lavivo's here too!" she beamed, "That would be the best!"

"—No!" opposed Aviva as Kara jumped with her hands, "I would never want her to be here! None of my family!"

Kara chuckled, "But your Lavivo's little sister, which makes you my idol!" she smiled, "Everyone hears how you two heal and battle Sinners across all the Districts!"

Aviva groaned, "But that doesn't—"

"—Kara stop praising her," spoke another participant from across the hall, "You can't really be serious about saying both of them protect Sinners around the world, we all know Lavivo does all the work."

"—Marubee!" smiled Kara as she turned her head back, "Can you believe Aviva's here?! Someone from the Kallent Family! Lavivo's blood relative! She has seen all of Lavivo's Abilities up close which makes her just as great!"

But Marubee eyed away, "Just because she's Aviva doesn't mean she's high above everyone else," she remarked.

Marubee Tasuki was a Farmake Sinner who had wide green eyes and hair that curled up on the ends. She wore a black dress with long sleeves and low-heeled black shoes.

Zayden slowly got up as he stood by the wall and watched on.

"—And so what if she is a Kallent," went on Marubee, "That was all luck that she got born into such a family."

Aviva listened to her.

"It's so annoying," stated Marubee, "She's given every opportunity in the world and doesn't even have to work hard."

"But—"

"No, that's what you don't see," broke in Aviva, "Yeah I'm from the Kallent family, but I'm great because of my own Sin."

Marubee heard her. There was a moment as the two stared at each other from across the hall.

But then Marubee began walking forward, "...I've had enough," she spoke as she grabbed Kara's shirt.

"Hey I—" uttered Kara as the lollipop fell from her mouth.

Marubee dragged her away from the collar, "Never call Aviva your idol," she told her, "You always mention them as such a figure..."

Aviva saw them go, "Don't view me like that!" she yelled, "That's not what I want!"

Marubee stayed quiet.

"—No no my pop!" freaked out Kara as she was dragged away, "Someone give me my lollipop back!" but then the two turned the corner.

After a moment, Aviva eyed to the ground, "Kallent..." she muttered to herself, "It's been like this the whole time..."

There was a pause. Zayden got up from the wall and walked to her, "...Who's Lavivo?" he asked, "She must be a great Sinner from the way those two were talking about her."

Aviva looked to him, "Lavivo's such a good Farmake Sinner," she murmured, "And I'm just her little sister..."

"But why—"

"She's good at everything and doesn't have one negative aspect about her!" Aviva raised her voice, "And I—" but then she stopped talking.

Zayden waited.

"What am I doing..." realized Aviva, *"It's so annoying talking about her..."*

23

Zayden half smiled, "I'm sure if you do well in the competition," he remarked, "People might think you're great on your own, and not whatever family you're from."

After a moment, Aviva exhaled, "Maybe," she spoke, "We'll just have to see."
Zayden nodded, "Well thanks for healing me," he recalled, "But now I have a fight to get to!" he smirked as he burst down the hallway.

Aviva walked the other way in deep thought about the whole competition.

In another hallway, Marubee took Kara into a room.
"—Let go of me!" shrieked Kara, "I just—"
But then Marubee threw her on the bed.
"—Marubee!" screeched Kara as she rolled on the bed.
But then Marubee looked to her, "Kara," she spoke, "Tell me that'll you never freak out like that again."
"—I promise!" smiled Kara as she stood up on the bed, "You can always trust me!"
There was a pause, "You know it's so annoying seeing you cry your eyes out for people," remarked Marubee.
"—I was not crying!" denied Kara, "I was just super excited!" she took out a lollipop and put it in her mouth, "This whole competition has me ready for anything!"
Marubee heard her, "I know what you mean…" she spoke, and in her thoughts, *"But one day, you're going to praise me like you do with those other Sinners."*

By now, on the lower level, Reno had finished filling out the participant form and waited for Kaesar in the hallway.
"—How long is he going to take?!" he thought, *"I really have people to see!"*
There was a moment as Reno saw other people coming out of the Procedure room, but not Kaesar.
He turned his head to the right, *"Kaesar has a fight with Zayden anyways,"* he recalled, *"And I got a meeting with the Attendant!"* he burst away from the Procedure Room.

Reno sprinted through several hallways until he saw a sign in the end of one hall: *"Sinara Service Desk."* *"—That's it!"* saw Reno as he turned into the hallway and approached the Desk.

But there was also another participant walking down from the opposite end.

After a moment, Reno reached the Sinara Service Desk, he stood on the other side of the glass.

Flare was inside the room as she filled out letters.

Reno saw her, "F-Flare!" he called out, "—Here's my participant form!" he put his form on the desk, "Make sure you double check it," he winked.

"Thank you participant Reno," Flare grabbed the form and put it facedown.

"—She didn't even read it!" worried Reno.

"Attendant," called the other participant who walked from the other side. He put his form down on the desk.

There was a moment of silence.

"Attendant," called the participant again, "Take my form."

"One second," the Attendant turned, "—Oh" she was stunned at the sight of the participant, "Uh—t-thank you, participant Soro...just leave it on the table please."

Soro Uzara was the participant that hadn't ridden the ship to travel to the Academy. His most noticeable feature was his spiky black-colored hair along with his dark blue eyes. He wore a white and black slim coat.

"Soro..." noticed Reno, *"I've heard that name a few times now..."*

Suddenly the big black bag that was strapped onto Soro began to shake.

Flare looked to the bag, "—Participant Soro," she called out, "Is there something I need to be aware of?"

Soro gave his bag a tug, "No," he spoke.

There was a pause, "...Are you sure?" went on Flare, "If there's something that I need to know, you must—"

"—Attendant, there's no need to concern yourself with me," remarked Soro, "I told you it's nothing."

"—Her name is Flare!" yelled Reno.

Soro nodded up at him.

"…I shouldn't have said that," worried Reno.

Flare went back to writing, "…Hm, you can be on your way now," she murmured, "Don't forget to claim your room before midnight."

Soro heard her as he looked to the other side of the hallway, then walked passed Reno as his bag shook again.

Reno turned back, *"—His bag is still moving!"* he saw, *"What could be inside?!"*

Reno began following Soro. With every few steps Soro took, Reno tiptoed behind him, hiding behind walls, plants, or anything he can find.

After a moment, Soro entered a room as Reno watched him from the corner.

Soro dropped his bag on the bed as a noise was made.

"—Is that the bag?!" heard Reno as he quickly side stepped in front of the door.

But then Soro closed the door and confronted him, "…What's the matter?" he spoke.

The two were face to face.

Reno stood up straight as he took a deep breath, "—What's in the bag?!" he asked.

Soro was quiet as he gave him a stern look.

"There's something about him…" worried Reno, *"He doesn't mess around…"*

"…Alright then," murmured Reno, "But just for the future, call the Attendant by her name," he remarked, "Some respect wouldn't hurt."

Soro stayed quiet as he turned around and stepped into his room.

"—Hey!" Reno quickly reached for Soro's shoulder, "I'm talking to—"

But then a Blue light sparked and shocked Reno's hand, "—What the hell was that?!" he groaned.

Soro closed the door without looking back.

Reno quickly opened and closed his hand, *"—Was I just imagining things?!"* he thought.

After a moment, he slowly opened his hand again, *"How did he..."* he saw a burn on his palm, *"I didn't even see it properly..."*

After a moment, Reno walked away as he shook his hand, *"Soro..."* he thought, *"What Sinning was that..."*

On the lower level, Zayden made his way to the Sinara Procedure Room, *"I should fill out my—"*

But then he saw Kaesar come out the door.

"—Kaesar!" called out Zayden as he walked to him, "You know why I'm here."

Kaesar saw him, *"...I've always disliked filling out personal information,"* he thought about the participant form.

"Kaesar?" repeated Zayden, "You said I was nervous on the ship, but now you look confused..."

There was a pause, "...I'm fine," spoke Kaesar, "And if you want to fight me, let's go."

Zayden nodded, "Finally," he smirked.

The two walked down the hallway, *"I couldn't have escaped this one,"* thought Kaesar, *"I did agree to this back on the ship..."*

After a moment, Zayden and Kaesar made it out of the Academy and outside to the fields. The sky was dark as it was getting late, it was dim as the Academy's lights weren't too strong.

"Wait—where's Reno?" recalled Kaesar as he looked around, "I wanted him to see our battle."

Zayden took a moment, "I have no idea," he spoke, "But for now, let's just focus on you and me."

The two stood a distance away on the grassy field face to face. The time was nearing 10:30 P.M. as the winds swayed the leaves and dust around.

"...Five minutes," stated Kaesar.

"—What?" uttered Zayden.

Kaesar gave a stern look, "We're only going to do this for five minutes," he remarked, "I told you about this on the ship."

"—But that's so short!"

27

"Doesn't matter," denied Kaesar, "It's getting too late."

Zayden heard him, "Hm, if that's what you want," he agreed, "Then that's fine with me."

Kaesar nodded, "The timer is set!" he raised his voice as he started his watch, "Come at me whenever you're ready!"

Zayden quickly began to Sin as he had a red aura.

Kaesar saw him.

After a moment, Zayden breathed in and out as Fire surrounded his body, "—Uh," he groaned as he felt the heat.

"He's hurting," noticed Kaesar, *"The Fire isn't in full control."*

"Come on Kaesar!" urged Zayden, "When are you going to Sin?!"

Kaesar stayed quiet as he had a Blue aura.

"—What can his Sinning Ability be?!" watched Zayden.

Ice appeared around Kaesar's fists and shielded his arms, "Didn't want Sin too early," he spoke, "But this battle forced me to," his white hair flowed with the wind.

Zayden smirked, "—Now that's out of the way!" he yelled as he charged forward.

Kaesar waited, "As expected," he murmured.

"—We can finally have some practice before the competition!" shouted Zayden as he went in with a punch.

But then Kaesar evaded to the side.

"—Another one!" yelled Zayden as he turned back.

Kaesar saw him, "You're doing the same—"

But then Zayden's body disintegrated into ashes.

Kaesar was stunned, "When did you—"

"I'll get the first hit!" yelled Zayden as he reappeared behind Kaesar and swung his arm.

Kaesar quickly turned grabbed Zayden's wrist, *"—That was close,"* he realized.

"But you didn't see—" uttered Zayden.

Kaesar tightened his hand as he swung and threw Zayden away.

Zayden was sent through the air but caught his balance and landed on his feet, "Wait—" he freaked out, "—My hand is frozen!"

Kaesar took a moment, "I know," he remarked, "Let's continue, a minute already went by."

Zayden bent down as he put out his right hand towards and lit up a few leaves on Fire.

Kaesar watched him.

"This should work," murmured Zayden as he put over his frozen left hand as it melted.

That shouldn't have been too hard to figure out," thought Kaesar.

But then Zayden quickly burned more leaves in the ground with his fingers, "—I bet you haven't seen this before!" he yelled out loud.

Zayden picked up the inflamed leaves and put them in his mouth.

"—What are you doing?" spoke Kaesar.

"Hm," smirked Zayden. He quickly burst through the field.

Kaesar put out his hand as he Sinned an Ice path underneath.

Zayden looked down, *"—That's too predictable!"* he thought and jumped up.

But then Kaesar Sinned a heavy Ball of Ice in his hand, "—Cough those leaves out!" he yelled as he whipped the Ball.

Zayden quickly spit out two of the inflamed leaves as it rapidly cut the Ice Ball down.

"—What kind of move is this?" uttered Kaesar.

Zayden landed on the ground and charged forward again.

Kaesar put out his arm.

But then Zayden disintegrated into ashes.

"—Not again," saw Kaesar as he turned back.

Zayden reappeared behind, "—I've got it now!" he shouted as he swung his arm.

Kaesar quickly caught his wrist again with his hand.

But then Zayden spat out several inflamed leaves from his mouth.

Kaesar let go of Zayden's wrist, *"I should've saw that,"* he thought as put his arms up shielded in Ice. Zayden's Fire grew bigger as he went in with a punch, "First touch!" he yelled as he punched into Kaesar's stomach.

"—Uh," groaned Kaesar his stomach went in. Zayden rapidly went in with punches.

But Kaesar stepped side to side as he had his arms up.

Zayden angered, "—I can't get through!" he yelled as he went in with a heavy punch to the arms. Kaesar was hit as he was forced back.

Zayden's breath was heavy, *"Seems unbreakable,"* he thought.

But then the Ice cracked on the arms, "...Are you serious," murmured Kaesar.

After a moment, he looked back up to Zayden, "You're not bad," he spoke, "Better than I expected for sure." Zayden smirked, "Thanks," he spoke, "I haven't fought anyone else aside from Reno, so you're the best I've ever fought."

Kaesar listened, "But now," he muttered, "Let's finish off this little practice." "—Hm?" saw Zayden.

Kaesar put out his arm as he Sinned a streak of Ice towards Zayden. Zayden saw it coming as he dodged to the side.

Kaesar swung his hand to the right as the Ice came back around. *"—That's so much control!"* thought Zayden as he turned his back.

Kaesar quickly put his arm to the ground as he Sinned a rapid Path of Ice. "—What?!" uttered Zayden turned back around.

But then his feet were caught and stuck in the Ice, "I can't—" he tried to move. Kaesar burst forward as he went in with a punch.

Zayden's eyes widened as he saw him coming.

Kaesar's fist shielded with Ice as he bashed Zayden's stomach.

"—Uh," groaned Zayden.

With the same hand, Kaesar Sinned an Ice Ball and swung his arm up forcing Zayden in the air.

"—He doesn't look that strong at first!" thought Zayden as he went up.

Kaesar tightened his hand as he whipped the Ice Ball into Zayden's stomach.

"—Uh," Zayden's mouth dropped as he grimaced.

"Hm," saw Kaesar.

Zayden held his stomach as he landed on the ground.

He then put out his arm as Fire surrounded his fist.

Kaesar's hair rose as he quickly reappeared beside Zayden.

"You were just—" Zayden turned his head.

Kaesar swung his arm as he punched into Zayden's face.

Zayden was sent flying and fell rolled on the ground, he caught his balance as he was on one knee, "There's no way he moved that quick," he recalled, "I know I saw him!"

Kaesar remained standing from across the field.

Zayden rubbed his face as he slowly stood up, "Kaesar..." he thought, "You're showing a lot more than I expected..."

There was a pause as Kaesar looked to his watch. But then Zayden groaned, "—The time is running!" he yelled, "The battle won't have a winner if we wait! So let's go all out!"

Zayden's Sinning Power began to rise as two spots of Fire lit up on his hair. The red wristband he wore shined in dark red.

Kaesar saw him, "That's a lot of Power," he remarked, "One of us might actually get hurt before the competition."

Zayden burst towards Kaesar as he scorched the ground beneath, "This might be too much!" he realized but swung with a punch.

Kaesar quickly dashed to the side.

31

But then Zayden swung his arm again to the right.
"—Oh," uttered Kaesar as he put up his arms up.

Zayden's fist clashed with the Ice, "Now I'll—"
But then the Ice rapidly went over his hands, "What—"

Kaesar quickly grabbed onto both of Zayden's arms and jumped a knee into his stomach.

"Uh," groaned Zayden as he stumbled back.
Kaesar put out his hand as he Sinned an Ice streak freezing Zayden's arms.

"Stop with this—" Zayden tried to move.
Kaesar burst forward, "I got to end this for the both of us!" he shouted as he kicked Zayden up the chin.
Zayden was sent flying up the air as the Fire around him lowered.
Kaesar looked up as he charged and jumped in the air, *"I'll restrict him before this gets out of control!"* he thought.

Kaesar was near Zayden in mid air as his arms surrounded with Ice, "We're finished here," he remarked and reached for him.
Zayden's eyes widened, "—No!" he yelled out loud, "This isn't how I want it to end!"

Zayden's wrist shined in dark red.
"Wait what's—" saw Kaesar, a bomb-like detonation exploded on his shoulder.

Zayden landed on the ground and looked up.
Kaesar held his shoulder as he fell through the air, *"What just happened?!"* he thought.

Zayden smirked as he saw him, "—This is a change up!" he yelled as he burst forward, "Now I'll come out on top!"
Zayden soared through the air as his fist inflamed in Fire.

Kaesar saw him, "—I didn't want to bring it out!" his eyes began turning Dark Blue, "But you left me no other choice!"
Zayden swung his arm as Kaesar widened his dark eyes.

But then a beep was heard as Zayden's fist stopped in front of Kaesar's face.
Both of them landed on the ground a distance from each other.

There was a moment of silence.

Kaesar's white hair went back down as his eyes turned back to normal, "...Why didn't you continue?" he asked.

Zayden's breath was heavy as he stopped Sinning, the Fire around him was gone. He pointed forward.

Kaesar paused, but then heard the beeping as he looked to his wrist, "The watch..." he murmured as he stopped the timer.

"The five minutes were up," spoke Zayden, "You made it clear that's how long you wanted to go for." After a moment, Kaesar stopped Sinning as the Ice went away, "Hm. You're right about the time," he recalled, "But I didn't think you'd actually listen to me."

"What? Why wouldn't I?" went on Zayden, "It wouldn't be fair."

Kaesar heard him, "...Yeah," he murmured, but in his thoughts, *"That bomb-like detonation on my shoulder,"* he recalled, *"It couldn't have been him."*

Zayden began walking forward, "Thanks for staying true to your word!" he remarked, "I needed this practice before the real thing tomorrow!"

Kaesar listened and turned back facing the Academy.

"Now I think the both of us will do well," determined Zayden as he walked up to him, "Right?" he turned his head and smiled.

Kaesar looked back, "Sure," he spoke, "We'll see."

After a moment, the two walked back inside the Academy for the night.

Zayden and Kaesar stepped onto the red carpeted main foyer.

Reno quickly walked passed them, "Imma prove Soro wrong," he repeatedly murmured to himself.

The two of them watched him go, "...What happened now," exhaled Zayden.

Reno marched up the stairs, *"Nobody disrespects Flare!"* he thought.

Kaesar turned his head to Zayden, "And he's the one you sparred with?" he recalled.

"Yeah," snickered Zayden, "Reno's something else."

Kaesar shook his head, "What can you do," he murmured as he went up the stairs, "That's enough things for today," he spoke with his right hand in his pocket, "I'm off for the night."

Zayden looked up, "I'm also going to—" but then stopped, *"—Oh yeah the participant forms!"* he remembered, *"I forgot to fill them out!"*

Zayden burst down the main foyer and into the hallways to find the Procedure Room.

Kaesar continued to walk by himself through the hallway heading to his room.

He was in deep thought as he recalled a moment with Zayden on the ship: *"I promised her back then that I would become a Full-Fledged Sinner in place of my Father!"* he remembered Zayden's words.

Kaesar made it to his room as he opened the door, *"If someone like you really wants to go through with that,"* he thought, *"Then I shouldn't be too quiet about what I want to do."*

He went inside his room and closed the door.

In a room on the other side of the hallway, Dedrian was inside with a red aura, "—Our tackle is sure to come!" he groaned, "I'll prove my worth to her and Zayden!" he thought about Zayden and another person.

"...It wasn't that bad," recalled Rajaul, "He just caught your—"

"—Little things like that tick me off!" remarked Dedrian as he turned his head, "Now everybody thinks he's that much higher than me, I won't allow it!"

Rajaul sighed as he saw small Fire coming out of Dedrian, *"There he goes again..."* he thought and walked to the room door.

"...Rajaul," called out Dedrian.

He turned his head, "Yeah?" he asked.

Dedrian gave a stern look, "If you see Zayden or any of his friends," he went on, "You have to show up stronger in front of them."

Rajaul nodded, "You don't have to remind me," he spoke, "I'll get it done."
Dedrian had a light smirk.

After a pause, Rajaul exited the room, *"I didn't want to mess with anyone this early,"* he thought, *"But if anybody screws around with Dedrian, I have to get involved."*

The night was late as most participants were in their rooms.
At the Sinara Service Desk, the Attendant, Flare, sat on a chair as she continued to fill out letters inside the glass.

But then Smoke appeared behind her as she turned around, "...Do you always have to enter like that?" she spoke.
After a moment, Adalo appeared, "...Its midnight," he remarked, "Let's get sleep before it all starts tomorrow."

There was a moment of silence.
"...Flare?" murmured Adalo.
Flare took a moment, "Stop acting like you didn't notice," she recalled as she turned around on the chair, "I know you can tell."

"What are you—"
"—Here's my form!" broke in Zayden as he put down his form down at the Desk, "You're Attendant Flare, right?"

Adalo quickly turned into Smoke and vanished.
Flare turned her head, "You can drop the attendant part, just call me Flare," she smiled, "And thank you participant Zayden."
"—No problem," assured Zayden, "But was there Smoke here just now?!"

Flare turned her head back, "I'm not sure," she murmured, "Could've been anything."
Zayden took a moment as he looked around inside the glass, "It's probably not important anyways," he spoke, "The night's getting too late for me."

"—Well have a good sleep," smiled Flare, "You'll need it!"

Zayden nodded then walked away, "Goodnight Attendant Flare," he spoke out loud.

"I said to drop the attendant part..." murmured Flare.

Smoke began to appear behind her again.

Zayden turned the corner out of the hallway.

After a pause, Adalo reappeared back inside the glass, "Does him calling you Attendant really matter?" he asked.

Flare heard him. "Hm, would you like to be called by your full name?" she reminded.

"...Good point," murmured Adalo.

"Wait—I'm not going to change the subject!" went on Flare, "You know exactly what I was talking about from before!"

Adalo saw a change in Flare's expression.

"You can't hide from it anymore," remarked Flare, "You have to confront it, this is your chance to redeem yourself!"

Adalo paused, "I have nothing to hide," he stated, "Come on, let's go to bed."

But Flare shook her head, "Adalo..." she muttered, "It's about participant—"

"—Flare!" broke in Adalo.

There was a moment as the two looked to each other.

"I know what you mean..." admitted Adalo, "I honestly never thought I would see him again..."

Flare saw him as she eyed to the floor, "So what are you going to do..." she muttered.

Adalo put his head up, "Give me time and I'll address the whole thing," he assured.

"—No! Let me get him now!" insisted Flare, "Everyone is asleep, this is the best time!"

"—Do you not understand how much of a burden this is for me?!" Adalo raised his voice, "I can't simply talk about it like it's another conversation."

Flare was stunned, "I-I"

Adalo took a moment as he relaxed, "I don't want to talk about this," he eyed away, "We'll further on if the situation ever arises."

36

Flare saddened, "But what you did to his life..." she spoke, "You changed everything...you owe some sort of explanation..."

Adalo looked to her, "You know I had too," he remarked, "Though you may even disagree."

Flare was quiet, she turned back around and began filling out the letters again.

"...He will know about everything eventually," assured Adalo, "Again, just give me time."

Flare stayed quiet, *"I trust you,"* she thought about Adalo, *"There's no reason for me to not believe you'll right this wrong."*

After a moment, Adalo spoke up, "It's been a long night," he recalled, "You're tired, just save that work for tomorrow."

"It's okay...I'm almost done with this," yawned Flare, "This whole competition, I'm excited we're doing it again," she snickered.

"We have to hold these competitions," stated Adalo, "The Power of Sinning is lethal, we need to make sure it stays in control."

"Yeah..." muttered Flare.

"Running this Academy will tire us eventually," added Adalo.

"Well it's been 3 years since the last one," half smiled Flare, "I'm sure we've had our fair share of rest."

"Exactly," yawned Adalo. He walked over to the exit door with his hand over his mouth, "—Oh and by the way," he turned, "Can you stop defending me in front of other people?" he recalled, "I have my own voice."

"—But that participant didn't know who you were!" reminded Flare, "That was so rude of him!"

"Regardless," stated Adalo, "Next time just leave it to me."

"—No!" she opposed, "Nobody talks bad about my Adalowala except for me," she told him as she filled out the letter.

"—I said not to call me by my full name," reminded Adalo.

Flare heard him as she chuckled, "...And done," she dropped the pen on the desk, "I'm all finished, let's get some sleep now Adalowala," she smiled.

After a moment, Adalo and Flare went to their room and slept.

With the clock striking midnight, everyone in the Academy were asleep. Day 1 of the Sinara Academy competition was to begin the next morning.

"—Rise and shine participants!" announced Flare through the speakers that outputted to all the rooms, "—The first stage of the competition begins this morning in 45 minutes!"

Zayden quickly sat up from his bed, *"—That speaker is so loud!"* he thought, *"But, Reno probably still ignored it."*

Zayden shook his head as he got up from the bed, he placed his hand on the side desk.

"Hm?" Zayden felt the desk again, "—Where is it?!" he quickly looked down, "Where's my wristband?!"

He jumped around the room searching for it, *"—Did someone take it?!"* he worried.

After a moment, he stopped in front of the window as he saw other participants outside preparing for the competition, *"I'll just have to check out myself,"* he thought as he went out of his room, *"That wristband is too important to not be with me."*

Zayden burst outside and onto the grassy field next to the Academy.

He walked up to two other participants, "—Did you guys see a red wristband anywhere?!" he asked.

The two turned around, "...That's not how you talk to us," one of them remarked, "It isn't respectful."

"Uh—what do you mean?" asked Zayden.

"You don't want to talk to Javarus with that tone," spoke the other participant, "The nature of him will be hurt."

"...The nature?" murmured Zayden, "What are you talking about?!"

There was a pause, "...Is he serious?" asked Javarus.

Javarus Hanzen was a muscular man with a well-built body, he was the tallest participant in the competition. He had long, spiky, shoulder-length light green hair.

"—It doesn't make a difference!" yelled the other one.

"—It makes a major difference Veny," explained Javarus, "Being nice and respectful to one another goes a long way."

"Why do I even be around you," wondered Veny. Veny Ikanu is tall as well, but not as muscular. He's also bald and wore a long black robe.

"Oh," went on Zayden, "I didn't mean to disrespect you or anything."

Veny looked to him, "Then you're going to have to repeat yourself," he stated.

"What do you want me to say?!" uttered Zayden.

"You can't ask us to help you without proper introductions," remarked Javarus, "I can't help a stranger."

"Proper greeting?" thought Zayden, "Oh so—I'm Zayden," he introduced himself, "Who are you?"

"I'm Javarus," he smiled, "Good morning, isn't it?"

"Yeah it is," nodded Zayden, "Alright—so I need so help," he went on, "Would you be able to lend a hand?"

"Yeah, why not," smiled Javarus, "Veny and I can certainly help you, what is it?"

"...That's all it took," Zayden was surprised.

"—The both of us?!" heard Veny.

Zayden looked to Javarus, "I had a wristband that was in my room," he recalled, "But now I seem to have lost it, I have no idea where it could be, would you be able to help me search for it?"

"I see," nodded Javarus.

Zayden went on, "And I really need it back—"

"Then we'll help you until we find it," smiled Javarus.

"Huh?!" uttered Veny.

"Just tell us where to look," said Javarus.

Zayden looked to the both of them, "—Thanks guys!" he nodded, "Let's separate and look everywhere. Ask other people if they've seen it—Oh and remember, the colour of the wristband is red!"

"Got it!" understood Javarus, "Let's go," he patted Veny on the back.

Veny put his head down.

After a moment, the three went separate ways to search for Zayden's wristband.

By now, all the participants were awake preparing for the competition.

In his room, Kaesar took a moment as he stood by the door, *"His last attack was so close..."* he recalled the fight with Zayden last night, *"How could I have let it get to that point..."*

After a moment, he opened the door and went down the stairs.

Kaesar walked through a hallway heading to the side door.

But then Rajaul came up from behind and saw him, *"—That's one of Zayden's pals that sneered Dedrian!"* he remembered.

Rajaul smirked from across the hallway, "Hey Zayden's buddy," he called out.

Kaesar turned his head back.

"You guys messed around with Dedrian!" remarked Rajaul, "So by association, I have to get involved!"

Kaesar looked from across the hallway, "No," he spoke and turned his back, "There isn't a point to this."

"—Turn around!" yelled Rajaul, "I'm talking to you!"

But Kaesar continued walking away, "I'm really not in the mood to deal with your type," he spoke.

"—What?!" uttered Rajaul, *"What does he mean my type?!"* he thought.

"Just don't bother me," stated Kaesar, "You should be focused on the first stage instead."

Rajaul shook his head and began Sinning, "You should be focused on me," he remarked as Water overflowed around his body.

Kaesar paused as he stopped walking, "I know you're Sinning," he spoke, "Stop."

"—And what are you going to do about it?!" yelled Rajaul.

There was a moment of silence.

Near the confrontation, Kara turned the corner into the same hallway, "—Oh," she caught a glimpse of the two and stepped back, *"—What's going on here?!"*

Kara quickly moved behind the wall, *"I'm ready to see this!"* she thought as she carefully watched on.

"—I may not be as strong as Dedrian!" went on Rajaul, "But you and I are a different story!" he charged towards Kaesar with his fist surrounded in Water.

Kaesar stood with his back turned.

"—Stop disrespecting me!" shouted Rajaul as he swung his arm.

But then Kaesar quickly turned around and caught his fist, "You're the one coming at me," he spoke.

Kaesar's hand turned Blue.

"—Uh," groaned Rajaul as he forced his hand out.

"—Huh?!" saw Kara, *"His hand got bigger!"*

Rajaul looked down to his hand, "What?!" he uttered as it was frozen in a block of Ice. He looked back up to Kaesar, "—This isn't funny!" he yelled.

Kaesar stayed quiet.

Rajaul burst towards him again, "—This is for Dedrian!" he shouted as he rapidly went in with one hand punches.

Kaesar moved side to side avoiding each fist.

Rajaul swung his arm, "How am I missing him every time!" he yelled as went in with another punch, "—I can't even get one on him!"

Kaesar stepped back as he dodged his fist.

There was a distance between them, Rajaul's breath was heavy, "—Now this is about me as well," he yelled, "—I have to show that I'm that much better than you!"

Water began rising behind Rajaul in a wave, "You won't be able to handle this one," he smirked.

Kaesar looked to him.

Rajaul turned his head behind as he saw the Water rising, "I don't care if I'm careless," he smirked then turned back, "As long as you're—" but then he stopped talking as Kaesar stared him down.

There was a moment of silence.

Kaesar's white hair lowered, "...I'm here," he spoke, "What's holding you back?"

Rajaul was stunned as he looked into Kaesar's eyes.

"What's happening now..." thought Kara as she watched on.

"I-I," stuttered Rajaul.

Kaesar looked to him with no expression.

"What's with this guy?!" saw Rajaul, *"He's not flinching at—"*

"Rajaul," broke in Kaesar, "You started a fight. Now finish it."

Rajaul was shocked, "—I-I will," he murmured, but in his thoughts, *"The way he's staring me down...it's so deep..."*

There was a moment of silence.

Kara continued to watch from behind the wall, *"What is this..."* she looked to Kaesar, *"His eyes...their super cold..."*

She looked back to Rajaul, *"—And he's frozen like a frozen lollipop!"* she saw.

Rajaul looked to Kaesar, *"I need to attack for Dedrian..."* he recalled, *"But this guy...he's too much."*

Rajaul slowly looked away, then looked back into Kaesar's eyes again.

He was stunned, "I..." he muttered, "I can't..."

Rajaul stopped Sinning as the wave of Water behind him splashed on the ground.

"Wait—" uttered Kara as the water splashed over to her on the side.

Kaesar took a moment, "We're done here," he spoke and turned around, "I told you there wasn't a point to this."

Rajaul eyed down, "B-But..."

Kaesar began walking down the hall again.

Rajaul was speechless as he saw Kaesar make his way outside, *"Why couldn't I finish the fight..."* he thought as he turned and walked the other way.

On the side, Kara's wet hair went over her eyes as she saw him go.

Rajaul didn't see her.

After a moment, Kara turned back to the side door Kaesar walked through, "He's a funny one," she snickered as she blew her wet hair up.

On the upper level, the last participant who got out of her room was Aviva.

She walked down the stairs to the main floor, *"...I'm wasting my time here in this Academy,"* she thought.

But then Smoke appeared beside her when she stepped on the ground.

Aviva turned her head, "I knew you were going to show up..." she murmured.

After a moment, Adalo appeared, "...I just wanted to make sure you were up and ready," he stated.

Aviva was quiet as she walked over to the front door.

"Aviva," called out Adalo as he walked behind her, "Your family expects big things from you, and so do I."

"—But why don't you say that to the other participants?" asked Aviva.

"I have connections with your family," recalled Adalo, "I wouldn't want them to be disappointed with you, nor do I want to see you not succeed."

Aviva listened, *"Adalo and Papa are close,"* she remembered, *"But it's not like that makes me any difference."*

Adalo went on, "You and I both know that you have what it takes to possibly make it into the winning circle," he remarked, "Only the effort is what holds you back."

The two stopped at the front door inside the Academy.

"What if I don't even want to do this whole thing," murmured Aviva, "Why should I?"

Adalo heard her, "Because you're going to surpass Lavivo," he referred to her older sister.

"—But I don't care about Sinning!" Aviva raised her voice, "Especially in this competition!"
"You can't be serious," remarked Adalo, "Sinning is what makes the world go around. Without Sinners, there would be chaos with no order."

Aviva looked away, "You're talking a lot like Papa..." she murmured.
"It can't be helped," spoke Adalo as he opened the front door, "I spent a lot of times with your Father."

The two of them looked outside to the Academy's fields, "I believe Lavivo is deep within your motivation for Sinning," spoke Adalo.

"Yeah, okay," muttered Aviva as she closed her arms.
Zayden quickly sprinted through the Academy's fields as small Fire flowed around his body.

Aviva saw him, *"He's going to hurt himself again,"* she thought.
Zayden looked back, "Oh hey—"

But then he bumped into someone and fell on the ground.
"—I found the wristband!" informed Veny.

"Wait what—" Zayden sat up.
"—Get off the ground!" yelled Veny, "I said I found the wristband!"

"—You did?!" tensed Zayden as quickly stood up, "Where is it?!"
"Follow me," he ordered, "Someone else is wearing it."

Zayden nodded, *"Who could have taken it?!"* he worried.
Veny turned and ran down the field as Zayden followed behind.

"There are just 15 minutes before the first stage begins!" announced Flare through the speakers that were connected on the walls of the Academy.

Veny stopped running.

44

Zayden was forced to stop just behind.

"Look," Veny pointed at someone, "He has it."
The two of them hid behind bushes watching the participant whose back was turned.

Zayden saw him, "...We need to get closer," he whispered, "I want to know who it is."

Veny paused, "Let's just confront him and go from there," he smirked, "It'll save a whole lot of time."
"No no," denied Zayden, "Let's just wait it out a bit."
The two quietly moved closer to the participant with the wristband.
Zayden began, "Alright let's—" but then he turned to his right, "—Where'd you go?!"

Zayden put his head up, "What the—" he saw Veny running forward.
"—This'll save time!" yelled Veny.

But then the participant with the wristband quickly turned around, "—What the heck is going on?!" he freaked out.
Zayden's eyes widened as he jumped over the bushes, "Wait!" he yelled as he realized who it was, "—That's Reno!"

But Veny put out his arm, "—You stole something that wasn't yours!" he yelled as he Sinned boulders of Rocks out of the ground and forced it forward.

Reno saw the boulders coming, "—Wait what?!" he worried as he ran away, "I'm not ready to—"

But then Zayden jumped into Reno and crashed with him to the ground, "—Stay down!" he yelled.
The Boulders of Rock rapidly passed by above them.
"—Zayden?!" saw Reno, "What's the problem?!"

After a moment, Veny walked over to him, "Hand back the wristband," he ordered.
Reno saw him, "—W-Why?"

But Zayden stood up, "I'll take it from here," he assured, "He's a friend."

There was a pause as Veny looked to him and Reno, "…Why did I even bother," he murmured, "Javarus is always getting me stuck in his business."

"Uh—" uttered Reno.

"See you later Veny," waved Zayden.

"Sounds good to me sir," mocked Veny as he jumped over the bushes, "I'll let Javarus know to put a hold on the hunt." Zayden nodded then turned back.

Reno slowly stood up, "So I was—" But then Zayden quickly grabbed his wrist with the wristband.

"—Let go!" shrieked Reno as he struggled, "—It's not what you think! I just need to borrow it!"

After a moment, Zayden released the hold on Reno's hand, "…You know that's important to me," he recalled, "Why would you take it?"

Reno paused, "First of all, why are you so angry?" he asked as he rolled his wrist.

"—Because you know that wristband is important to me!" yelled Zayden, "I just said that!"

"Oh yeah…you did just say that," remembered Reno, "Hey Zayden, can I borrow your wristband?" he asked.

"—What?!" uttered Zayden, "Reno! You're so—" but then he stopped talking.

Reno waited, "…I'm so what?" he asked. There was a pause as Zayden relaxed, "You're really something else," he snickered.

"—What do you mean?!" asked Reno, "I'm just asking to borrow your wristband!"

"Yeah…" spoke Zayden, "Right after you took it without my permission."

"Oh," heard Reno, "You're right," he admitted, "Sorry about that, but can I borrow it?"

"Why?" asked Zayden.

"Because of that whole thing with your Dad's Sinning Power within this wristband," recalled Reno, "I think if I wear it, I'll have a good shot at passing the first stage!"

46

"Oh…" murmured Zayden.

"—So please!" begged Reno, "I really need it to pass the competition! Specially to teach someone a lesson in respect!" Reno began punching the air.

"What did you get yourself into?" snickered Zayden. "Some wannabe cool guy named Soro!" recalled Reno, "He disrespected my lady! You believe that?!"

"Soro…" thought Zayden, *"He was Reno's roommate on the ship if I remember right."*

Reno stopped punching the air, "But Soro's not to be taken lightly," he spoke, "He's really strong," he thought about the blue spark that occurred when he put his hand on Soro's shoulder.

"Okay…let's just ignore this Soro guy," Zayden brushed if off, "But what if I'm in a situation and I—"

"What situation?!" uttered Reno, "You're already strong enough! Has the wristband ever protected you before?!"

"…Well—no," answered Zayden, "I've never really seen it do anything…"

"That's because you never truly needed it," remarked Reno.

"But my Mother gave it to me…" muttered Zayden, "And if you wear the wristband during the first stage and it works, you'll be disqualified…"

"Yeah, so?"

"I don't want the risk of you leaving…" murmured Zayden, "I need you here more than anyone—"

"Come on man!" broke in Reno, "Don't worry about me, this whole competition is one step closer to your dream of becoming a Full-Fledged Sinner! Remember that!"

"—Hey but don't you always remind me that people say becoming Full-Fledged is impossible?!" recalled Zayden.

"Well—" snickered Reno, "I said that because I was jealous of how strong and determined you always were…" remarked Reno, "But now I realize that it's possible that you could become Full-Fledged, because you want it that bad!"

There was a pause, "Oh," heard Zayden, "Thanks!" he smiled.

"—Will all participants make their way to the southwest side of the field!" announced Flare through the speakers, "The first stage is beginning in two minutes!"

"—Oh man only two minutes?!" freaked out Reno, "Zayden please?!" he asked again, "I really need the wristband, it might work for me!"

Zayden took a moment, "…Okay fine," he allowed, "Just know the wristband is your responsibility to keep safe, so please don't lose it."

Reno smiled, "—Thank you!" he celebrated as the two of them made their way back to the Academy's southwest field.

"—You're going to learn today Soro!" Reno was confident.

After a moment, all the participants were scattered on the field facing Adalo and Flare.

"Good morning to everyone!" smiled Flare with Adalo beside her, "Welcome to the first stage! I will begin by calling out everybody's name to see if they are here or not!"

Kaesar came up from behind the participants, *"Zayden's wristband is now on Reno…"* he saw.

Zayden turned back, "Oh hey Kaesar," he spoke. Kaesar paused as he looked to his wrist.

"…What are you looking at?" asked Zayden.

"…Nothing," Kaesar eyed back up, "I wonder what Flare has to say about the first stage."

Reno turned to the right, "Hey Kaesar—Wait, did you say Flare?!" he realized.

Reno looked forward far ahead, "—Hey Flare!" he yelled and waved to her, "Make sure you watch me closely when I start Sinning okay!"

"Reno…" sighed Zayden, "Focus on what she has to say instead of her appearance, alright?"

"Yeah sure," giggled Reno as he continued to wave, "No problem."

Kaesar looked to him, "He's not focused at all," he murmured.

By now, Flare called out most of the participants' as she got a response back.

She continued, "—Participant Rajaul!" she called out.

There was a moment of silence.

"—Is participant Rajaul here?" addressed Flare. Again, it was quiet.

Small Fire arose from the side, "—What the heck?!" angered Dedrian looking around, "Where did Rajaul run off to?!"

"Well that is unfortunate!" announced Flare, "Participant Rajaul is officially disqualified from the competition!"

My luck is getting better by the day!" thought Reno, *"Another one is out before the competition even begun!"*

"Wasn't Rajaul with Dedrian from before?" recalled Zayden.

"...I don't remember too well," spoke Kaesar, "Maybe..."

"Who cares!" rejoiced Reno, "He's out and that's fine with me!"

"—Hey Zayden!" shouted Dedrian as he marched over to him and grabbed his collar, "What did you do to Rajaul?!"

"—What do you mean?!" asked Zayden as he was held by Dedrian.

Everyone turned to them.

"—You must've done something!" remarked Dedrian, "You were reckless interrupting my fight with your pal! And you act without thinking!"

The grip on Zayden became tighter as he struggled, "I have no—"

"—You're lying!" shouted Dedrian as Fire appeared around his body, "—Where's Rajaul?!"

"—Uh," groaned Zayden.

"—Kaesar, do something!" yelled Reno, "He's Sinning now!"

But then Adalo vanished into Smoke beside Flare and reappeared in front of Zayden and Dedrian.

"—Adalo?!" the others saw him.

49

Kaesar's attention was caught.

Adalo broke up Dedrian's arm from Zayden's collar, "—What do you think you're doing," he looked to Dedrian.

Kaesar was stunned as he saw Adalo up close in that position, *"I've seen something like this before..."* he recalled, *"—But where?!"*

"He did something to Rajaul!" yelled Dedrian as he pointed to Zayden, "I'm sure of it!"

"No I—"

"It doesn't matter what happened before," remarked Adalo, "We have to begin this stage now."

Fire began surrounding Dedrian again.

"Save your heat for the days to come," insisted Adalo, "If you make it that far."

"I will make it that far!" stated Dedrian, "You can bet on it!"

Adalo paused, "...Are you sure?" he spoke.

Dedrian's aura was red, "I'm confident!" he tensed.

Zayden took a few steps back to Reno and Kaesar.

"Hm," heard Adalo, "For that reason, you are the first to begin the stage."

"I don't even know what this stage is about!"

"—Flare will explain," remarked Adalo, "So till then, I suggest you keep quiet."

Dedrian looked away as the Fire around him stayed.

"Will all the participants stand in a circle!" addressed Flare.

Adalo looked to Dedrian, "And you go to the middle and wait," he spoke.

The participants followed Flare's orders and made a circle with Dedrian in the middle. Adalo walked back to Flare on one end of the circle.

"With Rajaul being disqualified!" addressed Flare, "That means there are 24 participants competing in the first stage!"

The participants listened.

"I'm counting 23," Adalo spoke quietly to her right.

"...It's Soro," informed Flare, "He told me early in the morning that he would like to go last in the first stage," she recalled, "...And I told him that's perfectly fine."

50

"Hm, understandable, that would be good for everyone," accepted Adalo, "It would cause less tension." "Exactly..." muttered Flare, "Though I'm not going to lie, it's going to be uncomfortable when he arrives..."

"Really?" Adalo was surprised, "I thought you talked to him when he handed in his form."

"I did," recalled Flare, "But it's not like I wasn't nervous...I was shaking on the inside..." she remembered, "And now since I know he's going to be more serious, I don't know what to expect..."

There was a moment of silence.

"—Can we go on with this!" shouted Dedrian from the middle.

Adalo looked to him, "Go on Flare," he spoke. Flare nodded and took a step forward, "Welcome to the first stage!" she greeted and went on, "This stage is quite simple, same goes for the other two but anyhow, this stage consists of two parts!"

The participants listened.

"The first part will take place here!" addressed Flare, "We will test your combat awareness as one of our instructors will attempt to tag you in however way they feel fit, and you must evade all of their attacks for 5 minutes! If the instructor comes into contact with you in any way, you are eliminated and you must leave the Academy at once!"

The participants nodded.

"Then once all the participants have had their turn," continued Flare, "The ones who have passed will come back inside the Academy to do the second portion to complete the first stage! With all that said, good luck!"

There were some claps given.

Zayden was feeling out his collar at the side of the circle with Reno and Kaesar.

"Are you good Zayden?" Reno asked him.

Zayden took a moment, "...I'm great," he smirked, "Better than ever!"

"That's what I like to hear!" tensed Reno.

Zayden heard Reno and smiled.

51

He then turned and saw Kaesar lost in thought, "...What's gotten you so confused?" he asked.

"—I-I'm fine," snapped Kaesar, but in his thoughts, *"...I know I've seen something like that with Adalo before,"* he tried to recall, *"The same kind of scenario too...I...I just can't remember it..."*

"Alright, we're ready to begin," addressed Flare, "Will the instructors come out!"
Exactly 25 instructors jumped over the participants and stood in a straight line. All of them covered in black clothes aside from their face.

"Will one of you please start out the first stage with this young Sinner?" asked Flare.
One of the instructors came forward and stood face to face in front of Dedrian.

There was a pause as everyone watched on.
"And the 5-minute timer..." went on Flare, "Has started!"

The instructor quickly burst forward and went in for a grab.
Dedrian quickly stepped to the side and put out his arms, "—I'm not in a good mood right now!" he shouted as he Sinned a wave of Fire out of his hands.

But then the instructor jumped over the Fire and landed a distance away.
Dedrian smirked, "You're not coming near me at all," he stated.

The instructor burst again as the two continued the stage.

Javarus walked behind Zayden, he put his hand on his shoulder, "Dedrian is as focused as ever," he spoke.
Zayden looked to his right, "Oh Javarus," he saw, "And yeah I can tell he's serious."

Veny came up to his other side, "And he wants to hurt you," he stated, "You must be worried."
Zayden looked to his left, "...Not really," he spoke, "The competition is serious, so Dedrian probably felt a lot of pressure when his friend didn't show up," he went on, "I don't think it's anything more than that."

Everyone watched on as Dedrian excelled in the first stage.

"—And the five minutes are up!" announced Flare, "Participant Dedrian, you have passed part one of this stage!"
Some participants clapped for him while others remained silent.

Dedrian stopped Sinning. After a moment, he walked to one end of the circle, but stopped beside Zayden, "I'm hoping you pass," he remarked, "I'm itching to tackle you down," he then continued walking.

Zayden turned back and glared at Dedrian, *"He's actually a lot more serious,"* he thought as he saw him walk to the other side of the circle.
"Flare..." giggled Reno, "—Hey Flare, you should spend five minutes with me!"

But then Kaesar gave a friendly hit on the back of Reno's head, "That's enough!" he told him, "Don't say stupid things like that!"

Reno rubbed the back of his head, "—You didn't have to hit me!" he yelled.
"You deserved it," exhaled Kaesar, "I'm only doing what's good for you."

"—Yeah right!" Reno eyed away.
Flare called out another participant. She was doing well for a few minutes, but eventually got tagged, two others followed and failed the stage being sent home.

"—Next we have participant Aviva Kallent!" called out Flare.

Adalo waited for her inside the circle.
"Make your way into the middle and may the instructor please come out!" addressed Flare.

Some participants began clapping for her, "It's really a Kallent!" one cheered.

Aviva heard the others, "—I don't want to do this!" she agonized.
"Aviva," called out Adalo, "Come here."

Aviva looked to him. After a moment, she walked to the middle and stood face to face.

53

Adalo leaned over and whispered something in her ear.

"—Tell me the secret!" beamed Kara outside on the circle.

"—Really?!" screeched Aviva as she heard Adalo, "Is she watching?!"

Adalo nodded.

Aviva then turned to the instructor, "—Start the timer Flare!" she tensed, "Now I have to win!" she began to Sin as she had a pink aura around her.

"My belief for her motivation was correct," recalled Adalo as he walked away.

"And the timer..." addressed Flare, "Has started!"

The instructor quickly charged forward.

But then a pink flash appeared as Aviva Sinned five clones of herself.

"—What's this?!" uttered Reno.

The five clones of Aviva surrounded the instructor, "This'll take more than 5 minutes," she determined.

The instructor looked around at all the clones, "—Of course a Kallent would have a move like this!" he groaned. He ran towards Aviva as he went in for a grab.

"—She isn't going to move?" a participant saw.

But then one of the clones Sinned a pink barrier in front herself.

The was forced to stop, "I have a tough one today," he murmured as the two continued the stage.

"Farmake Sinners are always fun to watch," snickered Flare next to Adalo.

Zayden recalled the Power behind her Sinning: *"We usually don't have any abilities like Fire or Ice, our powers are a different category,"* he remembered what Aviva told him, *"It's hard to explain actually."*

But as everyone watched on, Kaesar made his way around the circle towards Adalo.

He stood behind him, "...Have we met before?" he spoke.

Adalo turned around, "Don't distract—" but then he stopped talking at the sight of Kaesar.

There was a moment of silence as the two looked to each other.

Flare turned her head and carefully listened.

"…What did you ask?" spoke Adalo.

Kaesar paused, "Have you and I met before?" he repeated, "We must've fought or did something with each other," he recalled, "When you broke the fight with Zayden and Dedrian, something triggered in my mind…"

Adalo took a moment, "…I've never seen you before," he stated.

"But—"

"—Adalo, are you sure?" broke in Flare, "You've travelled all around the world, there's always a chance you have encountered this young boy…think hard about it."

Kaesar looked to her, then back to Adalo.

"…*Flare,*" thought Adalo, *"You didn't have to say that…"*

Flare looked to him, "So did—"

"—Time's up!" addressed Adalo out loud.

Everyone looked to him.

"Good job Aviva," went on Adalo as he faced the middle, "You have passed part one."

"—That time went by fast!" uttered a participant.

"…Yeah it did," thought Kaesar, *"That was a quick a five minute…"*

Adalo began walking inside the circle, "There's no time for questions," he spoke out loud to Kaesar.

Kaesar saw him go.

Aviva stood in the middle and stopped Sinning, "That was fast," she murmured as her other clones popped.

Adalo looked to her, "Yeah I—"

"—Hold on!" yelled Marubee from the side.

Everyone quickly turned to her, "—What are you going to say Marubee?!" beamed Kara next to her with a lollipop in her mouth.

"—That wasn't five minutes!" remarked Marubee, "I'm not going to stay here and act like it was!"

There was pause as Aviva saw her.

"—I'm not letting her go just because she's a Kallent!" stated Marubee.

Marubee was the participant that argued with Aviva the night before about her being lucky to be Lavivo's sister.

"—Yeah!" someone else agreed with Marubee, "She's isn't lying! That couldn't have been five minutes!"

Some of the participants began yelling.

"Calm down calm down," assured Adalo.

"Why should I be calm?!" opposed Marubee, "This is clearly unfair, Flare had the timer anyways, so how would you know when the five minutes were up?!"

Adalo paused. Flare opened her mouth, but had nothing to say.

Marubee added, "Where's the—"

"—Let's be honest," broke in Adalo, "Was Aviva really going to lose this?"

There was a moment of thought amongst the participants.

"—Well of course not!" beamed Kara, "She's Aviva! She wouldn't lose!"

Marubee looked to her, "What are you—"

"—Exactly," agreed Adalo, "So let's not waste time and just pass Aviva for part one."

After a moment, a few began clapping for her.

"—What?!" uttered Marubee as she looked around, "...I get it," she muttered, "Just because she's Aviva, she get's a free pass, whatever..."

"—Adalo wait!" called out Aviva, "I didn't ask for—"

"You passed alright," Adalo turned and remarked, "That's all that matters."

There was a pause as Aviva saw a change in Adalo's expression. After a moment, she walked back into the circle.

"—You just had to be on Aviva's side, right?" Marubee complained to Kara.

"—Well Adalo isn't wrong!" smiled Kara, "No doubt Aviva would've won that!"

Marubee stayed quiet.

"...I'm super sorry if I made you mad Marubee!" apologized Kara with her hands together.

"—Participant Kara Cherry!" announced Flare, "Please make your way into the middle!"

"Wish me luck!" beamed Kara.

Marubee looked away with her arms crossed.

"—Well it's okay!" smiled Kara as she ran into the middle of the circle, "—I'm always ready to go!"

An instructor jumped from the line of instructors and faced her.

There was a pause, "—Five minutes on the timer!" addressed Flare, "Begin!"

Kara stuck out her tongue, "Na na try to get me!" she teased the instructor and ran away. She began to Sin as a bright orange aura flowed around her.

"—Farmake Sinners," groaned the instructor as he burst forward and jumped to her.

"—You're crazy!" chuckled Kara.

"How did I—" uttered the instructor as he went through Kara's body and fell to the ground.

Kara chuckled.

The instructor looked up as there were three clones of Kara surrounding him, "Not another one," he exhaled. All three clones took out a lollipop and put it in their mouths, "—Bet you can't stop my Kara clones!" they all snickered the as the stage continued.

Kaesar walked back from Adalo to Zayden and Reno, "She's a funny one," he murmured about Kara on the way.

"—Where'd you go?" asked Javarus as he put his hand on Kaesar's shoulder.

"—What?" turned Kaesar, "Oh, I just needed to talk to Adalo about something…"

"What was it about?" asked Veny.

"Why should I tell you," opposed Kaesar, "Who are you anyways?"

"Oh Kaesar," spoke Zayden, "They're just…people I've talked to."

Kaesar heard him, "Okay…" he murmured, "But still, can you get this big guy to keep his hands to himself."

"—Oh sorry," snickered Javarus as he took his hand off.

"You talk to odd people Zayden," muttered Kaesar.

Reno quickly stopped waving to Flare, "—What is that supposed to mean?!" he yelled and butted his head at Kaesar.

"—Back up," insisted Kaesar, "Go back to drooling over someone who's clearly not interested in you."

"—Don't say that!" Reno backed off and pointed, "I'll prove you wrong!" he declared, "Flare and me will be together! You're just a hater along with Soro!"

Many of the participants quickly looked to Reno as they were shocked.

"Did I hear that right?" one worried.

"I think I heard the same..." another one muttered.

"Hm, you said Soro," recalled Kaesar, "Right?" Zayden faced them, *"Why's everyone worked up over this guy..."*

"—Yeah!" nodded Reno, "And he insulted my lady!"

"—You talked to Soro?!" Veny burst to Reno, "When and where?!" he held him by the arms.

"—Veny?!" saw Reno, "What happened?!"

"—Tell me when and where did you see Soro!" yelled Veny.

"—Yesterday close to midnight!" uttered Reno, "Why are you guys acting so worried?!"

"Do you know who Soro—"

"I know who Soro is!" went on Reno, "I can handle him myself! You guys don't even have to get involved!"

Some of the participants began to worry, "I-I didn't know Soro was here..." one murmured "I don't feel like competing anymore..."

"—Are you that clueless?!" Veny shouted at Reno, "Do you really know who Soro is?!"

"—Let go of Reno!" yelled Zayden.

"—Yeah, I do know who Soro is!" shouted Reno, "Well-uh—"

"—He's the son of the only Sinner who has ever reached Full-Fledged," stated Javarus.

"—A Full-Fledged Sinner?!" heard Zayden as he tensed, "Are you serious?!"

Veny let go of Reno.

"Yeah Zayden," remarked Javarus, "It's understandable if you're—"

"—You don't know how good it is to hear that," smirked Zayden.

Most others were shocked to hear him.
Zayden put his fist up to his chest and clenched, "—That means becoming a Full-Fledged Sinner is possible!" he tensed, *"I'll reach that goal for the both of us!"* he thought about his Mother.

"Zayden..." muttered Veny, "Stop celebrating..."
"—Why?!" he asked, "Now I'm just waiting to see Soro!"

"How can you say that..." groaned Veny, "Why would you want to see him..."
"—Why not?!" opposed Zayden, "Because of him, now I know that—"

"—Just stop talking!" snapped Veny as he went in with a punch.
"What are you—" saw Zayden.

But then Javarus quickly grabbed Veny's arm.
Veny had small tears in his eyes, "—Don't ever celebrate the likes of Damon and Soro!" he yelled.
Zayden was stunned, *"—What happened?!"* he thought, *"I didn't mean for Veny to act like this!"*

"Relax Veny," assured Javarus as he held him back.

"I-I'm" uttered Zayden, "I didn't mean anything wrong, I don't—"
But then Dedrian burst up and punched Zayden in the jaw, "—I'll stop you right now if you have the slightest thought of becoming Full-Fledged!" he shouted with his fist inflamed in Fire.

Zayden was sent back as he crashed to the ground.
"—That wasn't fair!" yelled Reno as he rushed to him.

A small drop of blood came down from Zayden's mouth, "—Then try to stop me!" he yelled as he stood up, "Because I think about becoming Full-Fledged everyday!"

Dedrian's back was turned, but then he looked to Zayden, "—Why would you want to be Full-Fledged?!" he groaned, "Damon is a Full-Fledged Sinner, and do you see what he does with that Power?!"

Zayden took his hand off his jaw, "I don't know who Damon is!" he remarked, "But I'll control whatever Power that comes with me achieving my dream!"

"—You're so ignorant!" shouted Dedrian as Fire surrounded him, "—I make it my priority to cut down anyone who thinks of such things!"

Dedrian was in deep thought, *"For her, I will not allow this!"* he recalled about his Mother back home, *"I'll keep my word and make sure nobody tries to become a Full-Fledged Sinner ever again!"*

Back in the circle, the timer beeped, "Congratulations Kara!" addressed Flare, "You have successfully passed part one!"

Kara stopped Sinning as her clones popped, "You never got me!" she chuckled.

The instructor's breath was heavy as he was on one knee.

Adalo took a step forward.

But Flare stopped him, "—The participants are starting to find out Soro's here," she remarked, "And they're not taking it too well."

Adalo turned his head, "—Not again with these too," he saw as he turned into Smoke.

Zayden Sinned as Fire surrounded around him, "You make it your priority to cut down such people?!" he smirked, "What are you trying to say?!"

Dedrian's Fire grew larger, "—I think you already know!" he smirked back, "I've been itching to tackle you down!"

Zayden paused, "—So am I!" he tensed.

Outside of the circle, Zayden and Dedrian burst towards each other as they burned the grass beneath.

"—Somebody has to stop this!" uttered someone as everyone watched on.

"—You're mine!" Zayden and Dedrian shouted as they went in with punch.

But then Smoke appeared in the middle of them, "—It's gone far enough," groaned a figure.

"—It's Adalo!" saw the others.

Adalo had his hands out as he Sinned.

Smoke quickly enclosed Zayden and Dedrian. "—What the hell is this?!" angered Dedrian.

"—Where did it come from?!" coughed Zayden. The Fire around them was quickly faded away.

"—Dedrian," called out Adalo, "Go inside the Academy and wait for the rest of us to finish." Dedrian coughed and looked to Adalo, the two locked eyes.

"—No!" shouted Zayden, "We need to finish this!" "—You still have to compete!" Adalo told him, "You two can fight all you want after this stage, now's not the time."

There was a moment of silence. Dedrian turned to Zayden, "Hm, I was so close to tackling him," he groaned as he walked away from the circle.

There was a pause as Zayden saw him go. But then Dedrian stopped with his back turned, "I'm not going to allow you to become Full-Fledged," he remarked, "I have a promise to keep."

Everyone heard him, "...Why do you care," muttered Zayden.

After moment, Dedrian continued walking.

Zayden turned back facing the circle. Reno ran in front of him, "Are you okay?!" he asked.

Zayden opened his mouth feeling out his jaw, "I have to get him back for this one," he tensed, "He won't get the last say."

Reno nodded as the two walked back into the circle. Flare saw them, but then turned her head to Kara in the middle, "—You can walk back into the circle!" she smiled, "Wonderful job!"

Kara looked to her, "It was nothing," she chuckled. She turned and burst beside Marubee, "—Did you see that?!" she beamed. "Yeah, you did okay," Marubee brushed it off, "But did you hear about Soro?"

"—What about him?!" asked Kara. Marubee paused, "...He's here," she murmured.

61

"—Where where?!" Kara looked around, "I don't seem him!"

"I mean it's safe to say he's going to be here…" corrected Marubee.

Kara's eyes widened as she jumped, "Amazing!" she cheered.

"What?!"

"That's amazing I said!" repeated Kara, "Soro comes from a strong family, he's the son of Damon after all! He's super famous!"

"I'm telling you this for your own well-being," advised Marubee, "Don't go touchy touchy with him like you did with Aviva."

"—You can't stop me!" denied Kara.

All the participants continued talking about Soro.

"—Will everyone settle down," addressed Adalo. There was a moment as all the participants quieted.

Adalo went on, "As you may have found out, Soro is in fact here," he revealed, "But that does not mean we're going to put a halt in the competition," he pointed to a participant, "You there, you're next."

"—M-Me?!" uttered the participant whose legs were unsteady, "I-I don't want to go…" he murmured.

"What did you say?" asked Adalo.

"—You heard me!" shouted the participant, "—I'm out! This competition isn't worth the risk of my life!"

Everyone heard him, *"You can't be serious that Soro is this strong?!"* worried Reno.

"That's surprising…" muttered Adalo, "Go back to the academy, pack your stuff, and leave immediately."

The participant turned and walked back inside the Academy.

Another participant raised his hand, "I-I would like to leave too…" he muttered.

"Another one?" groaned Adalo, "Follow the other one who quit, and that goes for anyone else who has doubts, leave now."

After a moment, two other participants quietly walked out.

"Hey Reno..." murmured Kaesar, "You can leave if you want."

"Uh—" uttered Reno, *"—Should I?!"* he thought.

"—Reno isn't going anywhere!" assured Zayden, he put his arm around Reno's shoulders, "Am I right?"

Reno snapped, "Uh—yeah you're right!" he tensed, "—I'm here to stay!"

Kaesar saw the two, "I wonder how you'd be if Zayden wasn't here," he spoke.

"—What?!" uttered Reno, "'What's that supposed to—"

"—Reno!" called out Flare, "Please make your way into the circle!"

"—Flare!" shrieked Reno as he took Zayden's arm off him, "Coming!"

"Good luck!" wished Zayden as Reno ran off to the middle.

But then Zayden turned his head back, he saw Javarus and Veny outside the circle.

"You can't act like this," spoke Javarus, "You have to calm down," he advised Veny who was sitting down.

"—You want me to calm?!" groaned Veny, "This is my chance," he stated, "When Soro comes, I'm going to kill him...and nobody will stop me."

Zayden walked over to them, "Hey...is Veny okay?" he asked.

Javarus turned back, "Now's not the best time Zayden..." he spoke.

But then Veny stood up and wiped his eyes, "Oh it's you," he spoke and turned around.

Zayden looked to him, "About the whole thing about becoming a Full-Fledged Sinner..." he recalled, "I didn't mean to—"

"—Don't say anything," broke in Veny, "I shouldn't have raised my hand to you."

"No, that's fine," assured Zayden, "I shouldn't have been so loud about it."

There was a pause, "Yeah..." murmured Veny, "Let's just move on from this..."

Zayden heard him as he nodded, "But if it's okay with you talking about it..." he spoke up, "Do you have a history with Soro or something?" he asked, "I should've been more careful of my words..."

"Yeah, I do," remarked Veny, "But it's my issue and I'll take care of it."
Zayden listened.

"...Let's go watch your friend Reno," spoke Veny.
"Yeah, for sure," Zayden turned back to the circle.

"Yeah..." exhaled Javarus, "But he's supposed to go to the middle of the circle...".
Reno burst all the way to Flare on the other end, "—So how bout that five minutes I mentioned earlier!" he recalled.

"—Participant Reno," addressed Flare, "I said go to the middle, not to me."
"But—"
"—Go to the middle," broke in Adalo.

"But I need to tell Flare something!" whined Reno.
He kept it up as he faced Adalo and Flare.
Adalo shook his head, "Will an instructor come out?" he spoke up.

An instructor quickly followed the call and stood a distance behind Reno.
"You're still not going to pay attention?" thought Adalo.

Reno didn't see the instructor.
"—Well!" went on Flare, "The timer is set, begin!"

"—Oh, you mean the timer for our 5 minutes?!" smiled Reno looking to Flare.
"—He can't be serious?" uttered Kaesar.
"He needs to focus now!" thought Zayden.

But then the instructor charged towards Reno from behind.
"—Reno turn around!" yelled Zayden.

"—Looks like I got an easy one!" smirked the instructor as he went in for a grab.
But then the wristband on Reno had a quick spark.

"—Turn around you idiot!" shouted Kaesar.

"—Who are you calling an idiot?!" yelled Reno as he turned to his right.

Suddenly the wristband shined in green as two Boulders were Sinned out of the ground.

"What the—" uttered the instructor.

The Boulders rushed in from both sides and smashed the instructor in between.

Kaesar's jaw dropped as everyone was shocked.

After a moment, the Rocks fell apart as the instructor fell on his back unconscious.

"I hope nobody noticed anything…" worried Zayden.

Adalo squinted, *"Interesting,"* he thought.

Reno quickly turned around, "—Alright let's do this!" he tensed as he punched the air, "Start the timer Flare!"

"…I already did," she murmured.

"Huh?!" uttered Reno looking around. After a moment, he put his head down, *"Who did this?!"* he thought as he saw the instructor laying in front of him.

Reno kneeled as he put his hand on the Boulder beside him.

"Y-Yeah—good job Reno!" cheered Zayden as he clapped, "Y-You did the right move there!"

After a moment, some of the other participants began clapping.

Reno patted the Boulder of Rock a few times, but then he noticed his wrist, *"Oh wait—this was the wristband's doing,"* he realized.

Reno quickly stood up and turned to Flare, "—How was that?!" he smiled, "Pretty impressive right?!"

There was a pause, "Reno passes," Adalo whispered to Flare, "The instructor is unconscious."

"—Congratulations participant Reno!" announced Flare, "You have passed part one!"

"Yes!" cheered Reno as he quickly burst to her, "Hey so—"

But then Zayden rushed in and pulled him outside the circle.

Everyone turned to them, "…Just call out the next participant," spoke Adalo.

65

Flare nodded as she called for the next one.

Outside the circle, Zayden grabbed Reno's collar, "—What did I tell you?!" he shook him, "The wristband is too risky, you're going to get caught!"

"—Relax!" assured Reno, "Nobody noticed!"

"I'm sure everyone noticed!" yelled Zayden.

"I told you before!" went on Reno, "You have your own goals to aim for! Don't worry about me okay?!"

"But—"

"I'll be fine!" smiled Reno.

Zayden took a moment, but then he let go of him, "One day I'm really going to get mad at you," he snickered, "Then you'll see it coming."

Reno tensed, "—But then I'll use this wristband against you!" he remarked.

"—Do you not listen?!" yelled Zayden as he grabbed Reno's collar, "I just said to be careful with it!" he shook him again.

Reno's head bobbed up and down as he brushed Zayden off.

Aviva had her head turned as she watched on, *"I think I have an idea on what's happening…"* she thought.

The next two participants were eliminated as the instructor quickly tagged them.

In the circle formation, Javarus was with Veny, "Is everything okay now?" he asked him.

"I told you I'm fine," spoke Veny, he then yelled, "—Adalo!" he called out, "I would like to go next!"

Adalo looked to him, *"What's gotten into him?"* he saw a change in his expression, "Very well," he spoke, "Make your way into the middle."

Veny slowly walked inside the circle.

"…This doesn't feel right," worried Javarus.

Zayden stopped shaking Reno, *"It's Veny's turn,"* he heard and turned to the middle.

An instructor stood a distance in front of Veny.

"—And the five-minute timer…" went on Flare, "Has started!"

There was a moment of silence as a dark green aura formed on Veny's body.

The instructor saw him, *"Is he even focused on the stage?"* he thought.

Javarus' eyes widened, "Veny you—"

Suddenly Veny Sinned the Rock underneath him as it lifted him high up the air.

"—We need to take steps back!" yelled Javarus.

Everyone looked up to the sky as Veny levitated on top of a Rock, he was as high as the Academy. But then Veny roared as he put out his arm and Sinned large chunks of Rock out of the ground.

"—Veny!" called out Javarus, "Don't think about—"

"—Soro!" shouted Veny as pieces of the ground flew up the air, "—You're somewhere watching!" he yelled as he pushed his hand forward, "This is a statement for you!"

"—Take cover!" shouted a participant.

All the sharp large Rocks were rapidly Sinned towards the instructor.

"—This is too sudden!" uttered the instructor.

He dodged to the right, but then another one hit him and forced him down to his knee.

"—Adalo!" called out Flare, "Do you think this is too much?!"

Several Boulders of Rocks knocked the instructor on the ground, they crashed on top of him one by one.

"—He's lost it," remarked Marubee.

"What does he think he's doing?" thought Aviva.

Dust surrounded the field as the several more Boulders rushed down towards the instructor.

"—This is all about Soro!" recalled Zayden as he coughed, *"Every boulder is just for him!"*

Nobody could see the instructor underneath all the Rocks.

"—Veny!" shouted Javarus, "Stop!"

"—He's going to kill him!" worried Reno.

The participants' circle was broken as everyone backed away.

"—Adalo do something!" Flare raised her voice as she turned her head, "You have—"
But then Smoke covered the Rocks on top of the instructor and on the field.

"I've seen this type of Smoke before!" saw Kaesar, a quick flash of memory went through his mind, *"—What was that?!"* the images showed Dark Smoke flowing around a room, *"Does it have to do with—"*

"—Why are you interfering!" shouted Veny as he looked to the ground from high up and saw the Smoke. But then a figure of Smoke appeared behind him, "—Show yourself!" he yelled.

The Smoke went away.
"—Adalo?!" saw Veny.

Adalo levitated in the air as he put his arm forward. "Why are you—"

Adalo Sinned a heavy wind into Veny's stomach.
"—Uh," groaned Veny as he stepped back on the Rock. Adalo quickly rushed in and pushed Veny's shoulder with one hand.

"Wait—" uttered Veny as he fell off the Rock. Adalo watched him fall through the air, "You can't be so careless," he groaned as faced palm down and Sinned another heavy Wind.

Veny was bashed by the Wind as he was pushed rapidly down the air.
"—Veny!" yelled Javarus as he ran, "—Uh," he caught Veny on his shoulder, "I knew you were going to do something reckless!"

But then Smoke appeared around Veny's body, "What's this?!" uttered Javarus.
Adalo looked down from the air as he had a gray aura, "Javarus!" he called out.

Javarus and everyone looked up.
"Take Veny inside and leave him alone," spoke Adalo, "When he wakes up, tell him that he has passed part one."

Javarus was surprised, "But—"
"—However!" continued Adalo as he began coming down the air, "If anyone chooses to be careless again, you will

68

be disqualified with no warnings, do we understand?" he landed on the ground as he faced the rest.

There was a moment as the participants slowly nodded.

Javarus took Veny on his shoulders back inside the Academy.

Zayden watched them go as he recalled a moment with Veny: *"Don't ever celebrate the likes of Damon and Soro!"* he remembered his words, he then paused, *"...Just what happened to Veny?"* he wanted to know.

Adalo walked back to Flare, "It's essential that you have control of your Sinning Abilities," he spoke out loud, "Lose control, and you're bound to kill someone you don't intend to."

The participants listened.

Flare saw Adalo, "You didn't have Sin such a strong Wind to him..." she murmured.

"It was a message to all of them," stated Adalo.

Flare paused, "Usually we would disqualify a participant for this type of action," she spoke, "So why did you pass him?"

Adalo stood beside her, "His reason for his anger is not for Soro..." he remarked, "It's for Damon, I found it understandable so I let it go."

Flare listened.

"Call for the next participant," spoke Adalo.

Flare nodded, "—Participant Marubee Tasuki!" she addressed, "Please come to the middle of the circle!"

"Finally," exhaled Marubee as she began walking.

Everyone turned to face her.

Aviva saw Marubee, *"You talked down to me,"* she recalled, *"Now let's see what you're made of."*

"—Let's go Green!" cheered Kara referring to Marubee's hair.

After a moment, the instructor stood a distance in front of Marubee.

Marubee saw him.

"And the five-minute timer..." went on Flare, "Has started!"

The aura around Marubee turned green.

69

"—What kind of Farmake Sinning do you have?" asked the instructor.

Marubee had a stern look, "You'll see," she spoke, "You wouldn't want to come near me that's for sure."
"Really?" snickered the instructor, "Why not?"

Kara was excited, *"I wonder what Marubee's going to do this time!"* she waited.
But then the instructor quickly charged to Marubee, "If you're not going to move!" he yelled, "Then you wouldn't mind me tagging you!"

But then the curls on Marubee's hair rose, "—Let's try fear," she murmured.

The instructor continued running, "You shouldn't—" but then he stopped.
"—What happened?" uttered someone watching.

The instructor looked around the grass, "—Where are they coming from?!" he worried.

"Come on," thought Marubee, *"Why are people always afraid of this animal."*
The instructor looked down, *"—Snakes?!"* he saw and slowly backed away, *"When did snakes come on the field?!"*

"—Why is he freaking out?!" uttered Reno, "There's nothing around him, and Marubee doesn't look that scary!"

Everyone saw the instructor as his eyes widened.
"—No," yelled the instructor out loud, "I can't act like a child!" he jumped over the Snake hallucinations and ran again.

"—Trying again?" saw Marubee as her aura shined brighter.
More snakes began slithering beside her.

The instructor was forced to stop running, *"N-No—"* he fell back on his bum, *"I can't—"* he panicked as he crawled away, "—I'm not going to touch snakes to get to you!" he yelled out loud.

"Snakes?" Adalo heard him, *"Marubee's Ability must have something to do with illusions."*
The instructor was freaking out.

Marubee saw him, *"Just one more push,"* she thought.

The instructor heard slithers as he turned his head back, *"—These ones are darker!"* he saw.
The dark snakes opened their mouths and jumped onto him, "—I can't do this stage anymore!" panicked the instructor, "—Give her the win!" he quickly stood up rubbing his body, "—These Snakes won't go away!"

The participants watched on as they shocked, *"He's going to give up just because of Snakes?"* Kaesar was surprised.

The instructor sat on the ground with his eyes widened, "I-I-I can't d-do this..." he stuttered.
"—And the time is up!" announced Flare, "Participant Marubee has passed!"

Some participants began clapping for her.
"—Yes!" cheered Kara as overly clapped, "—Now Orange and Green have passed part one!" she smiled as she referred to their hair colours.

Aviva was in awe, *"She didn't even move,"* she thought, *"I've never seen something like that before..."* Marubee stopped Sinning as she walked back to the circle.
"—You scared the daylights out of him!" beamed Kara.

Marubee looked to her, "Yeah, I did," she recalled, "But I wanted to do other effects," she sighed.
"—Now you're getting ahead of yourself Marubee!" snickered Kara.

Marubee heard her, but then looked over to Aviva on the side, *"I wonder what I can do with her..."* she tensed.
After a moment, Flare called for the next participant as the stage was coming to its last turns.

Aviva looked to her right, *"Now time to find out something,"* she thought as she saw Zayden and Kaesar. "It should be our turn soon," Zayden spoke beside Kaesar, "You think we'll both make it?"

Kaesar heard him, "What makes you think we won't?" he asked.

"Oh I—"

But then Zayden was pulled from the circle, "Who's—" he uttered as he fell on his back.

Kaesar turned, *"It's probably nothing important,"* he thought and looked back to the middle.

Zayden opened his eyes, "—Aviva?!" he saw, "What do you want?" he sat up.

"—Cut the greetings," she remarked, "I want to know how Reno pulled off that Rock attack a while ago."

Zayden worried, *"—I can't let her know about the wristband!"* he thought and yelled, "How am I supposed to know?!"

"—Don't play dumb with me!" broke in Aviva, "Tell me the truth, I know that Reno is not that great of a Sinner, yet he pulled off that stunt with ease—especially with his back turned!"

"He just—" uttered Zayden as he stood up, "—Ask him yourself!" he blurted.

There was a pause.

"You're right…" murmured Aviva, she took out a strand of her hair.

"What are you—"

But then Aviva quickly whipped her strand of hair towards Reno's back, "—I will ask him myself!" she yelled as the hair attached to him.

"Wait—" saw Zayden.

"—Uh," Reno was pulled from the circle.

"That might not be the best idea!" worried Zayden.

"—Watch it!" shrieked Reno as he fell on his back beside the two, "—Zayden?!" he looked up and saw.

"Yeah I—"

Reno quickly stood up and turned to Aviva, "—And who are you?!" he asked, "Are you after me?!"

There was a pause, "Reno, this is Aviva," Zayden introduced the two, "Aviva, this is Reno."

"—I don't care about her name!" uttered Reno, "What does she want from me?!"

"—Nothing really," broke in Aviva, "I was just curious on how you Sinned back there, I believe there's more than what—"

72

"—I see!" smiled Reno, "So you're a fan?!"

"What—no, I'm not," denied Aviva, "I wanted to—"

"—No worries!" Reno put his fist up, "I'll tell you exactly what I did!"

"—And you're eliminated!" announced Flare as a participant got tagged, "Thanks for being a part of this competition!"

"It should be my turn anytime now..." thought Zayden.

But then Reno put his hand with the wristband forward, "I use this—"

"—No!" Zayden quickly came up from behind, "Don't even think about telling her anything!" he whispered as he put his hand over Reno's mouth.

Aviva saw the two, "Stop this—"

But then Reno swiped Zayden's arm off, "—I'm only going to say the truth!" he remarked, "Just trust me!"

"But you—"

Aviva put her hand in front of Zayden, "—That's what I wanted to hear," she looked to Reno, "So how did you Sin against the instructor?"

There was a pause as Zayden and Aviva looked to Reno.

"I'm a simple Sinner!" went on Reno, "I work hard everyday, I don't get distracted by anything, not even girls!"

Zayden heard him, *"What is he saying..."* he worried.

"My Sinning Ability is Rock, and I know just about everyway to use it!" went on Reno, "I have an awareness of a lion! I see and hear everything on any position of the battlefield! I won because of my skill! I am Reno, the great one!"

Zayden put his head down, *"Anything else would've been better,"* he sighed.

"Reno—the great one?" murmured Aviva.

"—Yeah!" smiled Reno.

Aviva gave a blank look.

"Well—I like that you're interested in me!" blurted Reno as he took steps back, "But I want to see the rest of the stage!"

"—Huh? Who said I was interested in you?!" denied Aviva, "I didn't even get the answer I was looking for!".

But then Reno quickly turned his back as he faced the circle, *"—I think that answer is also the truth!"* he thought, *"Sure the wristband helped, but I'm great too!"*

Aviva saw him.

After a moment, Zayden spoke up, "Well, there you have it," he snickered scratching his head.

There was a pause as Aviva turned back, "I have my ways," she stated then walked away, "—And I will find the truth about Reno's Sinning Ability!"

Zayden saw her go, "That was close," he murmured to himself, "And Reno thinks she's a fan."

But Aviva heard him and quickly turned around, "Tell him I'm not his fan," she exhaled, "That thought never crossed my mind."

Zayden snickered, "Alright, I might let him know," he spoke.

"Hm," Aviva turned back facing the circle.

Zayden relaxed as he walked back to Reno, "…Really?" he recalled, "Reno the great one…what were you even thinking?"

"--What do you mean?!" opposed Reno, "That's the perfect cover up!"

"Cover up for what?" spoke up Kaesar beside them.

"—Nothing!" they both uttered.

"—Participant Kaesar Kinnuan!" called out Flare, "You are next, please make your way into the middle!"

Kaesar turned to her, "About time," he spoke as he walked inside the circle.

"Good luck," wished Javarus as he came in from behind everyone.

"—Javarus?" Zayden turned around, "Oh yeah, you had to drop Veny back at the Academy…"

"Just following Adalo's orders," half smiled Javarus, "Did I miss anything?"

74

Zayden turned his head to the middle, "Nothing too important," he muttered, "But Kaesar was just called." Everyone looked to Kaesar in the middle.

But Kaesar had his head turned to Adalo, *"The moment with Zayden and Dedrian,"* he recalled Adalo's actions, *"The Smoke on the field and moves on Veny..."* he remembered, *"Why does it feels like I've seen it all before..."*

Adalo looked back at him, "—Will an instructor come out?" he spoke out loud.
An instructor walked on as he stood a distance in front of Kaesar.

But Kaesar had his eyes on Adalo.
"I suggest you turn and face the instructor in front of you," remarked Adalo, "It'll help you further onto the next stage."
Kaesar took a moment, "Yeah, you're right," he agreed as he faced the instructor.

"—And the five-minute timer," announced Flare, "Has begun!"
Kaesar put out his arm as he Sinned Streak of Ice out of his palm.

The instructor quickly jumped above it, "—Pretty straight forward!" he smirked.
But then Kaesar clenched his hand, "Thought to soon," he spoke as the Streak of Ice spiked up.

"Oh I didn't—" uttered the instructor as he barely avoided the Ice.
"That control," saw Marubee from the side, "He knows what he's doing."

"—That Ice is super pretty!" beamed Kara beside her, "And this time I don't see those mean eyes!"
"Huh?" heard Marubee, "What are you talking about?"

"I'll tell you about it soon!" chuckled Kara.
Kaesar's Sinning Ability was noticed by everyone.

"What do you make of this?" asked Flare beside Adalo.
There was a pause as Adalo stayed quiet and watched on
"...I'm glad you truly understand the situation now," remarked Flare.

The instructor burst forward.

Kaesar put his hand out.

"—That's what I thought you were going to do!" yelled the instructor as he jumped in the air.

"Did I get an easy one?" murmured Kaesar as he Sinned an Ice path underneath the instructor.

The instructor's eyes widened in mid air, "Oh no—" he uttered as he landed and slipped down on the Ice.

Kaesar saw the instructor coming as he jumped up and he slid underneath.

Kaesar landed on the ground and turned his head towards Adalo again.

The two locked eyes, *"...What does he know?"* thought Adalo.

Everyone saw the two, but then Kaesar turned back to the instructor as they continued the stage.

"What's going on between Kaesar and Adalo?" asked Javarus.

Zayden paused, "I have no idea," he spoke.

"—Who cares about that!" broke in Reno, "Are you guys seeing this?!"

"Yeah..." they murmured.

"Aren't you in awe?!" remarked Reno, "Ice Sinning looks so cool! It's so much better than Rock!"

"No, Sinning Rock isn't that bad," assured Javarus, "Every Sin is great, be thankful of yours."

"Nah I'd rather Sin Ice than dumb old Rock," muttered Reno.

Zayden looked to him, *"Kaesar's Sinning is taking everyone's attention,"* he noticed, "Hey Javarus?" he called.

"Yeah?" Javarus turned.

Zayden took a few steps back, "I need to know something," he spoke.

Javarus followed him as they stood a distance away from the circle.

"I know I've brought this up before..." recalled Zayden as he was face to face with Javarus, "But did I really say or do anything wrong to anger Veny?!" he asked.

There was a moment of silence.

"Zayden," spoke Javarus, "I already assured you that you did nothing wrong."

"—No," opposed Zayden, "Veny went all out against the instructor after the mention of a Full-Fledged Sinner," he tensed, "So—"

"—It's just that you seemed happy when you heard about the likes of Damon and Soro," recalled Javarus, "You were talking like you didn't know who they were."

"But now I do!" stated Zayden, "I know that Soro is the son of a Full-Fledged Sinner!"

"—And Damon is the Father who is the Full-Fledged Sinner," remarked Javarus, "He creates destruction wherever he goes."

"—But that doesn't explain why Veny and everyone else were so worried about Soro!"

"—Because he's Damon's son!" Javarus raised his voice.

Zayden was stunned.

Javarus looked around, "Sorry for yelling," he spoke, "We should keep our voices low."

"...My fault," muttered Zayden.

Javarus took a moment, "Don't you understand?" he went on, "It's been said that Soro has the same nature as his Father...the same Power."

There was a moment of silence.

"But for Veny, he isn't scared," recalled Javarus, "He wants to fight Soro, but I know that he has no chance of beating him..."

Zayden paused, "A Full-Fledged Sinner...this Power you're talking about..." he muttered, "Damon and Soro..." he looked up to Javarus, "I need to know everything behind Veny's fight against Soro, I brought his emotions out to begin with!" and deep in his thoughts, *"I also have a promise to keep to my Mother,"* he recalled, *"Anything that relates to a Full-Fledged Sinner is important to me."*

Javarus took a moment as he tensed, "Veny wants to fight Soro because of what Damon did..." he remarked.

"And what did—Damon do?" Zayden asked slowly.

"Damon had attacked Veny's hometown," recalled Javarus, "Many were hurt, the area was destroyed, and everyone lost their Sinning Abilities...including Veny's family."

"—*Losing your Sinning Ability?!*" Zayden was shocked, "*Is that even possible?!*"

Javarus continued, "Veny is the only one who can Sin in his family..." he explained, "His family depends on him to carry out their will of taking down Damon, that would be great for all the Districts."

Zayden listened, "But since Soro's the one who's here..." he spoke, "His anger for Damon spreads onto him instead."

"...It's reasonable," remarked Javarus, "But I'm hoping that Veny never confronts Damon or Soro, I don't want him to die against them...they're just too strong."

There was a pause, "Damon..." murmured Zayden, "Why would he attack Veny's hometown?"

Javarus looked to him, "That's just unfortunate," he stated, "Recently, Damon has been attacking places and families...nobody knows if they're random or calculated..." he recalled, "But following every attack, lives are lost and families lose their Sinning Abilities."

"—*And Damon is a Full-Fledged Sinner...*" remembered Zayden.

"Veny's hometown was caught in one of his meaningless attacks," went on Javarus, "And nobody knows why Damon does what he does."

Zayden understood, "That's a lot of weight on Veny's shoulder," he spoke, "I don't want his anger to get the best of him..."

"Neither do I," agreed Javarus, "But if the time arises when Veny and Soro clash, I won't interfere," he stated, "If Soro doesn't show up at all, that would be the best."

Zayden heard him, "...Yeah, I hope you're right," he murmured, but in his thoughts, *"It's not the right thing to admit right now,"* he tensed, *"But I need Soro to show up, I have to know how to become a Full-Fledged Sinner...and he may know how to do it."*

"—Congratulations participant Kaesar!" announced Flare back in the circle, "You have passed the first part!"

After a moment, Kaesar stopped Sinning as his blue aura faded.

Everyone was surprised, *"He doesn't show much,"* observed Aviva, *"There's more to him than he's letting on."*

Zayden and Javarus went back to the circle, "I'm glad you made it," half smiled Zayden.

Kaesar walked towards them.

Zayden gulped, "...Kaesar," he muttered, "Do you know anything about Damon?"

Kaesar looked to him, "Of course I do," he spoke, "...But he's not my issue to take care of," he turned back facing the circle.

"—Participant Javarus Hanzen!" addressed Flare, "Please make your way into the middle!"

"Clear your mind," advised Zayden, "Focus on passing this stage."

Javarus nodded as he walked to the middle.

After a moment, an instructor faced him from a distance.

"—And the five-minute timer..." went on Flare, "Has started!"

"I wish you luck," tensed Javarus.

"...Uh, you too," murmured the instructor, he charged forward and went in with a punch.

Javarus stepped to the side as he had a green aura.

"—How about this!" yelled the instructor as he swung a kick.

But then a Boulder of Rock quickly burst up in front of Javarus.

"—What?!" uttered the instructor as he kicked through the Rock.

Javarus jumped back a distance, "I'll use all this surface for my benefit," he remarked, "I cannot let you touch me."

"...Thanks for stating the obvious," exhaled the instructor, he charged again as everyone watched on.

"—How can he Sin Rock like that but I can't?!" yelled Reno out loud.

"It's because you don't try," spoke Kaesar.

"—But I do!" Reno turned to him. "Seriously!"

But then Zayden leaned into Reno's ear, "Then drop the wristband," he remarked.

"W-Wait!" uttered Reno, "You know I can't!"

Zayden backed off, "You know, you can learn a lot from Javarus," he spoke, "You both Sin the same Ability."

Kaesar turned towards them, "Even I agree with Zayden," he spoke, "And then you don't have to cheat with the wristband."

"—What?!" freaked out Zayden and Reno, "Who said anything about that?!"

Kaesar took a moment, "I know the wristband helped Reno against the instructor," he remarked, "It was obvious after I put the pieces together."

"What—no it didn't," blurted Reno, "I'm Reno the great! That's how I won!"

"—Yeah, he's great like that!" nodded Zayden.

There was a pause as Kaesar looked to them with a straight face.

After a moment, Zayden exhaled, "Okay fine," he gave up, "How did you know?" he asked.

"Like I said, I put the pieces together," recalled Kaesar, "On the way to Wavern, you told me some of your Father's Sinning Power was within the wristband."

"...Oh yeah," murmured Zayden.

"I didn't believe you at first," admitted Kaesar, "But after my battle against you last night, I know the wristband helped you with a bomb-like explosion in the end..."

"—It did?!" uttered Zayden.

"Yeah, and I got my confirmation when Reno easily took down the instructor," went on Kaesar, "He wore that same wristband he's wearing now," he pointed forward.

There was a moment as Reno looked down on his wrist, "But Kaesar..." he muttered then yelled, "—Please don't tell anyone!" he ran and shook him, "—I really don't want to leave!"

"—Let go of me," Kaesar swiped Reno's arms off, "I won't tell anyone."

"—Thank you!' smiled Reno.

"—And the five minutes are complete!" announced Flare, "Participant Javarus, you have passed the first part of the first stage!"

The instructor's breath was heavy he was on one knee.

Javarus walked to him, "Thanks for giving me tough test," he smiled as he offered a hand.

The instructor shook his hand as he was helped up.

After a moment, Javarus walked back to the circle. "Here, talk to him now," Zayden urged Reno, "He'll be happy to—"

"—Who said I'm giving up the wristband?!" denied Reno.

"—Next participant up!" announced Flare, "Will participant Zayden please make his way into the middle!"

Zayden heard his name as he turned to her.

"—Forget about me Zayden!" tensed Reno, "Put your focus into this!"

"—You're right," nodded Zayden as he ran into the middle.

Everyone looked to him, "Don't let the Fire hurt you again," snickered Aviva from the side.

"—It won't!" opposed Zayden, "Oh, and Reno still thinks you're his fan."

"—I told you to tell him I'm not!" yelled Aviva.

"—The circle has gotten really small!" screeched Kara.

Aviva looked to her, "...It has," she looked around. The circle only remained with the passed participants surrounding Zayden, as the others got eliminated.

"—Will the next instructor come out," ordered Adalo.

An instructor stepped up and faced Zayden a distance away.

"—And the five-minute timer," addressed Flare, "Has started!"

There was a moment of silence as nobody moved. "...Aren't you going to Sin?" spoke the instructor.

"Nope," Zayden shook his head, "It's best if I don't Sin to begin with."

81

The instructor burst towards him. "That's being overconfident!" he yelled.

Zayden saw him coming, "—Oh he's fast!" he uttered.

The instructor went in with a punch.

Zayden quickly jumped in the air, "—Too close!" he saw.

But then the instructor jumped up with his hand out. Zayden's eyes widened as his body disintegrated into ashes.

"—Where did he go?!" the instructor looked back. Zayden reappeared outside the circle with Fire around him, "...I guess I was overconfident," he murmured.

Everyone saw him Sinning, "Good for you to not be tagged," spoke Adalo, "But stay in the circle."

"Understood," nodded Zayden as he walked back to the middle.

"Well there goes that strategy," remarked the instructor, "You started to Sin pretty quickly there."

"Yeah, but now's not the time to be cocky," tensed Zayden, "After watching everyone else, I have no right at all."

"Hm, clearly," remarked the instructor, he burst towards Zayden again.

Adalo watched on, "Flare," he spoke, "Dedrian is the only Fire Sinner who has passed, right?" he recalled, "And if this boy passes, that'll make two."

"Correct," remarked Flare, "That would make Fire and Farmake the second most Sinned Ability passed, behind Rock Sinners who have three."

"How about the rest?" asked Adalo.

"—Just a little more time!" yelled Zayden as he dodged the instructor.

"Well, then we have Kaesar," answered Flare, "And he's an Ice Sinner."

Adalo nodded, "That's good to hear the variety," he spoke.

"Yeah," murmured Flare, but then worried, "And if the participant after Zayden passes..." her and Adalo continued talking.

"—*Come on!*" Reno saw them from the other side of the circle, *"This is really getting to me, Adalo always has Flare all by himself!"*

Reno took a step back, then began walking around the circle towards.

"Reno, where are you—" saw Kaesar, but then stopped, *"It's actually pointless with him..."* he thought.

After a moment, the instructor's breath was heavy, "You did well," he commended, "I won't be able to get you with a minute left."
Zayden shook his head, "—The timer isn't done yet!" he stated.

Reno made his way to Adalo and Flare, "—Hey!" he yelled, "I have something to say!"
The two turned back.

"What's the relationship between the two of you?!" asked Reno, "Is it serious?!"
"—What are you talking about?" spoke Adalo.

"—Oh, Adalowala and I!" snickered Flare, "We're just—"
But then a quick Static noise was heard throughout the field.

"—What's that noise?!" shrieked Reno.
Everyone looked around the field, the Static grew louder and louder.

"...This feeling," murmured Aviva, "The Sinning Power is so..."
Adalo and Flare turned back facing the middle, "...He's going to show up," worried Flare.

"—Who's here?!" asked Zayden as he turned.
"...Don't tell me," worried the instructor in front of him, "He's actually in this competition?!"

A quick Streak of Lightning appeared beside Reno.
"—Watch out!" yelled Zayden.

Reno stumbled back, "—I've seen this spark before!" he saw.
Everyone turned to the Sparks of Lightning appearing on the field.

"It took a while," thought Adalo, *"But his arrival was going to come."*

After a moment, a figure appeared.

Everyone was stunned.

Flare was nervous, as Adalo waited, *"Soro Uzara,"* he saw.

Soro appeared on the field. He stood up straight with his arms by his side, his head was faced slightly to the right. Quick flashes of Blue Sparks streaked across him. Everyone on the field had their eyes on him.

"...I-I was excited to see him in the beginning," worried Kara, *"But now..."*

The Lightning around Soro faded away as he looked straight.

"So, this is Soro..." grasped Zayden, *"The son of Damon...the son of a Full-Fledged Sinner..."*

But then the instructor saw Zayden, "—You shouldn't have lost your focus!" he yelled as he went in with a punch.

But then the Fire around Zayden's body quickly grew.

"—What?!" the instructor was forced to stop, *"I-I can't get through that!"*

"A-And the timer is up!" announced Flare with her head turned to Soro, "Y-You have passed the first part!"

There was a pause.

Zayden faced Soro as his Fire slightly turned Darker, *"You might know things I need to know,"* he tensed.

"Zayden," broke in Adalo, "You have passed, go back to the outside of the circle."

Zayden heard him as he stopped Sinning and walked to Reno.

The instructor saw him go, *"I thought he would be uneasy seeing Soro,"* he recalled, *"But he seems like he's being waiting the whole time."*

Kaesar saw Zayden coming back, then looked to Soro.

After a moment, Soro began walking to the middle as his every step was watched.

Reno's body slightly trembled.

"Don't act like that," spoke Zayden, "You're better than this."

"Y-Yeah," stuttered Reno, "I'll try."

"Will an instructor come out," ordered Adalo.

But the instructors in the line hesitated.

"—You go," one said.

"—I already went!" denied the other.

"Even the instructors are cautious about him," thought Javarus, *"And Veny thought he had a chance..."*

After a moment, someone stepped up, "...I-I'll take him," he tensed, "It's only right."

After a moment, the instructor stood a distance in front of Soro.

"P-Participant Soro Uzara," murmured Flare then paused.

"...I'm here," assured Adalo, "Go on."

Flare heard him and spoke up, "—The last participant for this part of the first stage!" she announced, "The five-minute timer has started!"

There was a moment of silence. Soro rubbed his left thumb and pointer together.

The instructor in front of him spoke up, "I know exactly who you are—everyone does!" he raised his voice, "Soro Uzara, the son of Damon!"

There was a pause.

"The amount of pain your family has caused is too much!" he yelled, "The entire world is against you, yet you don't stop."

"—They both did it?!" uttered Zayden.

"—You kill others, erase their Sinning Abilities, and destroy their homes!" shouted the instructor."

"—Javarus!" called out Zayden to his left, "I thought only Damon hurt people!"

"—There were never any incidents where Soro attacked others," Javarus raised his voice, "But people treat Soro like he does. Nobody can threaten Damon, so can you really blame the victims?"

Aviva stood near them, "It's like Soro is the outlet of all the hate people have towards Damon," she remarked.

Zayden was shocked, *"—How can he live like that?"* he turned back, *"Always on the lookout with*

85

everyone after him, people want to hurt him for crimes he didn't commit!"

"—Don't talk about my Father," spoke Soro.
There was a pause as everyone heard him.

"—How could I not?!" angered the instructor, "My younger brother lost his life to your Father!" he yelled, "There's been many warnings that you're going to follow the same path as Damon!"

Adalo looked to him, "—That's enough," he spoke, "Do your—"

"You're his blood!" shouted the instructor as he Sinned, "And if I can't stop you now! I'm sure one of these young Sinners will!"
Adalo raised his voice, "I said that's—"

But then a yellow flash shined from the instructor, "—It's fitting that I Sin Light!" he yelled.
Soro looked to the other participants on his left and right, *"So this is everyone at the competition,"* he saw as he had a light smirk.

The instructor burst towards Soro, "I have to try against you!" he shouted as he went in with a punch.
But then Lightning streaked across Soro's body.

"—Uh," groaned the instructor as his fists were sparked, "I must get through!" he shouted as he went in with rapid punches.
But the Lightning defended Soro.

"—You are prohibited from Sinning!" called out Adalo, "Stop now!"

"—That doesn't matter!" yelled the instructor as he jumped back, "—His death means so much more than this competition!" he charged again with as he went in with a heavy punch.

But then the Lightning faded as Soro stepped to the side, "Listen to Adalo," he spoke, "Don't continue."
The instructor saw him, "—T-That wouldn't make sense!" he yelled, "My brother didn't give up when he saw Damon!"

The instructor swung a kick.
But Soro ducked and jumped back.

Everyone was stunned watching the battle.

86

"—You're oblivious to everything," spoke Soro.

The instructor's breath was heavy, "—I won't back out!" he yelled, "I—"

But then Soro quickly pointed two fingers, "—It's over," he stated as he Sinned two rapid circles of Lightning.

"What are you—" saw the instructor as the Circles wrapped around his ankles, "—I-I can't escape!" he worried.

Soro put out his other arm, "Don't look at me like that," he groaned as Lightning formed in his palm.

Zayden looked around, "—Nobody's going to step in!"

The instructor saw Soro, "You're just like—"

But then Soro Sinned a Lightning Streak from his palm.

"What is—" yelled the instructor as his head hit back.

Everyone watched closely, Reno was scared, "Is he—"

But then a quick sharp Lightning sparked around the instructor, he screamed in pain.

Zayden was stunned.

After a moment, his clothes were torn and his aura was gone.

"That's what I expected..." muttered Javarus, "But to see it now..."

The instructor fell forward as his eyes closed, "Why did I try..." he murmured and landed on the ground unconscious.

There was a moment of silence.

"C-Congratulations participant Soro..." murmured Flare, "You have passed this portion of the stage..."

Smoke began to appear around the instructor's body.

"Hm?" saw Soro.

After a moment, the instructor's body vanished.

Reno's stomach dropped, "I-I should've quit..." he recalled.

Zayden eyed Soro, "Just how far is he compared to everyone else..." he thought.

"Flare," spoke up Adalo, "Go on as you would."

Flare took a step forward, "Congratulations to all the participants that have passed this part of the first stage!" she addressed, "There is one portion left that will take place inside the—"

"—Soro!" a voice was heard above.

Everyone quickly looked up, "—Veny!" saw Javarus, "Don't!"

Zayden's eyes widened.

"—I can't just hear Soro and not do anything!" shouted Veny as he went down towards Soro.

But then Soro turned around as their wrists clashed.

"—I'm taking you down for everyone that was hurt by your family!" yelled Veny, he took a jump back.

Soro looked to him.

"Adalo!" called out Flare, "Are you going to do anything?!"

But Adalo stayed quiet.

Soro put his head up at Veny, "…What are you looking for?" he spoke.

Veny's aura turned dark green as small tears filled in his eyes, "I'm looking for a sense of justice!" he groaned, "If I don't see Damon, then I take on the next danger."

There was a pause, "…So that's the reason," heard Soro, and in his thoughts, *"You're all the same…"*

Everyone was shocked as they watched on.

Kaesar looked to his right, "Zayden," he spoke, "You're not thinking of getting involved, are you?"

Zayden was stunned, "I-I don't know if I—"

"—You're not going anywhere," broke in Javarus behind them, "This isn't your fight."

Veny charged towards Soro, "—I'll be the one to beat you!" he swung his arm.

Soro stepped to the side and put out his arm.

But then the Rock underneath Veny quickly rose above the ground, "—I prepared for you!" he yelled as went up the air, "So I can—"

But then Soro put his arm up and Sinned a Lightning Streak towards the Rock.

"How did— saw Veny as his Rock was struck and broke down in mid air.

"—Hm," Soro jumped and punched into Veny's stomach.

"Uh—" groaned Veny as his stomach went in.
Soro opened his hand, "You can't take me," he spoke as
he Sinned a Lightning Streak.

Veny was sent down as he crashed into the
ground.
Soro landed and faced him, "How do you expect to beat
my Father if you can't touch me," he remarked.

"—You can't say that yet!" groaned Veny as his
body went through the ground.
"—He's still going?!" saw Kara.

Veny reappeared out of the ground with an
uppercut.
But then Soro leaned back as Veny's body went by him.

He grabbed and tightened his hand on Veny's
ankle, he Sinned a Lightning Spark through his fingers.
"—Uh," groaned Veny.

Soro then swung Veny in the air.
"—Veny can't do anything against him!" yelled Javarus,
and in his thoughts, "—Why won't Adalo stop this?!"

Soro Sinned a Lightning Bolt in his hand and
whipped it towards Veny.
Veny's eyes opened in mid air as he saw the Bolt rush
behind him, "What did you—"

But then Soro reappeared out of the Bolt behind,
"—So it worked," he smirked he swung a kick into Veny's
face.
Veny was knocked away as he rolled on the ground.

After a moment, he slowly got up to one knee as
Sparks of Lightning appeared on his face, "...H-He's too,"
he grimaced in pain.
Soro landed on his feet, "Did you find what you were
looking for?" he recalled.

Veny's breath was heavy, "You even look like him!"
he yelled as his legs went through the ground again.
But then Soro quickly appeared as he grabbed his arm.

"—How?!" uttered Veny.
Soro quickly raised up Veny and let him go, "—You don't
know what this fight is about," he groaned as he went in
with a heavy punch to his chest.

Veny was sent flying through the air.

"—I'm Damon's Son," spoke Soro as Sparks appeared and he vanished, "So like everyone says," he reappeared on the other side, "You can't overcome me," he swung his arm again and bashed Veny in the face.

"—Veny!" called out Javarus.

Veny was sent back as he laid on the ground, "S-Soro..." he muttered as his aura went away.

Clouds filled in the sky as the day became dim. Soro had a stern look, "...Like the other one," he spoke as he raised his arm up to the sky, "You're oblivious to everything."

Lightning appeared around the Sky as thunder was heard.

"—That's so loud?!" worried Reno.

"—Whatever's happening in the sky is overwhelming!" yelled Marubee.

Adalo crossed his arms tapping his fingers.

Lightning appeared around Soro, his black hair waved back, "I have to call for it," he spoke as sharp Sparks streaked across his body.

Veny struggled to stand up, "I-I..."

Soro's eyes widened, "Now you'll know—"

But then Smoke appeared in front of Veny.

"—What?" saw Soro.

After a moment, the Smoke went away as Adalo appeared, "—You're done," he spoke, "This stage is over."

Soro had his arm up, "Why are you interfering?" he opposed.

Adalo took a moment, "Veny passed this part of the stage, and so did you," he remarked, "It wouldn't be fair if any of you were to be hurt before the next portion."

Zayden angered, *"—He says that now?"* he thought, *"Look at Veny! He's not moving and his aura is gone!"*

Everyone was shocked.

Adalo gave a stern look to Soro, "I said we're done," he repeated.

The two locked eyes for a moment.

90

After a pause, Soro put his arm down, "I'm not here to kill empty lives anyways," he spoke and turned his back, "They're already worse off as it is."
Everyone saw Soro as he stopped Sinning.

"...And with that," remarked Adalo, "Everyone go back inside the Academy for the second part of this stage." But then Zayden, Reno, and Javarus ran over to Veny who was unconscious.

Kaesar walked behind them as he eyed Soro, *"It looks like everyone knows about you,"* he thought, *"I wonder how that would feel..."*

Javarus went on his knees, "—Veny!" he shook him, "Tell me you're fine!"
Reno saw him, *"It didn't look like Soro tried at all..."* he was stunned.

"—Stay calm," assured Adalo, "He'll make it," he put his arm out.
After a moment, Adalo's and Veny's body turned into Smoke and vanished.

"—Now will all the participants follow me inside the Academy!" addressed Flare, "We must finish this stage!"
There was a pause.
Marubee looked to Kara, "Don't change your mood now," she told her, "We still haven't passed yet."

The two went with Flare inside the Academy as most others followed.

But Zayden stayed behind as he stood a distance behind Soro.
The two remained on the field, "...Unlike everyone else," spoke up Zayden as he turned to Soro, "I needed you to show up."

Soro looked to him.
"I'm not afraid of you, or Damon," tensed Zayden, "To be honest, I want to meet your Father, and learn from him how to become a Full-Fledged Sinner!"

Soro stayed quiet for a moment, then began walking away.
"—So, before this whole competition is over!" urged Zayden, "You have to take me to Damon!"

Soro stood in front of the Academy's door, but then he turned back, "I don't owe you anything," he remarked, "Would you talk to me, if I wasn't related to him?"

Zayden was stunned, "—What?" he uttered, "I need to—"

But then Soro went inside the Academy and closed the door.

There was a moment of silence as Zayden saw him go, *"You'll have to answer me at some point,"* he thought, *"I'll do anything to learn from Damon…no matter what people may think of him…"*

Inside the Academy, Soro stood at the corner of the red carpeted room a distance from everyone.

Adalo and Flare stood on a platform in front of the room, Veny laid on the ground next to them.

The participants stood and watched on, "Who's that person on their knees?" asked Reno.

"I'm not sure," spoke Javarus, "But she's healing Veny's wounds at a fast rate."

Aviva sat on the ground leaning on the side wall.

Reno turned to her, "It kind of looks like—"

"—It's Lavivo it's Lavivo!" beamed Kara.

Aviva looked up, *"And it begins,"* she knew.

Lavivo Kallent was a Farmake Sinner who had long pink hair that tied up to two buns on each side of her head. She was Aviva's older sister. She also wore a pink and white dress with a rose necklace.

"—She's really here!" Kara ran towards the platform, "I need to meet her!"

But then Adalo appeared in Smoke in front of her, "Lavivo is busy," he denied, "Stand back with the other participants."

"—I know she's busy!" screeched Kara, "But she's also super strong! And she can teach me a few things!"

Dedrian leaned on the back wall watching on, "Why is Lavivo here?" he saw.

But then Zayden came in from the door, the two locked eyes for a moment.

Zayden slowly put his hand on his jaw, "Don't think it's over between you and I," he spoke, "I'll remember your cheap shot."

"—I wouldn't you to forget," smirked Dedrian, "I did it for the right reason."

After a moment, Zayden turned to the front as he saw Lavivo with Veny.

"Back up," Adalo told Kara, "You can't see her right now."

"—Oh please?!" beamed Kara, "Let me see Lavivo's—"

"—Kara," Marubee pulled her collar, "I told you before not to cry over people."

Kara was pulled back, "—But Marubee!" she opposed, "Lavivo's my idol!"

Aviva heard her and recalled a moment: *"But your Lavivo's younger sister which makes you my idol!"* she remembered Kara's words to her, she slowly stood up.

Marubee turned back.

"...I thought I was your idol," Aviva murmured her thoughts.

"—You actually thought Kara meant that," spoke out Marubee.

Aviva faced her.

"Nobody would look up to someone that doesn't do anything," stated Marubee.

But then Aviva tensed and walked to her.

"—What are you guys doing?!" Kara turned to them.

Marubee had a light smirk, she was face to face with Aviva, "You're just Lavivo's little sister," she remarked, "You don't—"

"—No I've had enough!" broke in Aviva, "What's your deal with me?! Ever since yesterday, you have this urge to talk down to me! Who are you to talk down to me?!"

"—I'm Marubee Tasuki!" she yelled back, "And you will know me as the greatest Farmake Sinner of all time!" she remarked, "So who are you to talk down to me! Just because you're a Kallent doesn't make you better than anyone else!"

Everyone saw them.

"—I never thought of it like that!" opposed Aviva, "I work hard on my Sinning and you can't take that from me!"

"—You work hard?!" smirked Marubee, "This thing you call work is nothing more than having coffee dates with your butlers and being Lavivo's cheer leader!"

"You don't—"

"—Aviva," softly called out Lavivo, "Please lower your voice, I need to concentrate on this young boy."

Aviva turned to her and irritated.

"Weren't you going to say something?" tempted Marubee.

Aviva stayed quiet.

"...Oh yeah, you can't," Marubee shrugged her shoulders, "Not without your sister's stamp of approval, right?"

But then Aviva's aura turned Pink as she opened her mouth.

Adalo quickly appeared in Smoke in front of her as they vanished.

After a moment, the two reappeared on the other side of the room.

"...That wasn't very nice," muttered Kara beside Marubee, "A lollipop won't taste that good with all this negativity."

But Kara still took out a lollipop and put it in her mouth, "—I have to change you Marubee!" she smiled.

Marubee exhaled, "I don't even know how we're friends," she spoke, "You're so bubbly all the time."

"—No I'm not!" screeched Kara, "I can be serious sometimes!" she shook her head.

"Adalo," called out Lavivo, "Will you please come here?"

Adalo was with Aviva, "I'm not letting you Sin for no reason," she told her and vanished.

Aviva saw him go, "...You don't know what it's like," she muttered.

Adalo reappeared in Smoke with Lavivo and Flare, "What happened?" he asked.

Lavivo stood up, "Soro's strikes on this boy will leave him unconscious for a few hours," she remarked, "Don't let him do anything until tomorrow."

"But he may want to prepare for the next stage," spoke Flare, "Can you heal him up to his full Power?"

Lavivo paused, "I healed him just enough so he wouldn't die," she explained, "I won't go further otherwise that would not be fair to the rest of the participants."

"What do you mean?" asked Flare.

"Remember?" spoke up Adalo, "If Lavivo were to heal someone to their fullest health, they become stronger then they were before."

Flare listened as she understood.

"I'll place him in the Medical Room for now," remarked Adalo.

After a moment, Veny's body turned into Smoke and vanished.

"—Wait a second!" broke in Javarus, "Is he going to be okay?!"

Lavivo turned to him and smiled, "He'll be fine," she assured, "You no longer need to worry."

Javarus relieved, "...Thank you," he half smiled, and in his thoughts, *"Maybe now Veny won't go after Damon or Soro anymore."*

Flare faced all the participants with Adalo and Lavivo beside her, "—We will now move onto the final part of the first stage!" she announced.

All 9 participants in the room carefully listened.

"—Will everyone please stand side by side facing forward!" addressed Flare.

Most of the participants followed the instructions, but Soro didn't move.

"That includes you," Adalo look to him, "You're not any different."

Everyone looked to Soro as he moved to the end of the line.

After a moment, Adalo spoke up, "I will ask each one of you the same question," he stated, "And you must have a genuine response."

The participants listened, "—What's this about?" uttered Reno.

"I will tell you," remarked Adalo.

Most of the participants nodded.

95

"The question that you will answer is," went on Adalo, "What is your ultimate goal?" he revealed, "What dream do you wish to become a reality?"

The participants heard him.

"In other words," explained Adalo, "What do you aspire to be, or to do, or to know?" he asked, "Answer this genuinely, and you pass."

There was a moment of silence. The participants remained facing Adalo, Flare, and Lavivo.

"I will ask you in order of which you are standing in," remarked Adalo, "So Zayden, what is your answer?"

Some of the participants turned to him.

Zayden closed his eyes and took a deep breath, *"My dream may seem like a bad thing,"* he thought, *"But it's my promise to my Mother!"*

Zayden opened his eyes, "—My ultimate goal is to become a Full-Fledged Sinner!" he determined.

There was a pause.

Adalo look to him, "So you want to be the next Full-Fledged Sinner after Damon?" he spoke.

Zayden paused, "...Yes, I do," he answered.

Adalo had a stern look, "Prepare for the next stage," he stated, "You pass."

Zayden heard him, "Sounds good," he smirked.

Some of the participants were uneasy, *"...After all the things he heard about being Full-Fledged,"* recalled Javarus, *"He still wants to become one..."*

Dedrian angered, *"I can't let him follow this path,"* he thought, *"Or else it'll be like before..."*

"Moving on, Aviva!" called out Adalo, "What is your goal?"

Marubee turned her head to her as she carefully listened.

Aviva took a moment, she glared at Lavivo, "—My goal is to be recognized for my own Power and Abilities instead of just a Sinner from the Kallent Family!" she answered.

Adalo listened, "That's good," he stated, "You pass."

Aviva nodded and stared at Lavivo.

Reno looked to the both of them, *"Oh right..."* he remembered, *"They're sisters."*

Kaesar heard Aviva, *"She wants to be recognized outside of her family..."* he thought, *"How can you get into that mindset..."*

Adalo looked to the next person, "Reno," he called out, "What is your dream?"

"M-My dream?!" uttered Reno.

There was a pause.

"Be honest," advised Adalo.

But Reno worried, *"—I can't say that!"* he thought about his answer, *"That's so embarrassing!"*

"Participant Reno," called out Flare, "Please answer, or you will be disqualified."

"—Oh that's Flare calling for me!" heard Reno, *"I have to pass this stage for her!"*

Flare saw him, "Participant—"

"—I want to learn how to Sin Rock!" yelled Reno.

Zayden worried, *"Everyone thinks you already know how!"* he thought.

Adalo spoke up, "If you don't know how to Sin Rock," he recalled, "How did you pass against the instructor?"

"Oh, I mean—I want to learn how to Sin Rock to the fullest extent!" smiled Reno.

Everyone looked to him.

"Well then..." spoke Adalo, "You have passed."

"—Yes!" cheered Reno, and in his thoughts, *"I don't wan to pretend anymore how to Sin Rock!"* he determined, *"I actually have to learn it!"*

"Next one, Javarus," went on Adalo, "What do you want to do with your life?"

There was a pause, "I wish to spread peace around the world by teaching people how to Sin positively," answered Javarus.

Adalo heard him, "That's a tough one," he remarked, "Many use Sinning for battling...there are wars, hate, and pain because of Sinning."

Javarus listened, "I am aware of this," he stated, "And I must spread positivity to end this!"

Adalo looked to him, "I understand," he spoke, "You pass."

"Thank you very much," nodded Javarus.

Adalo eyed to the next person in line, but he stayed quiet.

After a moment, Flare turned to Adalo, *"You can't be like this forever,"* she thought.

Kaesar saw the two, *"...What's the hold up?"*

"—Participant Kaesar!" addressed Flare, "What is your ultimate desire?"

Everyone looked over to Kaesar in the middle of the line.

Kaesar eyed down, "...My desire," he muttered, and in his thoughts, *"I don't even know how to go about it..."*

There was a moment of silence.

"...But if everyone speaks their mind," thought Kaesar, *"Then I shouldn't hold back."*

Kara was beside him as she turned.

Kaesar looked up to Adalo and Flare, "—I desire to know everyone about my life!" he answered.

There a pause in the room as everyone heard him, *"What does he mean..."* thought Zayden.

He recalled a moment on the ship heading to Wavern: *"Forget about my story,"* he remembered Kaesar's words as he saw change in expression.

"You're being honest," spoke up Adalo as he looked to Kaesar, "You have passed."

"...Adalo," Flare was surprised.

Kaesar's white hair went over his eyes as he slightly faced down.

"—Hey what do you mean by that?!" screeched Kara beside him, "You have to put more energy into your answer!"

Kaesar slowly turned his head.

"Err, you gray-haired person!" snickered Kara, "What do you mean by wanting to know everything about your life?" she asked.

Kaesar saw her and paused, "It's white hair..." he muttered.

"—I can't hear you!" beamed Kara, "Speak louder!"

"...You called me gray-haired," spoke up Kaesar, "When my hair is actually white."

Everyone looked to the two.

"—That can't be right!" denied Kara, she went in and felt the top of Kaesar's hair, "Your hair is—"

"—Wait!" Kaesar quickly backed off, "Don't get so close to me."

There was a moment as some snickered in the room. Kaesar eyed away.

Kara looked to him and smiled, "I'm just trying to tell you something!" she chuckled, "You don't have to be embarrassed!"

"—Moving on to Kara!" addressed Adalo.

"—Yes Sir!" Kara faced him.

Adalo took a moment, "What is your goal in life?" he asked.

"That's super easy," went on Kara, "I want to be someone anyone can look up to!" she beamed, "I really want to be an idol for everyone!"

Adalo nodded, "That's interesting," he stated, "You pass."

"Thank you!" smiled Kara, "—And its gray hair!" she turned to Kaesar.

Kaesar exhaled, "Believe what you want," he murmured.

"—Marubee!" Adalo called out the next one beside them, "What is you goal?"

"—Get em Marubee!" cheered Kara.

Marubee looked to her with a half smile, then looked back up to Adalo.

"My goal is a goal that anyone would love to see accomplished," tensed Marubee, "I Sin for the people who strive to be better a Sinner on their own, people who have nothing and become something out of it," she raised her voice, "—My goal is to prove that reputation doesn't matter and that anything can be achieved through hard work!" she turned and looked over to Aviva.

Aviva stared back, *"How does this have to do with me,"* she thought.

Adalo understood, "Good answer," he stated, "You have passed."

"—Now both of us made it!" beamed Kara.

Dedrian stood beside them, "She's so loud," he groaned.

"—Dedrian!" continued Adalo, "What is the goal you wish to achieve?"

Zayden glared at him, *"What goal can he have…"* he waited.

Dedrian smirked, "—My goal is to one day have a Sinning Academy of my own!" he remarked, "Where only the strong participate and the weak get tackled down!"

Adalo listened, "That would be intriguing," he spoke, "So you want to be a Sinegious?"

Dedrian tensed and nodded, *"I think Mother would like that too,"* he recalled.

Adalo looked over to the last participant in the line. There was a moment of silence as everyone eyed him.

"…And finally," spoke Adalo, "Soro, what is your ultimate goal?"

All the attention went onto him.

Soro had a stern look, "My ultimate goal is to become a Full-Fledged Sinner," he remarked.

There was a pause, *"—That makes two of us!"* heard Zayden.

All the participants were uneasy, *"I have Zayden's back on him becoming Full-Fledged…"* thought Reno, *"But when Soro says it, I-I'm scared…"*

Adalo looked to Soro, "You're being genuine," he stated, "You have passed onto the next stage."

Some of the participants murmured to each other.

"…Zayden," spoke Aviva, "Do you really want to be a Full-Fledged Sinner?"

Zayden turned, "…Yeah, I do," he answered, "I have a promise to keep."

Aviva paused, "It's just that…" she spoke, "Damon, a Full-Fledged Sinner himself, is going against the world and nobody knows why…" she went on, "That kind of Power leads to darkness…"

100

But then Zayden tensed, "I'll be a different Full-Fledged Sinner," he remarked, "I can't turn back now, this is the only reason why I Sin."

Aviva listened, *"...Two Sinners in this competition that both want to be Full-Fledged,"* she recalled, *"You never here talks like this."*

After a moment, Adalo looked to all the participants, "I commend you for answering the question," he spoke.

All the participants quieted as they faced him, Flare, and Lavivo.

"Each one of you should do whatever you must to reach your goal," stated Adalo, "The 10 of you were the deserving participants to move closer to the top 3 winner circle."

"He said 10," heard Javarus, *"So that confirms Veny made it."*

"—And just to clarify!" addressed Flare, "The 10 participants who have officially made it onto the second stage are participants Aviva Kallent, Dedrian Bellard, Javarus Hanzen, Kaesar Kinnuan, Kara Cherry, Marubee Tasuki, Reno Rossard, Soro Uzara, Veny Ikanu, and Zayden Fareno!"

The participants were eager to hear their names.

"—Now Lavivo will explain the second stage that'll begin tomorrow!" addressed Flare.

"—Tomorrow?!" freaked out Reno.

Lavivo took a step forward, "Good afternoon," she greeted, "I'm Lavivo Kallent, and I will be slightly involved in the second stage," she spoke in a soft voice.

"Just hearing her voice bothers me," irritated Aviva.

"—So, for the second stage," continued Lavivo, "You will be paired up with another participant, and will go 2 on 1 against Adalo Shuesi himself."

"—Really now?" smirked Dedrian.

"This battle will go on until either one of the sides can no longer fight, or one side gives up," went on Lavivo, "Or, until the timer set for 30 minutes runs out."

The participants listened.

"This stage will be test your overall offense, defense, and teamwork," remarked Lavivo, "As you are facing a very wonderful Sinner in Adalo, so you must be prepared."

"Why'd she use wonderful?" heard Adalo.

"—Then how are you involved?" spoke up Marubee.

"Oh, I'm just going to heal Adalo after each battle," snickered Lavivo.

"I see…" murmured Marubee, then turned, "—Kara!" she declared, "You're with me!"

"—Of course!" beamed Kara, "Nobody can stop Green and Orange from—"

"—Only 6 participants!" broke in Lavivo, "Again, only 6 participants will pass and move onto the third and final stage."

"—Zayden!" Reno turned to him, "You're going to be with me, right?!"

"I'm not finished—" uttered Lavivo.

"—But Reno," tensed Zayden, "You have to try and there's no easy way out."

"—I'll try my best!" nodded Reno, "You can count on—"

"—Why would anyone team up with someone who has trouble with the basics," murmured Kaesar.

"—What?!" uttered Reno, "I'm working on it okay!" Zayden chuckled, but then paused. He looked over to the far end of the line, *"…Soro,"* he saw him, *"Are you not going to—"*

"—This isn't right!" yelled Dedrian out loud, "I still have no idea where Rajaul went off to?! If he passed, he would've been my partner!"

Everyone saw him as he marched over to Adalo and Flare.

"—You guys should know why Rajaul didn't show up!" Dedrian raised his voice, "Me and him would've been dominant!"

Adalo looked to him, "Lower your voice," he spoke.

Dedrian angered, "Not until you—"

"—Participant Rajaul was disqualified for not being present," recalled Flare, "We do not know anything else."

"—But that's not like Rajaul!" opposed Dedrian as he had a red aura.

"These participants have their own agenda," snickered Lavivo, *"I didn't finish the explanation yet."*

Javarus made his way to her, "Hello Lavivo," he called out, "I know Veny isn't here right now, but will I still be able to choose him as a partner?"

Lavivo heard him, "Oh I see," she spoke, "This is what the commotion is about," she then nodded to Flare.

"—Will all the participants please let Lavivo finish!" addressed Flare.

"—Oh," the participants quieted and faced her.

Lavivo laughed quietly, "Everyone is in such a rush," she smiled, "But there's an important part you must know."

"—And what's that?" uttered Reno.

Lavivo paused, "The pairings have already been selected beforehand," she remarked, "And Flare will announce the teams who will each have their turn against Adalo."

"—Aw, but I better be with Marubee!" saddened Kara.

"Not to worry," assured Flare and smiled, "These teams are very suitable."

There was a moment of silence as the participants listened.

Flare took a step up, "—There will be 5 teams!" she addressed, "Team A is Javarus and Veny!"

"—Solid," nodded Javarus, and in his thoughts, *"I just hope Veny will be at 100% by then."*

Flare went on, "—Team B is Kaesar and Kara!"

"—Oh the gray haired boy?!" beamed Kara, "Now I can teach him the colour of his hair!"

Kaesar eyed her, "...What can I say," he exhaled.

Kara put a lollipop in her mouth, "—I'm super ready for this!" she smiled.

Flare snickered, and then continued, "—Team C is Dedrian and Reno!" she announced.

103

"—Come on!" groaned Dedrian.

Reno slowly turned his head to him, "T-This might not be too good..." he muttered.

"—I need a better tackling partner!" angered Dedrian, "Why did I get put with him?!

Zayden nudged Reno, "I think this is actually good for you," he spoke.

"—How?!" uttered Reno, "This isn't a joke!"

Flare went on, "—Team D is Aviva and Marubee!"

"—But why?!" opposed Aviva, "I know for a fact Lavivo had something to do with this!"

"—Aviva," called out Lavivo, "That doesn't matter, but I truly believe the two of you will make a remarkable team."

"—Hey I don't want to team up with princess Aviva either!" denied Marubee, "Plus, we're both Farmake Sinners!" she remarked, "We're not entirely meant to go against a Combat Sinner in Adalo!"

"—However, Marubee," addressed Flare, "Winning or losing does not translate to passing or failing," she explained, "Try your best, work with your partner, and you can make it to the next stage."

Lavivo looked to Aviva, "Don't be so quick to judge," she assured, "You may learn a thing or two from Marubee."

"—Heck no," denied Aviva.

"Exactly!" agreed Marubee, "I'm sure all of her high-end butlers taught her everything she needs to know."

"—That isn't true!" yelled Aviva, but then paused, "...I have an idea," she spoke.

There was a moment as everyone turned to her. Aviva had a light smirk, "How about this..." she tensed, "Marubee and I will team up if we don't go up against Adalo."

"—What?!" uttered Marubee.

"—But instead," Aviva pointed at Lavivo, "We do this second stage against you!"

"—Huh?!"

104

Lavivo heard her, "I'm...not too sure about that," she spoke.

Marubee took a moment, *"On second thought,"* she realized, *"This way I get the chance to prove myself against two Kallents instead of one!"*

"—So how about it?!" urged Aviva.

"—I completely agree!" broke in Marubee, "Aviva and I should go against Lavivo!"

Kara turned to her, *"Marubee,"* she thought, *"I hope you don't have any bad intentions."*

Lavivo stayed quiet.

"Lavivo," spoke up Adalo as he took a step beside her, "I understand what Aviva and Marubee are saying," he went on, "The best approach to testing two Farmake Sinners is by having them go against another Farmake Sinner, and with that being you, it seems fair."

There was a moment of silence.

"What's your answer?!" Aviva kept it up, "Will you—"

"Okay I'll do it," agreed Lavivo, "I'm looking forward to it," she smiled.

"—Yes!" rejoiced Aviva, "Now you'll see how far I've gotten, I'm not just a little girl from the Kallent family!"

Marubee tensed, *"And everyone will see how far a girl like me can go,"* she thought, *"You don't need to be given everything to be great."*

There was a pause as Zayden was anxious, "Then that means—"

"—And finally," announced Flare, "Team E is Zayden and Soro!"

There was a moment of silence as everyone heard her.

Javarus eyed Zayden all the way to left of the line, and Soro all the way to the right of the line, *"Both of them want to be Full-Fledged,"* he thought, *"And now they're partners?!"*

Zayden's eyes widened, *"—This is what I needed!"* he thought, *"Soro can help me realize my dream!"*

Reno put his head down, "Looks like we both got freaks as our partners," he sighed.

Zayden looked to him, "Now I wouldn't say that," he smirked.

There was a pause in the room as the participants understood the teams.

"—Thank you for listening to the announcements!" addressed Flare, "And with that said, tomorrow morning, there will be designations on the Academy's field for each Team. Both partners must show up for preparations before the second stage! It is a requirement!"

The participants listened.

"Hm, they must be doing that to see how we interact and prepare with one another," thought Kaesar, *"I wouldn't be surprised if they judged us during this preparation portion before the actual 2 on 1 battle."*

"—And then from there!" went on Flare, "The second stage will begin in the evening at the Sinara Examination Building located in Wavern City! We will direct all participants over there when the time comes!"

The participants nodded.

But then Adalo spoke up, "Locking hands with most of you will be worth the watch," he put out his hand with a small tornado on his palm.

"—Are you trying to make a threat?!" yelled Dedrian, "That's pathetic!"

"—Ouch!" chuckled Flare.

Adalo groaned, "I'm going to make sure I go hard on that one," he remarked, "Now let's leave them be."

After a moment, Adalo, Flare, and Lavivo began turning into Smoke.

"—I'm glad I met all of you," waved Lavivo as the three of them vanished from the room.

Only the participants remained.

Dedrian had a red aura as he made his way to the exit door, "—Rajaul's not here," he groaned, "And I get stuck with him."

Reno saw him go, "I-I'm not—"

But then Dedrian stopped and turned to him, "Just my luck that I get paired up with you!" he yelled, "You can't tackle with me! It won't work!"

Reno froze up, "B-But I—"

Dedrian marched towards him, "—And I know for a fact that you got help in your turn against the instructor!" he recalled, "That's how I know you can't do anything!"
The two were face to face, "—That's not what happened!" shouted Reno.

The other participants watched on.
"—Oh really?!" groaned Dedrian as he took a step closer, "Then prove you can fight by yourself! I'll give you the first hit against me!"

Reno saw Dedrian up close, "I-I don't have to fight you," he muttered.
Zayden walked over to the two, "Stop trying intimidate him," he remarked.

Dedrian angered, "—This isn't about you!" he turned, "It's between me and my partner!"

"—Actually, it is about me!" yelled Zayden, "If you're attacking Reno then you're attacking me too!"

There was a pause.
Lightning sparked appeared around Soro as he vanished from the room.

Dedrian turned to Zayden as began to Sin, "If I am attacking you," he smirked, "Then are you going to attack back?"
After a moment, Zayden began to Sin, "I'll have no other choice," he smirked.

The two stood face to face with Fire surrounding them.
Reno worried as he took steps back, "H-Hey, you don't have to—"
"—Oh look a fight Marubee!" beamed Kara with two lollipops in her mouth, "Let's watch it!"

"—Not right now," denied Marubee as she grabbed Kara's collar.
"—But I really wanted to see it!" screeched Kara, "—Oh," the lollipops fell out of her mouth, "—No no!" she freaked out, "My pops fell—Let me go Marubee!"

But Marubee dragged her away, "You have plenty more in your pockets," she murmured.

"—Every pop matters!" shrieked Kara.

Kaesar walked over and looked down at the fallen lollipops.

"—Oh my gray-haired partner!" called out Kara, "Please toss me my pops!" she asked putting her hands together.

Marubee was near the exit door.
Kaesar picked up one lollipop, "…If you say so," he spoke as he whipped it to Kara.

"—Yes gray haired!" beamed Kara as the lollipop landed in her mouth, "—Now the other one too!"
Kaesar picked the other lollipop, "…My hair's white," he murmured as he whipped it.

Kara's eyes shined as she saw lollipop coming, "Thank you so—" but then the lollipop got stuck onto her nose, "—This isn't the right way!" she freaked out, "Kaesar you—" but then Marubee left the room dragging away Kara.

Kaesar half smiled as he saw Kara go, *"That's actually the first time she said my name,"* he realized.
He turned back to the other side of the room.

Zayden and Dedrian smirked at each other as their Fire grew bigger.
Javarus saw them, then walked to the exit door.

But then Reno rushed to him, "—Javarus!" he called out, "You got to stop Zayden and Dedrian!" he begged, "I don't want a fight to happen because of me!"

"Sorry Reno," spoke Javarus, "But it isn't my duty to stop fights."
"—Please!" asked Reno, "This is my fault and I can't—"

"—And what if I get hurt?" opposed Javarus, "Then I'll get hurt because of you asking me to stop them."
Reno opened his mouth, but quieted, "Y-You're right…" he muttered.

Javarus took a moment, "Look, if you truly want to defend yourself and not rely on others," he remarked, "Then I'll take the time to teach you to Sin Rock better, I don't mind it."
Reno put his head up, "—But will that even help someone like me?!" he yelled.

108

Javarus nodded, "It will," he turned, "But for now, I have someone to check on."

After a moment, Reno saw Javarus exit the room.

"...I don't know where Javarus is going," murmured Reno, he then turned back, "But is anybody going to stop the two here?!"

"—Come on Dedrian!" urged Zayden, "I thought you were itching to tackle me!"

"—Don't get me wrong, I am!" stated Dedrian, "But there's something I must know first."

Zayden paused, "And what's that?" he asked.

Dedrian jumped back creating a distance between them, "...Just tell me why," he spoke and shouted, "Why the hell would you want to become a Full-Fledged Sinner?!"

Zayden took a moment, "—It's for my Mother!" he remarked, "I promised her that I will become Full-Fledged!"

"—To your Mother?!" Dedrian was stunned as the Fire around him lowered.

"—Yes, to my Mother!" yelled Zayden, "Is there something wrong with—"

"—I also made a promise to my Mother!" broke in Dedrian.

Zayden heard, "What are you talking about?" he asked.

There was a pause as Dedrian had a stern look, "My promise to my Mother was different than yours," he remarked, "I gave her my word that I will not allow another person to become Full-Fledged."

"Why?!" uttered Zayden.

There was moment of silence.

"—For the reason that my Father tried to become a Full-Fledged Sinner," recalled Dedrian, "And he died in the process..."

Zayden was surprised, *"Your Father passed away too..."* he heard.

"—He left me and my Mother alone!" angered Dedrian, "My Father should've never attempted to become Full-Fledged!" he recalled, "After that, my Mother told me to never allow anyone else attempt it, and that's when I gave her my word!"

Zayden took a moment as he listened, "It may be hard to hear, but you're going to have to break your word to your Mother," he opposed, "Because my Mother counts on me to become a Full-Fledged Sinner because my Father didn't..." he recalled, "And after my Father passed away in battle..."

Dedrian's eyes widened, *"So your Father's not here either..."* he heard.

"—My Mother told me to become a Full-Fledged Sinner in replace of him!" tensed Zayden, "And that's when I made my promise to her!"

Dedrian tensed, "—I'll have to show you my word is stronger," he stated, "You and your Mother's dream is just stupid."

Zayden was stunned.

Reno, Aviva, and Kaesar remained in the room with the two.

"...This is becoming serious," saw Kaesar. He raised his hand up, *"Let's get a better view,"* he Sinned an Ice platform high above on the wall.

"Hm?" Aviva turned to him.

Kaesar put his hand to the ground, "Icesarus," he spoke as he Sinned a Streak of Ice levitating him up onto the platform.

There was a moment as Fire surrounded Dedrian again, "—Enough talking!" he yelled, "Let's get on with this!"

"—I agree!" shouted Zayden as his Fire grew, "—I owe a fist to your jaw!" he quickly burst to Dedrian and swung his arm.

Dedrian stepped to the side.

"—I'm not stopping!" yelled Zayden as he turned and swung again.

Dedrian quickly caught his fist, "—I'm going to force you to stop!" he yelled.

But then Zayden roared as he forced the same fist forward, "—I'm going to show you that my promise is stronger!" he shouted as he swung the same arm.

"—Uh," Dedrian was pushed back against the wall, he put out his arms, "—I didn't think you would be this ticked off!" he shouted as he Sinned a wave of Fire.

Zayden evaded the Fire around the room, "—It's more than just being ticked off!" he yelled, "You called my dream stupid!"

"—This is getting reckless!" saw Aviva as she Sinned a Pink barrier around her.
The wave of Fire burst towards Reno.

"—I can't stop that!" freaked out Reno.
But then Aviva put her out her arm as she Sinned a Pink barrier around him.

"—Stop running away!" angered Dedrian as he Sinned more Fire.
Zayden quickly jumped in the air.

Dedrian looked up, "Now I—"
But then Zayden disintegrated in mid air.

"What the—"
Zayden reappeared behind Dedrian with his hand on his back, "—Incinerate!" he shouted as he Sinned Explosions of Fire from his fingers.

The ground broke in as Dedrian was sent crashing to the side wall.
Reno watched on from Aviva's barrier, "I-I want to do something like that..." he muttered.

Zayden stared down Dedrian from across the room, "I'm still not satisfied," he smirked.

Dedrian got up on one knee, "—You have no reason to be!" he shouted as he put his hand through the ground.
"What are you—"

But then a line of Fire erupted from the ground in front of him.
"Oh—" uttered Zayden as he jumped forward.

"—I got you now!" yelled Dedrian as he burst and punched Zayden in the stomach.
"—Uh," groaned Zayden as his mouth dropped.

Dedrian charged his shoulder into Zayden's chest, "—We're the only two Fire Sinners!" he yelled as he pinned Zayden to the wall, "—And I'll be the best one here!" Zayden coughed as his head knocked back on the wall, "What the hell are you—"

But then Dedrian swung his arm, "—This one's for my promise!" he punched across Zayden's face. "—Uh," Zayden fell over as he laid on his back.

Dedrian stood over him as he put his arms facing down, "—And this one's for embarrassing me the first night here!" he shouted.

But then Zayden's eyes widened, "—You mean when I caught your fist!" he yelled as he spat out an inflamed leaf.

"—What the hell?!" groaned Dedrian as the sharp leaf cut across his cheek, "—Uh," he was forced a few steps back.

Zayden slowly stood up.

Dedrian felt his cheek as blood came out.

"—Now who's tasting their own blood!" shouted Zayden.

Dedrian took his hand off his face, "—All these tricks you have!" he groaned, "Just like my partner, you can't tackle with the likes of me!"

The Fire around the two turned a bit Darker.

Aviva's eyes widened, *"—What's with these two?!"* she thought.

Kaesar looked down as he saw his Ice platform melting.

Zayden and Dedrian charged towards each other with Fire surrounding them.

"—I have a promise to keep!" yelled Zayden, "You're not going to come in the way of it!"

"—I have my word to keep!" yelled Dedrian, "I have to tackle you down!"

Reno saw them go, "—I caused this!" he worried, "Why can't I just fight for myself!"

Zayden and Dedrian swung their arms and shouted, "I have to beat—"

But then they froze on the spot as their Fire lowered.

"W-W-What happened?!" uttered Zayden as he tried to move.

Dedrian slowly turned his head, "W-What trick is this?!" he groaned.

Reno freaked out inside the Pink barrier, "—Who stopped them?!" he saw.

After a moment, the Pink barrier faded as Aviva walked towards Zayden and Dedrian with her hands were out.

Kaesar saw Aviva go on, "...Looks like its over," he thought, he Sinned an Ice path from the platform to the exit door.

"I-Is that—" Zayden tried to look up.

But then Kaesar slid down the Ice path and left the room.

On the ground, Dedrian slowly turned his head to Aviva, "Y-You," he angered, "I-Is this y-your doing?!"

"—Heck yeah it is!" remarked Aviva as her hands had a Pink aura, "I'm not letting you two blow up this Academy!"

Zayden angered, "B-But—"

"—Why do you care?!" opposed Dedrian, "This isn't about you!"

Aviva turned to him, "—Because I'm going to be one of the three to train with Adalo!" she declared, "And I need this building intact for that to happen!"

There was a pause.

"Hm, like a Farmake Sinner would win this competition," groaned Dedrian.

"—Yeah why would you stop us Aviva?!" Zayden raised his voice.

"What?!" Aviva looked to them, "What do you guys mean by that?!" she yelled.

"Isn't it obvious?!" groaned Dedrian, "A Farmake Sinner will not win this competition," he remarked, "They aren't nearly as powerful as Combat Sinners."

"—That doesn't make any sense!" yelled Aviva as she put her hands down.

Zayden and Dedrian were released as they fell to the ground.

Zayden uttered, "Aviva—"

113

"—Farmake Sinners are just as important as Combat Sinners!" she remarked.

Dedrian stood up, "I strongly disagree with that," he opposed, "Do you know the last time when a Farmake Sinner made into the top 3?"

There was a moment as Aviva stayed quiet.
"I'm sure you know it was your older sister Lavivo," went on Dedrian, "And that happened like what, 12 years ago?"

Aviva irritated, *"...Why is it always her,"* she thought.
"So tell me," smirked Dedrian, "How do you expect another Farmake Sinner to win?"

Aviva heard him, "I-I don't..." she muttered.
"—H-Hey Dedrian!" called out Reno from the other side, "S-She doesn't have to answer!"

"—Reno?!" saw Zayden.

"—My partner!" groaned Dedrian.

Reno tensed, "You're not as strong as you think you are!" he shouted.

"—You're kidding me!" Dedrian turned to him, "You're finally talking for yourself!"

Dedrian charged towards Reno as Fire surrounded him.
"—Wait no!" saw Reno.

Fire burst out of Zayden, "—Your fight's with me!" he yelled as he went in with a punch.
But then Dedrian quickly turned and caught his fist.

"—How did he block that?!" Zayden was stunned.
Dedrian tensed, "...Quit trying to get in my way," he groaned, "It's none of your business."

"—U-Uh," worried Zayden.
Reno's eyes widened, *"H-He just stopped Zayden!"* he saw, *"—But how?!"*
After a moment, Dedrian stopped Sinning as he let go of Zayden's fist.

Zayden stopped Sinning as he was in shock.
There was a pause, *"I have to be smarter than this,"* thought Dedrian as he walked over to the exit door.

Everyone in the room watched on.

But then Dedrian turned to Reno, "Better tackle well with me tomorrow," he demanded, "Or I'll make you disappear just like your buddy did to Rajaul."

Reno heard him, *"...How can I match up with anyone here,"* he was scared, *"They're all so much more above me..."*

"...N-Nobody knows what happened to Rajaul," muttered Zayden.

But then Dedrian turned and walked out the door.

On the other side of the room, Aviva angered, "I hate..." she muttered, "I hate this so much..."

Zayden and Reno looked back to her.

"Sinning...This Academy...This competition..." went on Aviva, "It's all so pointless..." she made her way to the exit door.

"Aviva..." murmured Reno.

"—Don't think about me," denied Aviva as she walked out of the room, "I don't even want to be in this competition."

Zayden saw her go as he tensed, "—I'll make Dedrian respect us!" he turned to Reno, "I'll make sure of it!"

Reno saw him, but then eyed down, *"...Is Dedrian right?"* he recalled, *"...Can I fight for myself?"*

There was a moment of silence.

"Reno?" called out Zayden.

Reno slowly shook his head, "No Zayden," he muttered, "I don't want your protection anymore..."

"Hm?" heard Zayden, "What do you mean by that?"

Reno took a moment, "...I have to go," he spoke as he walked to the exit door, "I-I'll see you later..."

Zayden saw him go.

Reno's expression changed as he walked out of the room, *"Zayden always talk to me like I need his help..."* he thought, *"I'm not just someone who needs protection all the time..."*

Zayden was the only one remaining in the room. He recalled what Dedrian told him: *"—I'll have to show you my word is stronger,"* he remembered his words, *"You and your Mother's dream is just stupid."*

115

Zayden slowly walked to the exit door and angered, *"—Calling my dream stupid?!"* he recalled as he punched into the wall, *"What does he know?!"*

There was a pause as a red aura formed.

"…This isn't over between him and I," remarked Zayden, *"If I want to win this competition, I have to be stronger than him,"* he went out of the room.

With the participants in different areas inside the Academy, on the upper level, Soro opened his room door.

But then Lavivo rushed to his hallway, "—Soro!" she called out.

Soro heard and faced her from across the hall.

Lavivo saw him, she took a few steps forward, "It's been a while…" she muttered.

Soro looked to her, "…What is it?" he spoke.

Lavivo stopped walking as there was a pause, "D-Do you know where your Father is…" she asked, "It's hard to believe what he's doing with his Sin…"

Soro had a stern look, "I have no answer to where he is," he remarked, "Find him yourself if you want, just don't get caught up in his mess."

Lavivo eyed down, "I wish I could…" she muttered, "But you know how he is now…"

There was a moment of silence.

"…Damon," Lavivo thought to herself, *"What happened to you…what's the reason for all the destruction you've caused lately…"*

Soro took a step inside his room.

"—Wait Soro," Lavivo called out again, "One more thing."

Soro looked to her.

"About your Mother…" spoke Lavivo, "Is she—"

But then Soro slammed the door shut.

Lavivo was stunned as she heard the door close, *"…He's been through a lot,"* she recalled, *"I shouldn't be pry on his personal life…"*

116

Lavivo turned back and walked away from his hall, *"Though this competition revolves around the stages,"* she thought, *"A lot more is going to happen than intended..."*

As a few hours passed by, the day went into evening.

In one of the participant's room, Reno laid on his bed. He was in deep thought as he put his arm up, *"...Would I have lost against the instructor if I wasn't wearing this wristband?"* he wondered and looked to his wrist.

He thought about what Dedrian told him: *"And I know for a fact that you got help in your turn against the instructor!"* he remembered his words: *"That's how I know you can't do anything!"*

After a moment, Reno shook his head and took off wristband, he placed it on the side desk.

He then stood up, *"Maybe it's about time that I stop taking the easy route..."* he thought, *"I need to be strong with my own Power, stronger than Dedrian...and Zayden."*

Reno walked out of his room and went down the stairs.

In the Sinara Medical Room on the main level, Javarus sat on a chair next to Veny who laid on a bed.

The room was dim in light, the walls were gray and the floors were white.

After a moment, Veny's eyes slowly opened as he sat up.

"...How are you holding up?' asked Javarus.

Veny groaned as he felt his shoulder, "How long was I out for?"

Javarus turned back to the clock, "About 3 hours," he remarked.

Veny heard him, he put his head down, "...I blew it," he muttered, "I-I couldn't get Soro back..."

There was a moment of silence.

"I'm sorry Javarus..." murmured Veny as he looked to him.

"For what?" asked Javarus, "You don't have to apologize."

117

Veny paused, "I assume you were here with me for those 3 hours," he spoke, "Probably waiting for me get up."

There was a pause.

"For that, I'm sorry," murmured Veny again and tensed, "But that doesn't mean I'm done with—"

"No, you listen to me!" yelled Javarus as he stood up, "You're done with Soro! You were so irrational against him!"

"—What did you expect?!" opposed Veny, "I had no other—"

"—Understand this!" went on Javarus, "You getting revenge on Soro is irrational in itself!" he stated, "First, he did not hurt your family, Damon did!"

"That doesn't—"

"Second!" broke in Javarus, "You could have easily died! Soro Sins on another level than you, and deep down, you know that too!"

Veny angered, "Then why didn't you stop me?!" he yelled.

There was pause in the room as the two looked to each other.

"—What's the point?" spoke Javarus as he sat back down on the chair, "You're going to do it again…and I didn't plan on dying that hour…"

Veny heard him as he calmed himself.

"Veny, I don't want you to die before you live your life without anger…" spoke Javarus, "Back at our town, you're always talking about taking down Damon and Soro…"

Veny looked away, "…And so what?" he groaned, "Damon took away my family's Sinning Abilities, permanently."

Javarus took a moment, "I know he did, and for this time I allowed you to go off against Soro," he remarked, "Now you've learned you're not ready to take him."

"—I've learned nothing!" denied Veny, "When I feel better, I'm going after him again!"

"But there's no—"

"You don't have to get involved in this!" yelled Veny.

There was a pause.

118

"I know I don't," spoke Javarus then shouted, "But if you ever want to get to Soro! You're going to have to go through me!"

"I said you don't—"

"—And me!" someone rushed through the room's doors.

"—Zayden?!" saw the two.

Zayden marched to Veny's bed, "Like Javarus said," he remarked, "You ever try fight Soro again, you're going to have to beat me!"

"Not you too!" yelled Veny.

"Zayden," called out Javarus, "How did you hear us?"

"—How could I not?!" Zayden looked back at him, "I was nearby and I heard all of your shouting!"

Zayden turned back to Veny, "—So are we clear?!" he asked, "You're not going after Soro anymore!" and in his thoughts, *"Not just for Veny's sake,"* he knew, *"But I need Soro for my own goal…"*

"—How are you going to stop me?!" opposed Veny.

"—Because me and Javarus will make it our duty to keep you grounded!" yelled Zayden, "I'll tackle you if you do anything stupid like that again!"

"—Tackle me?!" uttered Veny.

"—Yes!" tensed Zayden.

There was a pause.

"…Tackle is something Dedrian says," recalled Veny, "And you're so loud too…"

Zayden paused, "…Wait—I think you're right," he worried. "You're starting to talk a lot like Dedrian," snickered Javarus behind him.

"—Am I really?!" uttered Zayden.

Veny shook his head, "…What happened to you?" he asked.

"—Don't worry about me, you're the one who's in bed!" yelled Zayden, "And if talking like Dedrian gets through to you then that's fine!"

Javarus saw him, *"I'm grateful Zayden's helping Veny out,"* he smiled, *"Thank you."*

But then someone else rushed through the door, "—I heard you guys shouting!" a voice yelled.

"—Reno?!" saw the others.

"Why are you here?!" asked Zayden.

Reno stood in front of the Medical Room's door, "I'm going to do something for myself," he tensed and looked to Javarus, "You have to teach me how to Sin Rock better," he declared, "I have to get stronger to protect myself!"

There was a moment of silence. Javarus heard him as he stood up.

Zayden looked to Reno, "...This is about Dedrian," he spoke, "Isn't it?"

Reno looked back, "Maybe," he answered, "But it's also about you not defending me all the time..."

Zayden heard him.

Reno eyed back to Javarus, "You said you wouldn't mind teaching me how to Sin Rock," he recalled, "So I'm taking you up on your offer."

Javarus looked to him, "I'm glad you remembered," he half smiled, "I've always wanted to start my goal."

Reno listened.

"Spreading Sinning in a positive way," smiled Javarus, "That's what it's about, and I'll help you."

"—Yes!" cheered Reno.

Zayden saw him, *"I don't know what he means about me defending him,"* he thought, *"But it's good to see he's putting in the effort to improve."*

Javarus looked back to Veny, "I'm going to be outside with Reno," he remarked, "I want you to stay in bed and rest up, you'll need it."

Javarus then looked to Zayden, "We'll keep Veny grounded," he nodded.

Zayden nodded back.

"We'll see about that," murmured Veny on his bed..

After a moment, Javarus and Reno walked out of the Medical Room.

Zayden saw them go.

"Hm," Veny had a light smirk, "I still can't believe you said 'tackle,'" he recalled.

120

Zayden turned back, "Dedrian might be rubbing off on me or something," he spoke, "We are both Fire Sinners after all."

Veny heard him, "Something must've happened between the two of you," he remarked, "You look different when you speak about him."

Zayden slowly clenched his fists, "It's just that...Dedrian is as strong as anyone else here," he stated, "—I just can't let him have the last tackle!" his aura turned red.

Veny saw him, "Keep your heat out of this room," he told him, "I have to rest for now..."

Zayden snickered, "Yeah, you're right," he half smiled, "I'll leave you alone, I won't get anything done here anyways."

Veny listened.

After a pause, Zayden turned back, "Get better soon," he spoke, "You don't want to be hurt before tomorrow."

"I won't be," tensed Veny.

After a moment, Zayden made his way towards the door.

Veny carefully watched him exit out of the Medical Room.

He was in deep thought about Zayden, *"Is it just an act?"* he wondered, *"I mean, Soro wanting to become Full-Fledged is understandable..."* recalled Veny, *"But why would you want to, Zayden?"*

At the same time, Marubee and Kara were upstairs in Marubee's room.

Kara laid on the bed playing with her feet in the air.

"...And that's how I'll prove my case," remarked Marubee as she finished telling her plan for the second stage.

"—But Marubee!" beamed Kara, "That doesn't sound like a very good idea to me!"

Marubee paced back and forth, "I know what I'm doing," she spoke, "And it's going to make me look great against the Kallents."

121

There was a pause, "…It's way too risky," muttered Kara as she put her legs down.

Marubee closed her arms, "You don't understand, it's time for people like me to stand up for ourselves," she went on, "We can't let the people who are spoiled always be at the top! It's time for a change."

"—Yeah, I get that whole thing," Kara sat up, "But I know this isn't the best way to prove yourself, you'll be hurting your own chances of passing by a lot!"

"You don't get it—"

"—I do so!" nodded Kara, "Just please don't do this Marubee!" she begged, "It's going to make you look bad!"

Marubee took a moment, "Then think about it," she explained, "I'll essentially be out-doing two Kallents," she said, "Kallents I repeat, and if that's not enough to make it to the top 3 three…I don't know what is."

"—Well I'm not going to let you do it!" opposed Kara, "No way!"

"You won't change anything," denied Marubee, "I've already made up my mind."

Kara laid back on the bed as she shook her body around, "—You have to listen to me!" she yelled.

"—Stop that," demanded Marubee, "You look like a fool."

But Kara continued shaking, "—No!" she denied, "Not until you change your mind!"

Marubee shook her head, "Then you might as well go on for an eternity," she remarked.

Kara quickly stood up and stared into Marubee's eyes, "—I refuse to let you mess up!" she declared.

The two were face to face.

"…What am I saying," Kara gave up, "You're not going to listen to me are you," she laid back down on the bed.

Marubee saw her, "You know me too well," she snickered, "But enough about what I'm going to do," she went on, "What's your plan with you and your partner?"

Kara heard her, "Oh that gray-haired boy," she spoke about Kaesar, "He's funny…and really odd…"

"What? How so?"

Kara took out a lollipop and put it in her mouth, "Well..." she murmured.

There was a pause.

After a moment, Marubee spoke up, "Remember when your partner was talking about his goal at the end of the first stage?" she recalled, "How did it go again..."

Kara put her feet in the air, "...It was something about him wanting to know about his life," she muttered. Marubee recalled, "Yeah, what the heck was that all about?" she asked.

"—I really really wish I knew!" beamed Kara as she sat up, "He's so mysterious!"

"Hm, he's not that mysterious," spoke Marubee, "You probably think that because you two argue about the colour of his hair."

"Yeah—but," screeched Kara, "...There's something else."

"Hm?" heard Marubee, "What are you talking about?"

"Well...do you remember when Flare was doing roll call before the first stage," recalled Kara.

"Yeah?"

"And how someone didn't show up and so he was disqualified?"

"Yeah yeah, I think his name was Rajaul," recalled Marubee, "What about him?"

Kara quickly jumped as she put her finger up in front of Marubee's face, "—I think he didn't show up because of my gray-haired partner!" her eyes widened, "—He scared him off!"

"—And how would you know?" asked Marubee.

"—Because I saw what happened!" beamed Kara, "That Rajaul guy tried to attack my partner in the hallway!"

Marubee slowly shook her head as she put Kara's finger down.

"--And when my partner saw Rajaul Sin," went on Kara, "He basically asked Rajaul to attack him!" Kara's mouth dropped, "But then Rajaul froze like a frozen lollipop!"

"...You're over exaggerating," denied Marubee.

Kara quickly shook her head, then paused, "...I just don't know Marubee," she muttered, "He seems like he's hiding a lot..."

There was a moment of silence.

Kara recalled the moment with Kaesar and Rajaul: *"I'm here,"* she remembered Kaesar's words and stare, *"What's holding you back?"*

Marubee saw a change in Kara's expression, "Are you okay..." she murmured.

Kara eyed down, "...He gave Rajaul this stare that really sent off weird vibes," she spoke, "I didn't like his mean eyes at all..."

Marubee listened.

Kara was in thought, *"I really don't get my partner,"* she recalled, *"With his friends he's all happy and talkative..."* she noticed, *"But in that moment, he looked like a whole other person, his eyes were so cold..."*

But then Marubee burst into laughter.

"—Huh?! It's the truth Marubee!" beamed Kara, "Really!"

Marubee looked to her, "...You're making Kaesar out to be a real threat," she brushed it off, "And that's comical."

"—But he made Rajaul runaway!"

"That didn't change my opinion on him the slightest," stated Marubee.

"—Then we'll both show you!" yelled Kara, "He's super strong and we're going to dominate together!" she tensed.

There was a pause, "...Relax," spoke Marubee, "I didn't think you would get so defensive."

"—You better apologize right now!" screeched Kara.

There was a moment of silence.

Marubee saw Kara's emotion, "...Alright whatever," she murmured.

"—Thank you!" beamed Kara, she took out another lollipop and put it in her mouth, "It really means a lot!" she smiled.

Marubee saw her energy and forcibly smiled back.

By now, outside on the training fields of the Academy, the grass was moist with the sky partly cloudy.

Javarus and Reno stood away from each other. "—Alright I'm ready to learn!" tensed Reno as the wind blew his hair.

"Okay Reno," nodded Javarus, "First things first—"

"—This move always works on Zayden!" yelled Reno as he burst through the grass.

"—Reno," groaned Javarus as he stepped to the side.

Reno almost lost his balance, "—Take this!" he yelled as he turned with a punch.

"I knew you'd be like this," murmured Javarus as he began to Sin.

The ground beneath Reno shook, "—W-Woah what's happening?!" freaked out Reno.

A piece of ground quickly went up the air with Reno on top, "—W-Wait Javarus!" panicked Reno as he saw the ground becoming smaller, "—Let me down!"

Javarus looked high up, "If you want to touch the ground you're going to have to cooperate," he remarked.

"—How am I not cooperating?!" worried Reno, he was on his knees looking down, "Isn't this training?!" Javarus sighed as he put his hand out and closed it.

Reno yelled, "Hey I—" but then the Rock he was on broke apart as he fell through the air, *"—What do I do now?!"* he worried, *"This is going to hurt so much!"*

Javarus watched him falling, "Please show me that you know how to protect yourself in this situation," he hoped, "But then again, why am I worrying, I'm sure you know what to do."

Reno shrieked in the air and closed his eyes, *"I don't know what do!"* he panicked, *"I'm—I'm going to—"* but then his eyes widened, *"Hold on—I've been in a mess like this against Zayden before!"*

Reno Sinned in mid air as he had a light green aura.

"—There you go!" saw Javarus.

Reno turned facing towards the ground, "—I-I think this should work!" he uttered as he put his arms forward and back.

A thin platform of Rock Sinned and hovered over the ground, *"—This'll protect me!"* saw Reno and smiled. Javarus watched on.

"—This is the training I've been wanting!" cheered Reno.

But then he broke through the Rock platform and crashed into the ground.

"—Oh," saw Javarus, he quickly ran over to Reno, "—Hey are you okay?!" he asked.

Reno's eyes were half opened on the ground, "E-Everything hurts…" he murmured.

Javarus took a moment, "Maybe this whole training thing was a bad idea…"

"—No it's not!" shouted Reno as he stood up, "I'm tired of not being able to fight for myself!"

Javarus heard him, "If you want to learn," he went on, "You're going to have to be patient."

"Hm?" heard Reno.

"There's something I want to show you," went on Javarus, he sat cross legged on the ground.

Reno watched him as there was pause.

But then Javarus eyed to Reno to the ground in front of him.

"Really…" sighed Reno, after a moment, he sat down in front of Javarus, *"Yeah, this is exactly the training I was looking forward to…"* he mocked in his mind.

The two faced each other, "First things first," explained Javarus, "You got to know what your Sinning Ability truly is."

"—What?" uttered Reno, "You want me to know what Sinning Rock means?"

"Yeah," answered Javarus, "Do you know what a Rock is?"

"Uh—Y-Yeah…" muttered Reno, "It's…a part of the ground?"

"You're close," remarked Javarus, "To be specific, Rock is the solid mineral material forming on a part of the Earth's surface."

"I wasn't close at all..." Reno put his head down.
"So, you need to focus on the Earth's surface," taught Javarus, "Like the surface we are currently sitting on," he went on, "Feel it."

Reno knocked on the ground.
"Now close your eyes and carefully listen to everything around us."

After a moment, Reno closed his eyes, "...It doesn't hurt to try," he murmured as he waited.
"If you carefully listen and focus," went on Javarus, "You can hear the movement of the ground beneath."

Reno groaned, "The only thing I hear is the wind," he remarked.
"Keep concentrating."

Reno shook his head and focused again.
"Come on Reno," urged Javarus, *"Any Sinner who Sins Rock can hear the movement underneath the ground."*

There was a pause, "All I hear is a faint thumping noise," spoke Reno, "Is that you?"
"No—no it's not!" Javarus raised his voice, "That's exactly what I'm talking about, that is the surface being impacted!"

"—Really?!" rejoiced Reno as he kept his eyes closed, "A-And there's more!" he heard.
"—What do you hear?" asked Javarus, and in his thoughts, *"Please say what I want you to say,"* he hoped.

Reno took a moment, "...I-It's like," he spoke, "It's like a cracking noise—It sounds like Rocks tumbling down a hill!" he pointed to the ground on his right, "It's coming over there...I think."
Javarus heard Reno and smiled.

"—There's actually a lot of noise coming from that part of the ground!" Reno opened his eyes.
"That's because that part of the surface is weak," remarked, "That's why you heard many creaks and cracks coming from it. The weaker the surface, the easier to Sin that part of the ground."

127

"…Oh, I see," murmured Reno.

"Test is out," insisted Javarus as he stood up, "Try to Sin the ground you deem is weak."

"Okay," nodded Reno as he stood up. He had a light green aura.

He put arm forward to the ground on his right, "…Alright," he murmured, "Here goes nothing," he lifted his hand up.

A big chunk of Rock quickly Sinned out of the ground, "—T-That's so big!" Reno's eyes widened, "—Did you help me just now?!"

Javarus shook his head.

"—Does that mean I did it myself?!" Reno was shocked as he put his arm down.

The Rock crashed back to the ground, "Next time, please let it down gently," suggested Javarus.

"Sorry about that," chuckled Reno.

"Anyways," continued Javarus, "Try Sinning that part of the ground," he pointed out.

"Hm?" Reno followed Javarus' pointer, "—Sure!" Reno put out his arm again, "—I can do this!" he put his hand up.

But the ground didn't move.

Reno quickly put his arm up and down again, "—It isn't budging!" he worried.

"And vice versa," spoke Javarus, "If there's a part of the surface that you can't hear, it will be difficult to take control of it."

Reno took a moment as he understood.

"Any questions regarding this?" asked Javarus.

"Yeah, just one," went on Reno, "What was that thumping noise I heard earlier?"

"Hm, It can be anything that makes contact with the ground," answered Javarus, "It could simply be somebody walking on the ground around us, like someone on the other side of the Academy.

"—Really? I can hear that?!" Reno was shocked, and in his thoughts, *"—Sinning Rock is a lot cooler than I thought!"* he was surprised, *"Now I know everything about it!"*

"Other things you need to learn are—"

"—Hey let's have a friendly battle!" urged Reno. "But I still haven't—"

"—Nah I think I know enough!" remarked Reno, "And thanks to you, I'm stronger than ever!" he cheered. There was a pause.

Javarus saw him, *"He seems really happy after one lesson,"* he thought.

"—So can we?!" Reno asked again, "I want to prove myself to everyone that doubts me! Even people that should be on my side!"

Javarus heard him, "...Alright Reno," he nodded, "For the intention of you learning something through this battle, I will fight you."

"—Let's go!" rejoiced Reno.

Javarus walked away to create space between the two.

There was a moment of silence as they looked to each other from a distance.

"—Oh man I'm so excited!" thought Reno, *"I know this is exactly how Zayden feels! He's always eager to battle and maybe that's why he's so strong! And if I follow his way, I can be just like him!"*

The two faced each other.

The faint thumping noise Reno heard from the ground was caused by Kaesar, he was on the other side of the Academy's fields.

Kaesar walked around the field by himself, *"It's been a while since I took the time to do this,"* he thought. It was becoming darker outside as the Academy's lights slightly shined the field.

Zayden opened the side door onto the same field. Kaesar looked to the right as he saw light come through, he saw Zayden, "How did your fight go with Dedrian?" recalled Kaesar, "I didn't catch the ending."

Zayden looked to him, "He called my dream stupid," he groaned as he walked over.

Kaesar half smiled, "And so he did," he spoke.

129

"Yeah," went on Zayden, "He even stopped my last attack..." he stood in front of Kaesar and eyed away.

"And what are you going to do about it?" spoke Kaesar.

Zayden tensed, "—I'm going to have to be more prepared next time!" he declared.

Kaesar heard him, "How typical," he murmured.

"What—How else would you want me to go about it?!" asked Zayden.

"Calm down before you burn yourself," advised Kaesar.

"—I am calm!"

Kaesar stayed quiet, he looked to him as he slightly turned his head.

Zayden slowly breathed in and out, "Alright," he relaxed, "Now I'm calm."

Kaesar paused, "Thought so," he spoke.

"Come to think of it," went on Zayden, "Didn't you tell me that same thing before? How I should calm down before I burn myself."

"Yeah, I did," recalled Kaesar, "You tend to snap every time someone judges your actions."

Zayden took a moment, "I do, don't I," he agreed.

Kaesar nodded, "Sometimes you just need to walk around and clear your mind," he remarked.

"Is that what you were doing just now?"

"Well, I was..." answered Kaesar, "You're not walking with me if that's what your implying."

"—Why would I walk around?" opposed Zayden, "I'll get nothing done by doing that!"

"—It's something I like to do," defended Kaesar, "I always walk around with my—" but then he stopped.

There was a moment of silence.

"My..." Kaesar's voice lowered as his white hair went over his eyes.

Zayden paused, "...With who?" he asked.

———————————————

Back on the other side, Javarus looked to Reno, "I'm ready whenever you are," he half smiled.

Reno tensed, "—Here I come!" he yelled as he burst forward.

Javarus put his arm out, "Let's try it again," he spoke as he Sinned.

A piece of ground underneath Reno flew up the air with Reno on top, "Uh—Two can play this game!" yelled Reno as he put his arm out.

A piece of ground underneath Javarus flew up the air with Javarus on top.

The two were as high as the Academy as the time neared 7:30 P.M.

They levitated on Rocks a distance away, "—Looks like I improved huh?" boasted Reno.

"I guess you've made a little progress," remarked Javarus, he put his hand out and closed it.

"...What was that?" wondered Reno, "Why'd you—but then the Rock underneath him broke, *"—Not again!"* he panicked as he screamed down the air.

"—Come on Reno!" called out Javarus as he watched from above, "You should know what to do now!"

Reno freaked out, but then paused, *"He's right—I can feel that the Rock over there is weak!"* he saw, *"That means I can Sin a part of it to catch my fall!"*

But Reno was close to crashing on the ground, "—Reno!" worried Javarus as he quickly Sinned the same Rock Reno saw.

"—Uh," uttered Reno as he closed his eyes and landed on a platform of Rock.

After a moment, he looked down, "—How did I do that so fast?!" he was stunned.

Javarus landed on the ground and faced him, "You didn't do that," he spoke, "I did."

"—No why?!" groaned Reno, "Don't help me! How am I supposed to get stronger if people are always protecting me?!"

"You were so close to colliding with the ground again," remarked Javarus, "You were just too slow, I had to help you."

Reno looked down, "Yeah..." he saddened, "You're right about that..."

131

There was a pause, "…How exactly did you pass the first stage?" asked Javarus.

"Uh—" uttered Reno, "W-What do you mean?"

"I mean…" went on Javarus, "Well—don't get me wrong, from what I've seen up close, you're not a bad Sinner by any means, you just need practice," he assured, "But you passed the first stage faster than anyone else, the two huge boulders you thrusted onto the instructor made me assume you might even be stronger than me, so how did—"

"—You think I cheated, right?" broke in Reno. Javarus took a moment, "Well—"

"—I did," admitted Reno, "I cheated."

After a moment, Javarus smiled, "You're joking," he chuckled, "Aren't you?"

"—No, I'm serious," answered Reno, "I cheated, what's so funny?"

Javarus snickered, "It's just really strange that you confessed so quickly," he spoke, "I didn't expect that."

"—But that's the truth," repeated Reno, "I cheated."

"There you go again being so blunt," chuckled Javarus, "How did you manage to cheat anyways? Nobody suspecting you of it."

"—Oh, that was simple," Reno stepped off the platform and put out his arm, "I wore this—" but then he stopped.

"…Wore what?" asked Javarus.

"—I almost let it slip again!" recalled Reno, "I can't let anyone know about the wristband!"

"Uh, Reno?"

"Oh—It's nothing," blurted Reno, "I cheated and I know that's wrong."

Javarus paused, "Although I do disagree with the act of cheating," he spoke, "That's in the past and I hope you learned and grew from it."

Reno nodded, "—I did learn from it!" he stated, "And I will never cheat again!"

"As long as you stick true to your word, I'll continue to be involved with you," remarked Javarus, "Now let's finish off our training!" he declared, a thicker green aura formed around him.

The ground began shaking, "—T-This is too much!" shrieked Reno as his legs trembled.

But then Javarus ran towards him, "—Get a hold of yourself!" he went in with a punch.

Reno quickly put his arm to his chest, "—I'm trying!" he yelled.

A Boulder of Rock rose in front of Reno.

Javarus swung his arm and punched through it. "—Uh," uttered Reno as he was pushed back, he was shocked, "—*That Rock…actually protected me!*" he saw, "*I would've been done if I didn't Sin it in time!*"

"Hm," half smiled Javarus.

Reno burst towards him, "I can do this!" he yelled as he went in with a punch.

But then Javarus caught his fist.

"—No!" Reno went in with his other fist.

But then Javarus caught it as they both locked hands.

The two pushed each forward and back, "—Come on!" Reno urged himself.

"Keep going," encouraged Javarus.

Reno screamed as he swayed Javarus' hands way.

But then Javarus kneed him in the stomach.

"—Uh," groaned Reno.

Javarus turned and kicked Reno's side sending him back.

Reno rolled on the ground and laid on his side.

"—Was that too hard?" worried Javarus.

"—No!" denied Reno as he quickly stood up, "All this experience will make me stronger!'

Reno charged at Javarus again, "*I can't be looked down at anymore!*" he thought, "*I don't want anyone defending me! I can do it myself!*"

Javarus saw him coming.

On the other side of the Academy, it was quiet. "…Kaesar, what were you going to say?" asked Zayden, "Who do you like to walk around with?"

Kaesar put his right hand in his pocket, "...I like to walk around with the people at my home," he muttered as he brushed his hair up.

"Then you must have a boring family,' snickered Zayden.

Kaesar paused, "Yeah, whatever..." he murmured.

But then Zayden recalled a moment in the first stage: *"I desire to know everything about my life!"* he remembered Kaesar's goal.

"...So, what do you do at your home?" spoke Kaesar.

"Oh," went on Zayden, "I eat, sleep...and fight with Reno a lot..."

There was a pause, "...Makes sense," muttered Kaesar.

Zayden saw a change in his expression, *"...I shouldn't straightaway ask Kaesar about his answer to Adalo's question,"* he thought, *"It's too personal, but if I slowly talk more and more about his life, I'm sure he'll open up..."*

"—Yeah, that's what I do," Zayden put his head up, "A lot more exciting than whatever you do at your home!"

Kaesar had a stern look, "I..." he spoke, "I just want to beat Dedrian with my Fire."

"—What?!" uttered Zayden, "That's what I want to do! And you don't even Sin Fire!"

"I know I don't," smirked Kaesar, "But I actually want to see your Fire again," he jumped back.

Zayden saw him from a distance.

"I haven't forgotten about the ending of our battle last night," recalled Kaesar, "It's been slowly bothering me all day."

Zayden remembered their battle, "The wristband helped me back then..." he murmured then spoke up, "Are you serious about this?" he asked.

Kaesar stayed quiet as a Blue aura formed around him. His hair slightly rose with his eyes turning into a dark blue colour.

"...What's this?" saw Zayden.

"You don't have the wristband on," remarked Kaesar, "So this time, there will be no controversy."

After a moment, Zayden began Sinning as Fire surrounded his body, *"I'm still hurt from the fight with Dedrian,"* he groaned, *"But I'm not backing down from Kaesar."*

The two looked to each other from across the field.

Kaesar had an emotionless expression.

Zayden stared into his eyes, *"...Why does Kaesar appear so different,"* he felt a change.

Javarus and Reno stood a distance away from each other.

Reno's breath was heavy as his aura faded, "I-I can still go..." he grimaced.

Javarus saw him, "Doesn't appear so," he remarked, "And with the second stage tomorrow, we should head back—"

"—That'll be the same as running away!" shouted Reno as he ran forward.

"—What?!" saw Javarus.

Reno burst with 2 boulders of Rock behind him, "—My Sinning isn't done yet!" he yelled as he Sinned put his arm out.

The Boulders rapidly rushed forward.

Javarus' eyes widened, "How would that be running away?" he recalled as he avoided both Boulders jumping in the air.

Reno jumped towards him, "—Just let me continue!" he yelled as he went in with a punch.

But then Javarus caught his arm.

"—How?!" uttered Reno.

Javarus swung Reno and threw him down.

"—Uh," groaned Reno as he rolled on the ground.

Javarus landed and looked to him, "I'll be more than happy to continue this another day," he spoke, "But enough is enough."

"—No!" denied Reno as he got up to one knee, his breath was heavy, "I'm not running away!"

There was a pause as Javarus looked to him, *"It doesn't look like he's going to stop,"* he thought, *"And I also don't want injure him before tomorrow."*

Reno slowly stood up, "—Uh," he fell back down to one knee.

"Okay, but—unless I deliberately let you hit me," went on Javarus, "You won't be able to land one attack."

"—T-That's not true!" opposed Reno, "Please, let me continue sparring with you! I don't want anyone protecting me anymore!"

Reno burst towards Javarus again, "—I want to prove everyone wrong!" he yelled as he jumped in the air. Javarus looked up.

A Boulder went into Reno's arms, "—Just one hit!" he shouted as he crashed down with the Boulder.

"—Did I get him?!" uttered Reno.

There was a pause.

After a moment, Reno lifted up the Boulder, "Where did he go?!" he looked around.

Javarus saw Reno from behind, *"He just wants one hit against me?"* he recalled.

"Where are—"

"I'm right here," spoke up Javarus from behind, "And we're finished our session."

Reno turned around, "I said I—" but then he stopped, he slowly clenched his fists.

There was a moment of silence as Reno eyed down.

Javarus spoke up, "...What's this sudden change of attitude?" he asked.

Reno stayed quiet.

"I know you want to be a better Sinner," recalled Javarus, "But you continue to mention that you don't want anyone to protect you...why wouldn't you want protection?"

Reno heard him as he saddened, he dropped down onto his knees, "...I have to learn to protect myself," he muttered, "And once I do, I won't need Zayden anymore..."

Javarus listened.

"...All the time in our village," recalled Reno, "Zayden always defended me from anyone who picked on me...and even now he's still defending me..." Reno raised his voice, "—I don't ever want him to see his back ever again! I want

136

to change all of that! And in order to change, I have to get stronger!"

Reno tightened his fists as he had his head down. Javarus heard him, *"...I see how he feels,"* he thought, *"Maybe if he gets that feeling that he can fight for himself, he'll stop being so reckless."*

Reno closed his eyes, "Even other—"

"—Alright Reno," called out Javarus, "Last attack wins."

"—Huh?!" Reno opened his eyes.

Javarus smiled, "Whoever lands the next hit," he went on, "Will win this battle."

"—You got it!" rejoiced Reno, he stood back up.

There was a pause as Javarus waited.

But then Reno burst towards him with a light aura, "—For everyone that thinks I'm a nobody!" he yelled.

Javarus saw him coming and closed his eyes.

Reno swung his arm, "—I will get stronger!" he went in with a punch.

"—Uh," groaned Javarus as he was hit on the cheek and pushed back.

Reno's breath was heavy as he saw him.

After a moment, Javarus opened his eyes, "...Looks like you got me," he half smiled as rubbed his cheek.

Reno's eyes widened, "...I, did it?" he murmured then smiled, "—I really did it!"

Javarus snickered, *"Though I didn't think his punch would pack that much strength,"* he stopped rubbing his cheek.

"—I can't believe it!" cheered Reno, "I actually hit you! Clean too! I'm stronger than ever!" he put his fist up.

"—Reno," broke in Javarus.

Reno stopped dancing, "Yeah?" he heard.

"...Yes, you have gotten better," remarked Javarus, "But this thing with you wanting to be stronger so Zayden doesn't have to defend you..." he recalled, "It isn't right."

"Huh?" murmured Reno, "It's better to be able to fight for yourself..."

Javarus took a moment, "...I understand not wanting to hide behind Zayden all the time," he spoke, "But you're talking like you don't want him by your side…and that's the bad idea you're getting at."

"—Don't get me wrong!" Reno shook his head, "Zayden's my friend!"

"—Exactly," nodded Javarus, "And friends protect one another through anything and everything."

Reno looked up and listened.

"…Everyone needs a friend," spoke Javarus, "There will be times where you cannot defend for yourself, and those are the important moments when your friends lend you a hand."

Reno's expression changed, "…Oh," he muttered.

"So don't say you don't need Zayden," advised Javarus, "I'm sure the both of you need each other more than just for battling," he remarked.

Reno eyed down again, "…*Maybe I was thinking about it the wrong way,*" he reflected.

There was a pause as the wind blew his hair.

Reno looked up, "—Thanks for everything Javarus," he half smiled.

Javarus saw him, "No worries," he smiled back, "Let's go inside now, I need to check up on Veny anyways."

Reno nodded.

The two made their way inside the Academy through the front door.

Reno walked forward as Javarus walked to the right.

He took a step in the Medical Room, but then looked back, "—One second Reno," he called out.

Reno turned and faced him.

"…Speaking of Zayden from before," recalled Javarus, "This may seem random, but do you have any idea why he wants to become a Full-Fledged Sinner?"

"—Oh, yeah he…" murmured Reno as he took a moment.

There was a pause, Javarus continued, "It just seems like—"

"—I remember now!" went on Reno, "It's this promise he made to his Mom when he was younger, he promised her that that he will become a Full-Fledged Sinner."

Javarus heard him, "...A promise?" he repeated.

"Yeah," confirmed Reno.

There was a pause.

"And, this may seem random as well," spoke Reno, "But can I check up on Veny with you? I want to know something..."

Javarus opened the Medical Room's door, "Sure, why not," he answered.

Reno walked to him as they both went inside.

Javarus thought about Zayden, *"He made a promise to his Mother to become a Full-Fledged Sinner?"* he recalled, *"...Why would he ever want to make such a promise...the power is too much..."*

The only ones remaining outside in the night were Zayden and Kaesar.

The two were Sinning from both ends of the field. After a moment, they burst towards each other.

"—Attention all participants!" Flare announced through the speakers.

"—What?!" Zayden and Kaesar stopped on the spot.

"—It is now 8:00 P.M and the Sinara Eatery is now open for 20 minutes!" went on Flare, "We have burgers, noodles, rice, fruits, vegetables, pizza, and more!" she listed, "This is the only time you can grab a bite! So, come to the main foyer!"

Zayden and Kaesar listened.

"---That sounds so good," uttered Zayden as his Fire slowly went away.

Kaesar saw him, "Zayden," he called out, "We have to settle this."

But then there was a pause as Zayden's stomach growled, "...Kaesar," he murmured, "I think I'm going to go inside to eat."

139

"—We already started this," urged Kaesar, "Now we have to finish."

"We'll just got at it another time," tensed Zayden then smiled, "But for now, I haven't eaten for a while and I got to go!"

The two faced each other.

Kaesar saw Zayden's red aura fade away, "...Just when I brought out these eyes too," he muttered as he stopped Sinning.

Zayden saw Kaesar's eye turn back to normal colour.

But then Kaesar's stomach growled.

"You might even be hungrier than me," snickered Zayden.

"That isn't it," remarked Kaesar, "I wouldn't want to battle if you're not completely invested into the fight."

Zayden heard him, "I knew you'd see it my way," he ran off to the Academy's door.

Kaesar saw him go as he eyed away.

But then Zayden looked back, "—What's with that look on your face?" he asked.

"Hm?" Kaesar looked up.

"We have many battles waiting for us after this whole competition," remarked Zayden.

"Yeah but..."

"—You're my friend," went on Zayden, "And just like Reno, every time you and I fight, we're always going to improve each other."

Kaesar listened as there was a moment of silence.

"...I'm glad I got to know more about you and your home," recalled Zayden, "And since I told you about my family and home before..."

There was a pause.

"...I hope later you tell me more about where you're from too."

Kaesar heard him, "...Yeah," he muttered, "We'll see..."

After a moment, Zayden turned and walked inside the Academy.

Kaesar looked back, and walked towards the door.

———————————

Inside the Academy, Flare stood in front of big golden doors.

Most of the participants stood in front of her.
"Is everyone here?!" addressed Flare.

"We're here and ready to eat!" beamed Kara with Marubee beside her.

Javarus and Reno came out of the Medical Room on the side.
"Hello participants Javarus and Reno," saw Flare, "Is participant Veny coming to eat?"

Javarus shook his head, "No he will not," he spoke, "He just went back to sleep."

Flare nodded.
Zayden came up from behind Reno, "How'd the training go?" he asked as he stood beside him.

Reno turned, "—It was great!" he tensed, "I-I actually think I got better!"
Zayden half smiled, "That's good to hear," he remarked. After a moment, he looked around the room, *"Dedrian nor Aviva is here,"* he noticed, *"So isn't Soro."*

"—Alright participants!" addressed Flare, "You only have 20 minutes to eat!"

The participants were eager.
Flare turned around as she grabbed the big handle on the golden doors, "—W-Why is this always so difficult?!" she struggled to open it.

Reno saw her, "Hey Flare do you—"
But then Smoke appeared around Flare's hand, after a moment, the doors opened.

"Hm?" saw the participants.
Flare's breath was heavy as she had her hands on her knees, "I didn't need your help!" she uttered out loud, she then turned to the participants, "—Make use of your time in the Sinara Eatery!" she smiled.

"—Yes!" cheered Kara as the participants burst inside the room.
Inside the Sinara Eatery, there was a digital clock on the wall counting down from 20 minutes. The room had brown walls and a red carpeted floor. There was a long dinner

table with various foods on them, along with a yellow chandelier that shined from the top.

"—I'm glad I heard the announcement!" snickered Zayden as he ran to the table.

Outside of the room, Kaesar saw everyone preparing their plates from across the hall.

"Hm?" Reno turned with bread in his mouth, "—Hey Kaesar!" he looked out the door, "Come eat! It's really good!"

After a moment, Kaesar scratched his hair with his finger and walked inside the Sinara Eatery.

There was a moment as the participants filled up their plates.

Zayden, Reno, and Javarus, sat on one table, while Marubee and Kara sat on another.

Kaesar walked over to the two tables.

Zayden put his spoon in his rice, "—Come sit with us," he saw him.

Kaesar turned.

"—This soup is going to be so good!" beamed Kara to Marubee, "I'm super ready!"

"Okay okay just drink it," spoke Marubee.

Kaesar looked over to their table.

After a moment, Kara turned to him, "Oh it's my gray—"

But then Kaesar looked back to the boys.

"Hm?" saw Kara.

He walked over to the boys table and sat down. Both tables had white cloth over surrounded by four chairs.

The boys looked to Kaesar as their plates were filled to the top, "...Why didn't you grab a plate?" asked Zayden.

Kaesar looked up, "Oh, I'm not too hungry," he half smiled.

"—Well like Flare said!" broke in Reno, "I'm going to make use of my time before 20 minutes!"

"—Yeah!" agreed Zayden.

The two of them rapidly at their food.

On the other table, Kara quickly drank her soup.

Marubee swallowed her food, then looked around their table, "You know Kara…" she murmured, "You can sit with the other people if you want…there's only the two of us here…"

Kara had her lips on the bowl of soup in her mouth, "—No way!" she put the bowl down, "—I'm always going to stick with you Marubee!" she went on to eating rice.

Marubee heard her, "If you're happy," she spoke, "Than who am I to judge," she picked up her spoon.

On the boys table, Reno gulped, "—There's no time to waste!" he yelled as he continued.

"…Slow down," snickered Javarus, "20 minutes doesn't go by too fast."

Zayden drank his juice and put it down, "I admit, I do eat fast," he was stunned, "But Reno's going all out." Javarus exhaled, "You guys are treating like this is your last meal," he picked up his sandwich, "Well actually—this could be your last meal in the Academy."

"—Nope!" opposed Zayden, "There will be many meals to come once I'm in the top 3!"

"—Yeah!" Reno swallowed his food, "Me too!" Kaesar looked to the two as he stayed quiet.

"Then I can show you guys my recipes," smiled Javarus, "Because I'm also going to be here."

"—You can cook?!" asked Reno.

"Yep," he answered, "I use my Sinning to assist me as well."

"Really?!"

Javarus nodded, "It's really good," went on, "Just ask Veny."

"…It's actually not that great," spoke someone from the golden doors.

Everyone looked to the direction, "—Oh it's Veny!" uttered Reno with his mouth full.

Veny walked to the dinner table, he began filling out his plate, "…I really mean it guys," he looked to the boys, "Javarus' cooking is odd."

"—No it is not!" denied Javarus, "I make the best sandwiches."

143

"Yeah..." murmured Veny, "And while I ate one of them, I chipped my tooth on a piece of Rock."

Zayden and Reno chuckled.

"That...was a mistake," recalled Javarus.

Veny walked over to their table, "Not going to lie though," he went on, "The Rock wasn't bad compared to the rest of the sandwich."

Zayden and Reno burst into laughter.

"Alright now you're going overboard," uttered Javarus.

Kaesar looked to them and snickered.

"—Yeah Veny!" laughed Reno, "I think Soro knocked you down too hard!"

The plate Veny carried dropped to the floor.

The laughter quickly stopped, "...Huh?" paused Reno, "...What happened?"

After a moment, Zayden groaned, "Reno you—"

"—Everything's alright," assured Veny as he picked up his plate, "My hands just feel numb from the sleep I had."

Javarus looked on as he worried, "...Reno," he turned to him, "We just told you about his history with Soro in the Medical Room..."

Reno remembered, "...Oh," he looked down.

On the other table, "This Reno's an idiot..." murmured Marubee.

"—Marubee!" screeched Kara, "Why are always criticizing everything?!"

"—I'm sure anyone with the right state of mind would think the same way," remarked Marubee.

Kara looked to her, "Who said your mind is right though?" she asked.

"—What?" uttered Marubee, "You think it isn't?!"

The two locked eyes for a moment.

But then Kara took out a lollipop, "...Just kidding," she smiled as she put it in her mouth.

Veny pulled out a chair and sat down with the boys, "The water is pretty warm," he spoke, "Don't you think?"

"—I know right!" agreed Reno, "Someone needs to make it colder!" he picked up his glass and drank down the water, "It's always like—"

144

But then a quick blue flash appeared, "Uh—" uttered Reno as the water turned into Ice.

"—What just happened?!" saw Javarus.

Kaesar waved his finger up, "You get that for being too loud," he snickered as Ice shattered from the tip.

"But—" uttered Reno as his mouth was frozen on the glass, "I can't—" he struggled.

The group laughed, "I agree with Kaesar," snickered Zayden, "Watch your mouth."

Reno irritated, "I'm going to shove a Rock up your—"

"—Relax Reno," assured Zayden, he raised his finger, "I got you," the tip lit on Fire as he waved it over the glass.

Reno worried, "Just hurry—" but the Ice turned to Water, "Uh—" it went down his mouth as he choked on it.

"...I think you'll be fine," saw Zayden, he then looked to the boys, "—By the way, do you want go into Wavern City tomorrow?!" he asked, "After the partner training session of course."

There was a pause, "Hm..." muttered Javarus.

"It may be out last day together," swayed Zayden, "So why not?"

"—It'd be best if I don't come along," answered Veny, "I'd rather train and rest till the second stage. I don't want any distractions."

Zayden heard him, "How about you Javarus?"

"Same over here," he spoke, "The second stage is in the evening. I wouldn't want any distractions either."

Zayden listened to them.

"Plus..." went on Javarus, "Someone has to keep Veny grounded."

"—I don't need you for that!" opposed Veny.

Zayden exhaled.

There was a pause, "...I'll come," Kaesar looked to him.

"Oh really?" Zayden turned, "I was going to ask...but I didn't think you'd want too..."

Kaesar heard him, "I am the one who told you how popular Wavern was," he recalled, "I want to see it as well."

Zayden nodded, "Yeah I remember," he remarked, "That's what made me want to go."

"—Uh," Reno choked beside them, but had his thumb up front of Zayden.

"—Reno! You're still choking on the water?!" realized Zayden.

"Alright so the three of us will go," settled Kaesar. Zayden quickly hit the back of Reno's head, "Are you okay?!" he worried.

"—Uh," Reno took deep breaths, "—What took you so long?!" he yelled.

"—I was making plans!" Zayden yelled back, "But you're good now and that's all that matters!"

Reno shook his head as he stood up, "Yep, you helped me this time!" he remarked, "But with the training I got from Javarus, I won't need you anymore!"
Zayden paused, "...What?" he heard.

Reno walked over to the dinner table.
Javarus looked to him, "...Don't act like that again," he advised.

Kaesar also got up and walked to the dinner table, he stood beside Reno.

There was a pause as the boys watched.
But then Veny turned back, "—Javarus," he spoke, "Let's bring it up now."

"Hm?" Zayden looked to the two.
Javarus turned Veny, "I suppose so," he spoke.

"...What are you talking about?" asked Zayden.
Javarus tensed, "...Zayden," he spoke, "While it's just the three of us at the table..." he took a moment, "...Veny and I both want to hear it from you," he remarked, "How do you plan on becoming a Full-Fledged Sinner?"

There was a moment of silence.

"...I didn't expect to talk about this now," spoke Zayden, "I mean...I don't..."

"Don't even—" sat up Veny.

"—Zayden," assured Javarus, "Take your time."

Veny groaned as he slowly sat down and waited.

At the dinner table, "Reno…" spoke Kaesar beside him, "Let's go upstairs."

Reno burped, "—Why?" he asked.

"I assume that's where you left the wristband," went on Kaesar, "I'd like to check it for myself."

Reno put bread on his plate, "…Yeah, it's in my room," he turned to Kaesar, "But I'm still—" he burped.

"Then let's go," urged Kaesar, "What are we waiting for?"

"But I'm still—" Reno burped again.

Kaesar paused, "Doesn't sound like you're still hungry," he spoke.

Reno put his plate down, "Yeah, I think I've had enough," he snickered, "But why should I show you the wristband anyways?!"

"—Because I know that it exists," remarked Kaesar, "And I can tell anyone whenever and wherever I want."

"—Uh," worried Reno.

Kaesar stared at him.

"—Alright fine," he gave in.

"Hm, let's go," spoke Kaesar, he put a piece of bread in his pocket and walked out of the Sinara Eatery with Reno.

Back at the table, Zayden finally spoke, "I mean…" he went on, "Aside from getting stronger, I actually don't have any idea how to become Full-Fledged."

There was a pause, "So that's the case," went on Javarus, "That was unexpected, I assumed you would know."

Zayden eyed down, then looked to Veny, "…What is a Full-Fledged Sinner exactly?" he asked out loud, "My Mother never told me what it really was…but she kept telling me to achieve the state of it."

Veny looked up, "I'm not too sure myself…" he groaned, "But it's nothing you would want."

"…Neither do I know," spoke Javarus, "I—"

"A Full-Fledged Sinner is when a Sinner reaches the ultimate state of their Power and can control all Sinning Abilities," answered Kara from the other table.

All the attention went onto her.

"However," continued Kara, "The state of being Full-Fledged can be overpowering, which then causes one to lose their sense of thought and emotion."

"I—"

"—Furthermore," went on Kara, "The appearance of the Sinner considerably changes once he or she has reached Full-Fledged."

There was a moment of silence as everyone listened.

Marubee turned, *"...As much as I always think Kara knows nothing,"* she thought, *"In actuality, she knows more than what anyone expects."*

"—Well bye now!" smiled Kara as she stood up, her and Marubee began walking out of the room.

"—Should we go to Flare to say 'thank you' for the food?!" beamed Kara.

"I think she'll be fine without it," denied Marubee.

"—But Marubee!" screeched Kara as they walked out.

Javarus and Veny turned back.

Zayden leaned on his chair facing up, "...So that's what it is," he recalled, "—I'm going to have to Sin all the Abilities?!"

"...Yeah," muttered Veny.

Javarus looked to Zayden, "And did you hear the last part?" he asked.

Zayden nodded.

"...The state of being Full-Fledged will overpower you," remarked Javarus, "You won't be yourself anymore..."

But then Zayden tensed, "...I understand the facts about being Full-Fledged," he went on, "But this is my only reason for Sinning..." he yelled, "—So I'll just find a way to be me and still become a Full-Fledged Sinner! I have too!"

"—You hardly need to think about it!" shouted Veny as he slammed the table, "—The state of being Full-Fledged will be the guaranteed chaos on the world!"

"Veny—"

"Let's talk about the only Full-Fledged Sinner!" recalled Veny, "—Damon Uzara!" he stated, "He's on a massive war with himself against world! And soon enough—even Soro will!"

Zayden stood up, "—I'm going to become Full-Fledged!" he repeated, "But I promise I won't hurt anyone!"

The two looked to each other.

"You can't...promise that..." groaned Veny, "At first, I thought you were clueless about being Full-Fledged, I thought you just wanted to be strong ..." he muttered and yelled, "But you're really serious about this, aren't you?!"

Zayden slowly nodded, "I'm sure you know by now," he remarked, "There's nothing more important to me than my promise to my Mother."

But then Veny gave a stern look, "...I'm not playing around," he tensed, "You become Full-Fledged, I'll chase you down...and kill you."

Zayden was stunned, "What are you..." he muttered.

"—And that's my promise," ended Veny, he turned and walked away.

Javarus looked back, "...Why would you say that?" he was shocked.

Zayden watched Veny go.

But then as Veny walked towards the door, Dedrian passed by him to the dinner table.

Zayden looked up, "—You," he saw.

Dedrian picked up a plate, "...There's no need for Veny to kill you," he smirked at Zayden, "Because of my promise, there's no way in hell I'm letting you become Full-Fledged."

Zayden heard him as he slowly angered.

Dedrian shook his head, he turned and walked outside of the Academy.

After a moment, Javarus looked to Zayden, "...I didn't want that to happen," he murmured.

Zayden slowly clenched his fists, "I'm—I'm going to do it," he reminded himself.

"...Zayden," called Javarus, "I strongly suggest you reconsider this..."

149

But then Zayden had a stern look, "...With this many people against me," he smirked, "I have to become Full-Fledged more than ever."

Javarus worried, *"Even after hearing all of that..."* he was surprised.

Zayden closed his eyes, "...Maybe Soro's the only one that understands me," he spoke out loud, "After all, we share the exact same goal..."

After a moment, the buzzer went off on the 20-minute clock, and Zayden walked out of the room.

Javarus saw him go, *"...His determination won't change his mind,"* he thought, *"Yet, he may not even go far enough in Sinning to become Full-Fledged..."*

There was a pause, *"...But the same can't be said for Soro,"* recalled Javarus.

As the Sinara Eatery timer ended, Kaesar was in Reno's room as he held Zayden's wristband. He hanged it from his finger, "...So this is the all-important item you and Zayden cry over," he murmured.

Reno stood in front of him, "—We don't cry over it," he denied as he sat down on the bed, "It's just really important to Zayden."

Kaesar paused, "It looks like an ordinary rubber band," he remarked.

"Well—what'd you expect?" asked Reno.

"...I don't know," murmured Kaesar, "This red piece of rubber attacked me on night one...I want to know how it does what it does..."

Kaesar lifted his left finger, "...Let's see this," he murmured as he Sinned a streak of Ice.

"—What are you doing?!" freaked out Reno as the wristband froze, "—I promised Zayden nothing will happen to it!" he jumped towards Kaesar.

Kaesar put his arm up and blocked him, "Nice try," he shook his head. But then his eyes widened, "...What's this?" Kaesar saw as the Ice quickly melting off the wristband, "So it protects itself too..."

150

At this point, Dedrian was outside the Academy. He sat down a distance from the entrance door, he rested his feet on the stair below as his plate was not eaten out of on the side.

Veny came up from behind, "Thought I'd find you here," he saw.

There was a pause.

Veny looked to Dedrian, he sat down next to him, "...I know we've never talked before," he spoke, "But we share the same hate."

A red aura slowly formed around Dedrian, "I'm not in the mood for conversation," he stated.

"I'm not looking to pick a fight with you," assured Veny, "I wanted to talk to you about something."

Dedrian looked straight ahead to the field.

"Look," went on Veny, "I despise the idea of being Full-Fledged just as much as you do."

Dedrian smirked, "But you're senseless," he remarked, "Hm, attacking Soro head on back at the first stage. I didn't see what happened with my own eyes but I sure as hell saw your pain afterwards."

Veny remembered, "...You're right," he muttered, "All my built-up anger went to waste back there..."

"—Of course I'm right," went on Dedrian, "But my tackle with Zayden will have be the complete opposite."

"—That's what I'm counting on!" broke in Veny

"Hm?" heard Dedrian as he turned.

"—You're going to have to fight Zayden one more time!" urged Veny, "To finally shut him up!"

"You don't have to remind me about that," groaned Dedrian, "I've been itching to tackle him...one more time."

Veny saw his expression change, "...Things really have been getting serious between the two of you," he recalled.

Dedrian had a stern look, "...It's important to the both of us," he remarked, "—It's his promise vs mine!"

Dedrian's Father died in the process of becoming a Full-Fledged Sinner. So, after his Father's death, Dedrian

151

made a promise to his Mother to never let anyone else attempt to become Full-Fledged.

On the other hand, Zayden's Mother wanted his Father to become Full-Fledged. But after his Father died in battle, he made a promise to his Mother to become a Full-Fledged Sinner in replace of his Father.

"—But don't even have the least assumption that I'm tackling him because of you," remarked Dedrian, "I'm doing this for myself."

"...Do it for whoever," spoke Veny as he stood up, "I'm trusting you to knock him down...I have my hands full with Soro."

Dedrian heard him, "You're going after him again?" he went on, "You're going to be put down even harder than before."

"No, not this time," denied Veny.

Dedrian stayed quiet as he stood up and walked to the front door.

Veny turned, "—I'm counting on the both of us to take down Zayden and Soro!" he declared.

Dedrian opened the door, "You really are hopeless..." he spoke, "Just like my useless partner," he referred to Reno.

"You're comparing me to him?!" opposed Veny, "Why do you always talk like you're that much better than everyone else!"

"—Because I can tackle with the best," smirked Dedrian, "And there's a difference between hope and expectation."

There was a moment of silence as Veny listened. Dedrian went inside the Academy and walked up the stairs, *"...Isn't that right?"* he thought about his Mother, *"Father died becoming Full-Fledged leaving you and I alone..."* he recalled, *"So I have to cut down anybody who strives to follow the same way..."*

Veny remained outside, *"...His personal feelings may be enough to shut down Zayden,"* he thought, *"And no matter what...I have to beat Soro..."*

Back upstairs in the room, Reno tried to get over Kaesar, "—You can't do that without my permission!" he yelled.

Kaesar warded him off with his hand, "Or maybe—"

But then Reno quickly went over Kaesar, "—I allowed you to check it out" he snatched the wristband, "Not destroy it!" he rolled on the bed and and stood on the side.

Kaesar faced him.

But then Aviva had her hand on the room's door as she loomed by.

"Hm?" Kaesar and Reno turned to her.

There was a pause, "...Is the Sinara Eatery closed now?" asked Aviva.

"Yeah, it should be," answered Kaesar, "20 minutes must have passed by now."

Aviva sighed, "I should've ate..." she murmured.

"...Then why didn't you go?" asked Kaesar.

Aviva looked to him, ...I just had a lot of things on my mind," she muttered.

Aviva thought about when she stopped the fight between Zayden and Dedrian: *"Hm, like a Farmake Sinner would win this competition,"* she recalled Dedrian's words, *"—Yeah why would you stop us Aviva?!"* she remembered Zayden's words.

After a moment, Kaesar felt his pockets. He walked over to Aviva, "...Here," he spoke as he took out a piece of bread.

Aviva looked to the bread, "...You're not going to have it?" she gulped.

Kaesar shook his head, "Nope," he spoke, "I'm fine as it is."

Aviva raised her arm and got a hold of the bread. "...You should come in here and eat though," remarked Kaesar, "I don't know if there are any rules of eating outside the timer, but just to be safe."

Aviva nodded as she went inside the room.

"—I don't know who you are!" yelled Reno from the side, "But try to not to make a mess in my room!"

153

Aviva looked to him, "—I saw you in the first stage!" she recalled, "Is your memory lost?" she snickered as she sat down on the bed.

Kaesar heard her, *"...Memory,"* he thought.

"—It tastes so good," rejoiced Aviva as she took a bite, "It's warm."

Kaesar took a moment, *"...Now that she's here,"* he looked to Aviva, *"I could get some answers about Adalo..."* he recalled, *"Why did I see those images with him back in the first stage?"*

The first time these images occurred in Kaesar's mind was when Dedrian was holding Zayden by the collar, and then Adalo broke it up. The other time was when Veny attacked the instructor from the sky on the Rock, but then Adalo interrupted and stopped him with his Smoke.

"...Just who is Adalo?" thought Kaesar then spoke, "Here's a question," he went on, "What's your relationship with Adalo?" he leaned back on the drawers.

Aviva took a bite, "Why do you assume I have some type of relationship with him?"

There was a pause, "He speaks to you in a different manner compared to the rest of us," remarked Kaesar, "It's like he cares more about you."

Aviva swallowed her food, "...It's because I'm a Kallent," she muttered then spoke up, "I think he knew my parents."

Kaesar heard, "...And then that's how he knows you," he spoke.

"Basically," she went on, "I don't know how they met, but my parents and Adalo seem close, I think they grew up together or something," she took another bite from the bread.

"I see," went on Kaesar, "Where did they grow up?"

"They grew up where we live," remarked Aviva, "Korona Island."

"—Korona Island?" broke in Reno, "That's near Ayshan village, where me and Zayden live."

"Yeah, it's kind of close," Aviva turned to him, "You just have to get over a few kilometres of water..."

"—You don't have to brag about it!" yelled Reno, "Everyone knows how wealthy you have to be to live on Korona Island!"

"—I didn't mean it like that!" denied Aviva, she took a hard bite of the bread.

"But you—"

"—Whatever Reno," broke in Kaesar, "Aviva," he called out, "...That's your name, right?"

She nodded.

"Did you ever see me on that Island before?" asked Kaesar.

Aviva took a moment as she chewed on the bread, "Wouldn't you remember?" she asked.

Kaesar stayed quiet, *"This may solve a lot of things,"* he waited.

Aviva squinted at him, "But no, I haven't," she remarked and finished her bread.

Kaesar eyed away, *"...Did I see those images wrong?"* he wondered, *"Was that even Adalo?"*

"I didn't know you before this competition," went on Aviva, "Why are you asking all of this? Did you see Adalo and I before?"

Kaesar looked the other way, *"...Maybe it's all in my head,"* he thought, *"I guess I'll never know what it means..."*

There was a moment of silence.

But then Aviva stood up, "—Does this have to do with the answer you gave in the first stage?" she recalled.

Kaesar's hands tightened on the drawers.

"—Yeah Kaesar," Reno looked to him, "What was that all about?"

There was a pause.

"...Kaesar?" called Reno.

"—Come on, don't play dumb with me," continued Aviva, "What do you want to know about your life?"

Reno heard her, "...Wait a minute," he murmured, "—Don't play dumb?!" he recalled the words, "You're the fan that wanted my autograph at the first stage!" he pointed to Aviva.

"—What?!" uttered Aviva, "You said that! Those words never come out of my mouth!"

"—I remember you!" went on Reno, "You pulled me aside because you wanted my attention!"

"—Don't think of it like that!" denied Aviva, "I just wanted to know the about the wristband!"

"—You mean this?!" Reno held it up.

Aviva saw it, "Exactly," she nodded as he put her hand out.

The wristband shined in Pink, "What the—" uttered Reno.

The wristband levitated towards Aviva. She kept her hand open, "So this is the wristband you and Zayden cry over," she murmured as it landed on her palm.

"—I've never cried over it!" denied Reno.

Aviva took a moment as she felt the wristband.

Reno opened his hand to her, "Can I have it back now?" he asked.

There was a moment of silence.

"—Hand it over!" repeated Reno.

Aviva eyed him, "...You're persistent," she remarked, "Now I know how Flare might feel."

"—Huh?!" uttered Reno, his cheeks slightly turned red, "—What does that have to do with anything?!" he yelled.

Aviva snickered, then looked back to the wristband, "...Hold on," she noticed a tiny opening on the inner rubber, "I learned about these types of equipment..."

"—You and Flare are two different people!" screeched Reno.

But then there was a pause.

"...This wristband might be more than it seems," spoke Aviva.

"Hm?" Kaesar and Reno listened.

"...A few years ago," went on Aviva, "I was learning about the tools Sinners used in battle...and these wristbands were included in their equipment..."

"I never learned anything about that," sighed Reno.

"That's because—I learn a lot about Sinning through the teachers and lessons my parents set up for me..."

explained Aviva, "Aka my high-end butlers Marubee refers too..."

"Oh...that's what she meant."

Aviva took a moment as she wore the wristband, "Years ago, they used wristbands like these, so whoever wore the wristband would slowly absorb the life force from the teammate wearing the counter wristband," she remarked, "This would help the user of the wristband battle with a better health while their teammates may be resting or so."

Reno shook his head.

"...It's not that complicated Reno," murmured Kaesar.

"—You mentioned Zayden's Mother," recalled Aviva, "Is she the one who gave Zayden this?"

"...Yeah," answered Reno, "But I've met Zayden's Mom, I don't think she would give Zayden the wristband for that purpose..."

But then Aviva slowly took of the wristband, "I don't know about Zayden's family," she spoke, "But if this is that type of wristband I just talked about, it can take years off your life," she informed.

Reno was in deep thought, *"...What is she talking about?"* he doubted, *"Even if I told Zayden, he'd think I'm making some sick joke..."*

"Just destroy it," advised Aviva, "It'll only cause you harm," she dropped the wristband on the bed and walk to the room's door.

Reno watched on.

Kaesar had his head down, *"...Why do I care about my past so much,"* he thought, *"No matter how many times I feel I should forget about it...I always find myself trying to find out more..."*

Aviva looked to him, "Oh, and thanks for the food," she half smiled.

Kaesar snapped, "Y-Yeah, no problem," he muttered.

"—Wait Aviva!" yelled Reno.

"Hm?" Aviva turned.

Reno took a moment as he tensed, "...The wristband is important information to know," he murmured then yelled, "—But I'm sorry that I made Dedrian put you down from before! I think Farmake Sinners can make it to the top 3!"

"—Uh," uttered Aviva with her hands out, "You don't have to—"

"—And now since I trained with Javarus!" went on Reno, "Nothing like that will ever happen to you again!"

"—You fool!" denied Aviva, "I don't need you to look out for me!"

"—But I'm going to fight Dedrian tomorrow!" yelled Reno, "In our partner training session, I have to challenge him!"

Kaesar heard, "...One lesson in Sinning won't change the world," he spoke.

"—You'll see!" Reno pointed at him, "I can defend myself and others from now on!"

"—I don't need your protection!" yelled Aviva, "Seriously! I'm my own person and I don't want your help!"

"—Too bad!" opposed Reno, "Dedrian won't expect what I have in store for him!"

"—Do you even hear me?!" asked Aviva.

"Yep!" nodded Reno, "Loud and clear!"

But then there was a moment of silence.

Aviva exhaled, "...This passion to fight Dedrian is pretty dumb," she spoke, "But thanks for the apology I guess."

"—Anything for a fan!" recalled Reno.

"—A fan?!" uttered Aviva, "Not with that again!" she irritated and walked out of the room.

"—Huh?" Reno watched her go, "What happened?" There was a pause.

Kaesar looked to Reno, "...I don't see you changing your mind," he remarked, "And I can't stop it, so you do you."

"—Exactly," Reno turned to him.

"But don't comeback with broken bones," stated Kaesar, "We both told Zayden that we're going out to the city before the next stage begins."

"—I'll be fine," Reno brushed it off, "Dedrian is the one who should be worried!"

There was a pause, "Hm, you keep telling yourself that..."
spoke Kaesar, "Maybe one day it'll come true."
"—It will!" yelled Reno.

The night was late as the time neared 10:30 P.M. At the
Sinara Service Desk, Flare was inside the glass on her
chair writing out letters.

But then Adalo appeared inside the glass in
Smoke, "...Must you do this every time?" he saw.
"Uh huh," nodded Flare, "Just wait till the others find out we
have Damon's son in the competition..."

"—Don't' tell them anything," opposed Adalo, "No
other Academy should be informed of what is taking place
here."
Flare continued to write, "...I do this every year, why are
you so worked up about it now?" she asked, "It's important
that every Sinegious and Attendant stay connected with
the information on each other's Academy."

Adalo walked near her, "That's unreasonable," he
went on, "Considering we never get the information back."
"Well—we do get letters from the other Academies,"
corrected Flare, "You just never bother to read them."

"—Indeed," affirmed Adalo, "The only thing I care
about is this Sinning Academy and nothing else."
But then Flare stopped writing, "You're lying to yourself,"
she snickered, "You care about another Academy just as
much as this one."

"What makes you make say that?" denied Adalo,
"That Academy is not of importance to me, I despise him."
Flare looked to him, "I'll never understand your feelings
towards The Sinetity Academy," she shook her head.

But then a strong tornado appeared on the desk,
"—Okay okay!" uttered Flare as all the letters flew around,
"I was just poking fun!"

But Adalo shook his head as the wind grew
stronger.
Flare's hair was blown back, "—I understand all of it!" she
screamed, "With your brother, your history, everything!"

But the Wind continued.

159

"—Adalo!" shrieked Flare.

After a moment, Adalo closed his eyes as the Wind calmed, all the papers dropped to the floor.

"—Now I have to clean this up!" groaned Flare as she went on the floor to collect the papers.

Adalo pointed his finger as he Sinned slight Wind floating a few letters onto the desk.

"…Don't expect me to say thank you," murmured Flare as she put the papers together and aligned them on the table.

"My brother nor his Academy is to be spoken of," recalled Adalo.

"Is that the truth?" heard Flare.

Adalo nodded.

"…Well then," murmured Flare then yelled, "How's Juro and his Academy doing?!"

"—Flare," groaned Adalo.

Juro Shuesi is the younger brother of Adalo, they only differ in age by 3 years. Juro is also a Sinegious of a Sinning Academy called the Sinetity Academy.

"Oh be quiet," Flare brushed it off, "The two of you always talk bad about each other, but in the end, neither of you do anything about it."

"—He's the one who decides to begin this cycle by calling my Academy dirt every year," reminded Adalo, "And I must defend the honour of this establishment."

Flare exhaled, "…You just want to defend yourself rather than the Academy," she spoke, "You and your brother can't stand seeing the other one exceed in anything."

Adalo gave her a stern look, "You wouldn't get it," he remarked, "After fighting with Juro over my life, I realized the competitive aspect of being a Sinner is in my blood," he spoke, "Though I do respect my brother, I will never like him nor his Academy…I'm sure he feels the same way."

"—Meaningless banter," chuckled Flare, "I can see the both of you fighting in your graves, you two take things a bit too serious between this 'competitive aspect.'"

"No Flare," opposed Adalo, "This competitive nature is what pushes Sinners to go even further beyond

160

their powers," he stated, "He will eventually accept my superiority."

But then there was a moment of silence.

"...Okay there," murmured Flare, "Don't talk like you know anything about acceptance..."

"Hm?" heard Adalo.

"The participant in this Academy..." spoke Flare, "You still didn't talk to him..."

There was a pause.

Flare stopped writing as she turned her chair, "—Accept your past with him!" she tensed, "Resolve your issues with participant—"

"—Flare," broke in Adalo, "The topic will not change to that."

"—But I guarantee that he's already suspicious of something," she went on, "This is the best time to tell him about what he doesn't know..."

Adalo groaned, "...This isn't the best time," he stated.

"—Then when is the best time?!" yelled Flare, "It hurts me that you did that to him!"

There was a moment of silence.

"...When I see fit," answered Adalo, "I'll tell him everything he wants to know."

Flare eyed to the floor, "...Didn't his answer to your question mean anything to you," she muttered, "I wouldn't be too surprised if he leaves without ever knowing the truth..."

Adalo looked to her, "...I do care," he admitted, "I'm responsible for everything—I know that!" he tensed.

Flare looked up and saw a change in his expression.

"...So, like I told you before," advised Adalo, "Leave it to me, I'll handle all of it."

Flare took a moment, she turned back to the desk, "...You've never lied to me before," she started writing the letters again, "So I can't assume anything..."

Adalo heard her, "...Exactly," he agreed.

161

Flare saddened a bit, "...Just make sure everything turns out fine," she muttered, "Okay?"

Adalo listened.

Flare moved onto the last letter, "...I'll see you in a minute," she spoke, "If you're waiting for me."

"...Just finish this up," assured Adalo.

After a moment, Flare aligned the letters and put them in separate folders, "Okay I'm done," she yawned and stretched her arms.

But then Adalo opened his down hand in front of her.

"Hm?" saw Flare, "...Do you want me to give you something?"

Adalo stayed quiet.

"Oh, I see," remembered Flare, "It's been a long day Adalowala," she snickered, "Let's go now."

"Glad I don't have to tell you that," relieved Adalo, "But do not call me Adalowala."

Flare put her hand over Adalo's, "I can say it as I please," she smiled and stood up.

After a moment, the two began turning into Smoke.

"Wait," spoke Adalo, "What about the letters?"

Flare yawned, "I'll just mail them tomorrow," she murmured as she rested her head on Adalo's shoulder.

"—You know you should ask before you do that," groaned Adalo.

But Flare quickly fell asleep.

Adalo saw her, "...I'm not much for these types of things," he muttered.

The two of them turned into Smoke and vanished from the Service Desk.

By now, all the participants were in their rooms. In one of them, a participant laid back on the railing looking out the window. He rubbed his left pointer and thumb together.

There was also a big black bag beside the bed with cookie crumbs spattered on top. And to nobody else's knowledge, there was another person in the Academy; A little 6-year-old girl who sat cross legged on the bed.

The little girl put the half-eaten cookie down in front of her, "—Sowo!" she whined with crumbs over her face, "—You say we go today!" she tried to put a sentence together.

Soro faced her.

"—I want now!" water filled in the girl's eyes, "You said..." she began to cry.

Soro stopped rubbing his fingers. He stood up from the railing and walked over to the bed, "Not now," he spoke. He picked up the half-eaten cookie and held it in front of her.

The little girl wiped her tears and looked to him, "...You say that all time," she took the cookie and nibbled on it.

Soro took a moment as he walked back to the window, "...It's only a matter of time," he remarked, "I'm one step closer for the both of us, Cecelia."

Cecelia was the name of the little girl on Soro's bed. She had dark eyes and long hair with bangs. She wore a pink sweater along with a red scarf and mittens.

"—Huh?" uttered Cecelia, "Step for what?! You strong already!"

But Soro glared down at his left pointer and thumb, "...Not nearly enough," he saw his semi-dark fingers.

After a moment, Cecelia yawned, "...Sowo," she called out.

Soro looked to her.

"...Who that pink girl before?" Cecelia tiredly asked, she recalled about when Lavivo confronted Soro. She secretly watched their conversation through a little opening in the door.

Soro remembered, "...I hardly know her," he answered, "But she knows about us...or me, at least."

Cecelia's eyes began closing, "...W-What that mean?" she murmured.

There was pause.

Cecelia fell on her back as she went to sleep.

163

Soro looked to her, then back out the window, *"...Lavivo doesn't matter to me,"* he thought, *"My only concern is to become Full-Fledged like him..."* he recalled, *"...Nobody will stand in my way, that includes my partner..."*

With everyone in the Academy eventually falling asleep, day 1 of the Sinara Academy competition was completed.

Aviva Kallent, Dedrian Bellard, Javarus Hanzen, Kaesar Kinnuan, Kara Cherry, Marubee Tasuki, Reno Rossard, Soro Uzara, Veny Ikanu, and Zayden Fareno, were the 10 participants that made it onto day 2.

As the next morning arose, Zayden opened his eyes as he laid on his bed staring at the ceiling. *"...My only reason coming to this Academy was to come closer to becoming a Full-Fledged Sinner,"* he recalled, *"That was my only purpose."*

But then he recalled what Dedrian told him: *"I'm not going to allow you to become Full-Fledged,"* he remembered his words, *"I have a promise to keep."* Zayden was in deep thought, *"...Is my goal the right one to reach for?"* he had doubts.

Zayden slowly got up and sat to the side of his bed. He recalled when Kara defined a Full-Fledged Sinner: *"A Full-Fledged Sinner is when a Sinner reaches the ultimate state of their Power and can control all Sinning Abilities,"* he remembered Kara's words, *"The state of being Full-Fledged can be overpowering, which then causes one to lose their sense of thought and emotion."*

Then Javarus followed: *"The state of being Full-Fledged will overpower you,"* he recalled, *"You won't be yourself anymore..."*

After a moment, Zayden stood up and looked in the mirror, *"I'm only doing this for my Mother,"* he thought, *"But if I do become a Full-Fledged Sinner..."* he wondered, *"Just—who will I be?"*

There was a moment of silence.

"...I've always wanted to know why she wanted me to be Full-Fledged so bad," tensed Zayden, "...And why Father's death didn't affect her."

But then a loud knock was heard from the door, "Let's go Zayden!" a voice yelled.

"—Huh?!" turned Zayden.

"We have a whole day of Flare—I mean partner training to get to!" he shouted.

Zayden snapped out of his thoughts, he half smiled. He knew who was knocking and recalled what he told him: *"But now I realize that it's possible that you could become Full-Fledged, because you want it that bad!"*

"—You're usually up early!" yelled the voice, "What's gotten—"

"—I'm awake Reno!" Zayden opened the door, "You're going to break your hand if you continue!"

"—You should be thanking me!" remarked Reno, "We've been called to go on the fields! We're almost late!" he burst through the hallway and down the stairs.

"—*Is it noon already?!*" thought Zayden, *"We were told that we must train with our partners at this time!"* Zayden quickly went down the hallways and down the stairs, *"...And my partner,"* his eyes widened, *"...Is Soro."*

Zayden burst outside through the front door, but then bumped into someone.

"—Participant Zayden," Flare turned to him.

"—Attendant Flare!" saw Zayden, "Am I late?!"

"No, you're not," assured Flare, "But I already told you to not call me attendant."

"Okay yeah," Zayden brushed it off, "But where do I go to see my partner?!" he asked.

Flare looked to him, "You are Team E," she remarked, "Your designated area with your partner is on backside of the Academy's fields," she answered, "Your partner should already be there."

Zayden smirked, "—Sounds good," he nodded. He turned around and ran inside the Academy.

Zayden went through one of the many hallways and recalled the most important line his Mother told him: *"If you promise me to become Full-Fledged,"* he remembered her words, *"I'll promise you that I'll live long enough to see it."*

Zayden had small tears in his eyes as he thought about his Mother's smile. He wiped them away as he was on his way to the back fields of the Academy.

It was a bright day outside with little to no clouds in the air. The field surrounding the Academy had a vast amount of space. This partner session was planned so each Team had some time to prepare with one another before the second stage. All 5 Teams; Javarus and Veny, Kaesar and Kara, Dedrian and Reno, Aviva and Marubee, Zayden and Soro; must be present at their designated areas until Flare announces otherwise.

"Let's take it easy," advised Javarus, he stood a distance away from Veny on the right side of the Academy.

"You're caring suggestions are beginning to get on my nerves again," remarked Veny.

Javarus Sinned a Boulder out from the ground and took a seat on top, "Not only do I care about your injuries," he spoke, "Overall, we have to keep our strength at full for the evening bout with Adalo."

"—Then let's practice Rockora!" insisted Veny, "Adalo would not be able to withstand it!"

"—We can't," Javarus shook his head.

"What the heck—how come?!"

"Because I know the second stage isn't the only reason you want to perfect the attack," opposed Javarus.

"—What are you trying to say?"

There was a pause as Javarus got up from the Boulder, "You know what I mean," he put his arm forward as he Sinned the Rock forward.

Veny quickly put his arm up, "—You still think I'm after Soro?" he asked as he Sinned the Rock back.

Javarus Sinned another Boulder off the ground as both Rocks collided, "...Yes," he spoke as the Rocks crashed, "I still believe you're obsessed with him."

Veny paused, "I've changed," he spoke as he Sinned another Rock off the ground.

166

Javarus listened.

"All I can do is hope," went on Veny, "Hope that one day someone will get rid of Soro…and Damon," he sinned the Rock forward, "So nobody would have to go through what I did with them…"

Javarus put his arm out as the Rock stopped in front his palm.

"—What happened?" broke in Veny, "Swing the Rock back!"

"—Oh," uttered Javarus as he Sinned the Rock forward, "A-Are you serious about not going after Soro?"

Veny nodded, "I'm being honest," he assured, "After years of frustration…I've realized you were right…" he went on, "And from now on, I'm going to live my life with no anger."

Javarus heard him, "…I'm glad you came into the realization," he relieved, "Although you must feel hurt."

"I'm good," assured Veny, "That doesn't change the fact that we still need to beat Adalo."

Javarus nodded, "I'm with you there," he agreed, "Let's kick it up a notch."

Veny heard him as both of their auras grew bigger. "I'm ready," spoke Javarus.

"—Good to hear it," smirked Veny, he Sinned multiple Boulders forward.

Javarus Sinned a wall of Rock off the ground, "—Uh," The Boulders crashed into the wall, "Keep it going!" he yelled, "I need to withstand this!"

"—I won't stop till you tell me to!" yelled Veny. Veny carefully saw his Boulders attack the wall of Rock, "…This feeling of attacking someone is what I need!" he thought, "I'm sorry Javarus, but I have to feel this way when I go after Soro again…and I won't need you to use Rockora!"

The two continued their preparation.

Across from them on the same side of the field, there was Team B.

167

Kaesar sat down cross legged on the field, "...You've been doing that for a while now," he murmured with his hand on his chin.

Kara stood behind him quickly flicking his hair, "it's super annoying how clueless you are about colour!" she screeched, "This is white hair, not gray!"

Kaesar exhaled, "I don't think it matters too much," he spoke.

"—Of course it does!" beamed Kara, she bent forward as her head was upside down, "Does winning this competition matter?" she looked to him.

"Yes, it does," answered Kaesar.

"—Then so does this!" smiled Kara as she stood back up. Kara put a lollipop in her mouth, and then her hand on Kaesar's hair, "Now let's—"

"—That's enough," Kaesar quickly shook his head.

"—Kaesar!" freaked out Kara, "What are you—" the lollipop dropped out of her mouth.

"—What landed on my hair?" spoke Kaesar as he remained seated.

There was a pause.

"...Kara?"

"—No no no!" worried Kara, "—My pop is stuck to your gray hair!" she tightly grabbed the lollipop, "—Super sorry, but this is a must!" she tugged the lollipop.

"Wait—" uttered Kaesar as his hair was pulled up, "That's not going to work!" his face cringed.

"I don't care one bit!" screeched Kara as she pulled the lollipop again.

"—Stop that!" yelled Kaesar as his head was forced up.

"—I can't waste a pop!" cried Kara as an Orange aura formed around her, "That would be mean!" she pulled with all her Power.

Kaesar's head forced up again, "You'll—"

A quick ripping noise was heard.

"—Oh," Kaesar stood up rubbing his hair, "Was that the only solution you had," he spoke.

"—Oh well, it worked!" smiled Kara, she opened her mouth towards the lollipop, "Uh—What's this gray hair doing on my pop?!"

There were some strands of Kaesar's hair stuck onto Kara's lollipop. "—I can't eat this anymore!" she wept.

Kaesar snickered, "Hm, don't mess with my hair." "—That's fine!" beamed Kara, "If I can't have it, then I can just give it to you!" she held the lollipop in front of him.

Kaesar saw her, "...No," he denied.

"—Uh Uh!" Kara shook her head, "I'm not going to standby to watch this pop wasted, now eat it!"

Kaesar paused, "One lollipop isn't going to make a difference," he remarked, "Now can we go onto preparing at least one move for the—"

"—Move Shmoove!" Kara kept it up, "Just please finish this lollipop, it's cherry too! It's the best one around!"

Kaesar heard her, *"...Is she serious?"* he looked to Kara.

"—Every pop counts!" she beamed.

There was a moment of silence.

Kaesar put his right hand in his pocket and eyed away, "...How about if we practice one attack," he murmured, "I'll finish it."

Kara's eyes widened, "—Really?!" she smiled.

Kaesar eyed back to her, "...Yeah," he spoke, but in his thoughts, *"...Of course not, it's dirty."*

"—Thanks!" smiled Kara as she put the lollipop in her pocket, "—Okay now let's practice! Train! Make a move!" she cheered, "Whatever you want! Just as long as you keep your end of the deal!"

Kaesar nodded, "Let's just clear things out a bit," he spoke, "I'm an Ice Sinner, and you're a Farmake Sinner."

"Mm hm!" nodded Kara.

"If I recall," went on Kaesar, "You can create clones, right?"

"—Yes!" beamed Kara as she began Sinning.

Kaesar saw an Orange aura around her.

"—Come on out Kara clones!" she yelled as two clones appeared beside her.

169

"...I was right," saw Kaesar.

Kara and her clones pranced around Kaesar in a circle, "I love my Kara clones!" they smiled.

Kaesar slowly lifted his hand in the air.

"And nobody can—"

"—Found you," he spoke as he Sinned a Streak of Ice from his finger.

"Wait—" uttered Kara as two of the clones froze, "I didn't expect you to Sin without warning!"

Kaesar paused, "You got to mask your Sinning Ability," he remarked, "Or else your aura will give away which one's the real you."

"Aww," bummed Kara.

"It's okay though," assured Kaesar, "We can think of something."

"For sure," she beamed, "But—can you at least unfreeze my clones first?"

Kaesar put out his arm and closed his hand.

After a moment, the Ice on the clones shattered, "...We can control again!" smiled the three Kara clones as they stood a distance away.

Kaesar turned to them, "Yes you—"

"—Now watch this!" they burst forward towards him.

Kaesar saw the clones coming, "What do you think you're doing?" he spoke.

Two of the clones jumped in the air, "—Bet you can't stop this one!" they yelled while the other clone stood in the middle.

Kaesar eyed the two clones jumping from the side, then stared to the Kara in the middle.

"—He isn't going to move?!" wondered Kara.

The two clones in the air took their lollipops out of their mouth as they lollipops shined.

Kaesar was surprised.

The lollipops grew into a long pole-like figure with the candy increasing in size as well, "—This is super sweet!" they beamed as they went down for a strike.

170

But then Kaesar blocked both sides with his arms over his head, "—Those can be useful," he spoke as the lollipops snapped.

But then the two clones grabbed Kaesar by the arms, "We aren't finished yet!" they yelled as they quickly melted into sticky liquid.

Kaesar's arms stuck to his side, "H-How'd she—" he uttered as he tried to lift his feet, but the liquid covered them.

"I guess planned B worked," smiled the real Kara standing from a distance.

Kaesar looked to her.

Kara quickly burst forward, "—Super sorry in advance!" she beamed as she took out the lollipop in her mouth.

Kaesar shook his head as his white hair went over his eyes, *"You won't need to apologize,"* he thought.

The lollipop in Kara's hand extended, "—Plan B always works!" she yelled and swung the pole across.

But then Kaesar widened his eyes as it quickly turned dark Blue.

"Hey—" uttered Kara as her feet, hands and the lollipop froze, "W-When did—"

Kaesar's eyes turned back to normal, "That was close," he spoke.

Kara struggled to swing the pole, "I-I—" she stuttered.

But then Kaesar closed his eyes, the sparkly Ice on Kara and the lollipop shattered in the air.

Kara's mouth dropped as she saw the Ice fall, "Wow..." she awed, "—This is so pretty!"

Kaesar eyed to the ground as the Ice landed, "That was pretty good," he looked back to Kara.

There was a pause, "—Huh? That's all?!" screeched Kara, "Tell me what you did back there! You didn't move at all but my pop and I froze up!"

Kaesar snickered, "I might tell you," he answered, "Because I think I just figured out our combination attack."

Kara's eyes widened, "Did you really?" she smiled.

Kaesar nodded.

"Great!" she cheered, "Now we'll show Marubee and everyone else our dominance as the strongest team!" she took out a lollipop and put it in her mouth.

Kaesar half smiled as he saw Kara. After a moment, he began explaining the combination attack to her.

Back inside the Academy, Adalo and Flare were on the upper level as Flare watched the participants from a terrace. She looked down from above, "Looks like Team B has something planned," she saw.

Adalo stood inside the room from the terrace, "Are you speaking about Kaesar and Kara?" he asked.
"Yeah," answered Flare.

Adalo heard her as he was in deep thought, *"...Kaesar Kinnuan,"* he recalled, *"Our battle is going to bring me back..."*

"—Participants Javarus and Veny seem to be picking up the pace too," remarked Flare.
But Adalo stayed quiet.

After a moment, Flare turned her head back, *"...I suppose he's lost in thought again,"* she saw, *"He's been like this since he woke up..."*

Moments before all the participants began their training session, Zayden went out the back door of the Academy.

He saw Soro's back from a distance across the field, *"...There he is,"* he was nervous.
After a pause, Zayden slowly took steps towards him.

At the same time, on the left side of the Academy, one half of Team C was there.

Dedrian had his arms out, "—I can tackle better than this!" he groaned as he Sinned a wave of Fire towards a tree.
Reno saw him from a distance, *"...I know how to Sin Rock now,"* he thought, *"There's no need to be afraid!"* he took a deep breath and walked forward.

172

"—Don't think of stepping near me," Dedrian turned as he had a red aura.

Reno stopped, "...W-We're partners," he spoke up, "We have to work together!'"

"—Work together?" groaned Dedrian, "I only got along with Rajaul, and your pal Zayden took him out before the competition."

"—Why do you keep blabbing on about this Rajaul guy?!" asked Reno, "I don't even know who—"

"—I don't have to explain anything to you," broke in Dedrian, "Especially you!" he raised his voice, "You're the most weak-hearted one here! I'd be wasting my breath."

There was a pause.

"...I'm not pathetic," tensed Reno, *"I can defend for myself now, and I have that urge to fight just like Zayden!"*

"T-That's not true!" opposed Reno, "I can fight for myself and I don't need anybody!"

"—Look at you getting emotional," smirked Dedrian, "Does being protected by Zayden all the time make you this way?!"

"—I said I don't need anybody's help!" repeated Reno, "Including Zayden's!" he began Sinning as he had a green aura.

"—Hm?" saw Dedrian.

Reno quickly Sinned the Rock underneath him, "Look at my Sinning!" he yelled as the Rock hovered in the air with him was on top.

"—What are you planning?" tensed Dedrian.

"...I challenge you to a battle!" shouted Reno and pointed down, "You fought Zayden and attacked Aviva! That was all because of me!"

Dedrian smirked, "—Those are the words I've been waiting for!" he began Sinning as his body surrounded in Fire, "The only thing that I care about is the challenge!" he yelled.

Reno saw him, *"This...this is what Zayden must feel like,"* he thought, *"This energy to fight, I have to be like him!"*

There was a pause.

Dedrian looked up to Reno, "—It's not like you were going to tackle hard with me against Adalo," he groaned, "As my partner, it's embarrassing!"

"—No!" yelled Reno as he jumped off the Rock, "You're going to respect me!" he went down with a punch. "—Shut up!" Dedrian ran and jumped towards him, "You're not worth it!" he went in with a punch.

They swung their arms in mid air as their fist clashed, "—Uh," groaned Reno as Dedrian's Power pushed him back.

Dedrian smirked, "—I'm simply stronger!" he burst forward and bashed Reno in the face.

Reno quickly crashed and rolled on the ground. Dedrian landed and stared him down from a distance, "...What else did you expect?" he groaned with Fire around him.

Reno was shocked as he laid on the ground. He slowly sat up, "H-How did he just overpower me like that?!" he saw Dedrian, "—Uh," he felt the wound on his face. "—You can't do anything," stated Dedrian, "You'll always need someone's help!"

"—You're wrong!" denied Reno as he stood up, "Take this in!" he put his arm out as he Sinned a Boulder Sinned from the ground.

"Hm."

"—I learned this from Javarus!" yelled Reno as he Sinned the Rock forward.

Dedrian saw the Boulder coming, "—No use!" he shouted as he swung his arm and punched through the Rock.

"—What?!" Reno was stunned, "Y-You just can't—" he Sinned more Boulders towards him.

"—What did I just say?!" angered Dedrian as he punched and kicked down two of the Boulders.

"B-But—"

Dedrian put his hand into the ground, "—You won't be able to do anything!" he yelled as a line of Fire burst from the surface and burned the last Boulder, "—Will that be all?!" he looked back up at Reno.

174

Reno's eyes widened as he saw his Rocks turned to ash, "I-I…" he stuttered, and in his thoughts, *"—This shouldn't be happening!"* he worried.

Inside the Academy, Adalo and Flare went to the other side of the field on the terrace.

"—Why are the participants of Team C fighting?!" saw Flare.

Adalo stood next to her as they watched from above, "…He's making a mistake," he remarked.

On the field, Reno saw Dedrian from a distance, *"W-What did I just start?!"* he panicked.

Dedrian was on one knee, "—Now that you're done your tricks!" he yelled, "I'll begin mine!" his arm was on Fire as he roared.

Reno's eyes widened, "What are you—"

But then a thick line of Fire burst from the ground beside Reno.

"—Uh," groaned Reno as the Fire burned the side of his arm.

Dedrian stood up and watched.

Reno's breath was heavy, *"—This isn't good!"* he worried as another line of Fire burst up, "—Uh," he groaned as it burned his other arm.

Reno stumbled back, *"—These flames are just as hot as Zayden's!"* he grimaced.

Another line of Fire burst behind him, "—What?!" Reno jumped, "I have to stop running away!" he shook his head.

Dedrian saw him.

Reno charged forward as he put out both of his hands.

"—Still trying?!" groaned Dedrian.

Reno Sinned two Boulders out of the ground on opposite sides of Dedrian, "—I learned so I don't have to runaway!" he yelled as he put his hands together.

The Boulders came rushing in.

175

Dedrian looked left and right, "—Hopeless," he smirked as he jumped in the air.

The Boulders crashed into each other.

But then Reno jumped towards him, "—You're not that great!" he shouted as he went in with a punch.

Dedrian quickly caught his fist, "—What kind of tackle was that?!" he yelled as he grabbed Reno's collar in mid air.

The two landed back on the ground.

Dedrian still had a grip on Reno's caller.

"—Uh," struggled Reno as he tried to swipe his hands

"This reminds me when I held Zayden like this," recalled Dedrian, "—But Adalo interrupted!"

Reno struggled to face his arm to the ground.

"—I'll finish what he and I started with you!" yelled Dedrian as he punched into Reno's stomach.

"Oh—" Reno's stomach went in.

Dedrian's fist inflamed in Dark Red Fire, "—You're the one who challenged me in the first place!" he bashed Reno in the stomach several times.

Reno couldn't move as he grimaced in pain.

After a moment, Dedrian let go of Reno, "And you said you can tackle with me," he kicked Reno heavy in the stomach.

Reno was sent flying back a distance as he rolled on the ground.

Dedrian quickly ran forward.

"I-I can't," Reno barely stood up.

But then Dedrian punched Reno's face left and right, "—This isn't your tackle!" he shouted.

"—Uh," groaned Reno.

Dedrian put his hands in Reno's stomach, "—Give it up!" he Sinned a wave of Fire out of his palms.

Reno was sent flying back as he rolled on the ground again.

Dedrian's Fire lowered as he saw him.

Reno stopped rolling as he was on his side. His clothes were torn as he coughed, "...W-Why does this always happen to me," he muttered as he went on his knees.

Dedrian walked over to him, "You're covered in pain," he remarked.

Reno slowly felt his arms, "...Everything I said gone to waste," he saddened.

"—Come on!" yelled Dedrian, "Call for Zayden!"

Reno's head was down. He suddenly remembered a fight he had with Zayden back when they were younger. Reno recalled when Zayden would hold him by the collar like Dedrian did: *"Come on Reno!"* he remembered Zayden's words, *"You always find yourself stuck on my hand!"*

Dedrian looked down in front of him, "The night we landed here, we were set to tackle," he recalled, "But Zayden saved you..."

"He did...didn't he..." thought Reno.

"When I was angry at the fact of you as my partner," groaned Dedrian, "Zayden came in again...but now he's not here and you've found yourself on the ground."

Reno grimaced in pain.

Dedrian gave him a stern look, "—You really can't fight for yourself," he tensed.

Reno's eyes widened as he was on his knees. There was a moment of silence, "...No!" shouted Reno, he forced both of his fists through the ground, "I don't need Zayden's protection..." he saddened then yelled, "I don't need anybody's!"

A green Flash appeared from Reno's fists, "What—" saw Dedrian.

Reno was shocked, "—What is this?!" he panicked. Dedrian lifted his foot "—It won't change anything!" he shouted as he went down with a kick.

"Uh—" Reno closed his eyes as he quickly put his hands over his head.

But Dedrian's foot didn't make contact with him.

"—What the hell?!" groaned Dedrian.

"—Huh?!" Reno opened his eyes. He saw hard Rock forming around his hands, "—I-I can't feel them!" he worried.

177

"—These tricks you and Zayden pull are ticking me off!" angered Dedrian, he put his hands over Reno's Rock hands, "I'll get rid of them."

"No wait—Don't!" begged Reno as he was lifted off the ground, "I—"
But then Dedrian Sinned Fire out of his hands as he roared and forcefully closed them.

The Rock forming around Reno's fists broke apart. Reno was stunned, "...Just when I finally found my own move," he murmured as the Rocks crumbled in front of his eyes, "Why'd you—" he went in with a punch.

But then Dedrian caught his fist again, "—Because we're in a tackle!" he yelled as he pushed Reno, but then pulled him back as went in with a head-butt.

"—Uh," Reno was knocked back losing his balance. Dedrian saw him, "...You won't be able to take much more," he smirked.

Reno's mind was all over the place as he was dizzy. He remembered another time he fought with Zayden when they were 12: *"You know Reno..."* he recalled Zayden's words, *"We both act like dummies...we must be brainless..."* he remembered how hard Zayden head butted him right after, but while Zayden stood up, he landed on the ground, *"Get up Reno, unless you want to admit your brainless!"*
Dedrian put his arms out, "—Fight back or call for Zayden!" he shouted as he Sinned a wave of Fire from his hands.

Reno quickly turned around, "H-How can I—" he was bashed by the Fire as he was forced onto his stomach.

The Fire kept coming.
Reno looked back, "I-I can't—" he panicked as he quickly stood up and closed his arms.
Pieces of the ground were rapidly Sinned as it created a small sphere-like object around Reno.

"—I'll take this down too!" yelled Dedrian as he Sinned more Fire towards the Rock.

Reno was inside the Rock sphere. Small tears slowly appeared in his eyes, "...This is just like my battles with Zayden," he muttered, "...Has nothing changed?"

But then the sphere began to shake as it became hotter and hotter, *"I-It's getting tough to breathe..."* felt Reno, *"I-I'm..."*
The atmosphere inside the sphere heated up blurring Reno's vision.

But then the sphere cracked, "—You're always hiding!" shouted Dedrian as he punched through the Rock and bashed Reno's head.
The sphere broke into pieces and landed on the ground.
"—Uh," Reno crashed with the Rocks around him.

Dedrian stood in front a distance away.
Reno was out of breath as the heat from the Rock made his body oozy. He had trouble opening his eyes as he laid on his back.

There was a pause.
After a moment, Reno slowly opened eyes, he was stunned, *"...That doesn't look Dedrian,"* he saw an unclear image in front him, *"It looks like..."* an image of Zayden as a kid appeared.
He began hearing voices from a younger Zayden: *"Mark my word Reno!"* he remembered Zayden's words when they were little: *"As of this day, you're never going to beat me!"*

Reno thought to himself, *"Zayden was right..."* he knew, *"I still never beat him..."* he eyed away, then looked back.
Reno saw the real person in front of him, Dedrian. He saw a similar image, with the Fire and the same eyes staring down on him, *"This kind of reminds me of..."* he compared, *"Zayden..."*

"—Remember when I say this," remarked Dedrian, "You're never going to beat me," he stopped Sinning as the Fire around him went away.

There was a moment of silence.
Reno was stunned, *"I...I lost,"* he saddened, *"Zayden...and now Dedrian too..."*

"—And now Zayden's next!" shouted Dedrian out loud.

After a pause, Reno opened his mouth, "I deserved to win this one..." he murmured.

Dedrian heard him, "—Deserve?!" he opposed as he marched over to Reno, "Nobody deserves anything! Everything is earned!"

"—Just shut up!" Reno desperately Sinned one of the Rocks from the broken sphere.

The Rock slapped across Dedrian's face turning his head to the left.

Reno's breath was heavy, *"Oh no..."* he worried. In a flash, Fire surrounded Dedrian again. He turned his head and glared at Reno.

Reno had one eye open as he stared back. Dedrian approached him again, "—You really did that?!" he groaned. But then he saw Reno's ripped clothes, the burns and bruises on his arms and face, and his swollen right eye.

Reno opened his mouth, but then paused, *"...I'm not going to say sorry,"* he changed his mind.

Dedrian angered, "...The only thing that's keeping me from knocking your teeth down your throat," he clenched his fists, "Is that I need your pulse beating once the second stage begins," he groaned, "I can't have myself disqualified taking you out before that."

Reno laid on the ground as he couldn't move.

"—Sinning isn't a joke," Dedrian turned and walked away, "Get it through your head."

After a moment, Reno's eyes began closing as he saw Dedrian's back, *"...I'm not nearly as good as I think I am,"* he saddened, *"I'm a weak boy that uses a wristband and needs his friends to protect him...I'll never be able to fight for myself..."*

Reno's eyes closed as he went unconscious.

Back on the terrace, Adalo and Flare viewed Dedrian and Reno from above.

"...He never stood a chance," spoke Adalo.

Flare exhaled, "I thought maybe it would be more of an even fight," she spoke, "Though they shouldn't be against each other in the first place."

"No, not with Reno's mindset," remarked Adalo, "Combat Sinners like myself, need a strong reason to strive for power."

Flare turned, "Like I never heard that one before," she rolled her eyes.

"—I'll continue to say it until the entire world hears me," stated Adalo, "But this defeat Reno took may change him...and give him that reason to be serious and not carelessly jump into battles."

Flare listened, "Well that's your opinion," she spoke, "Reno's funny, and that's not bad."

"Hm?" heard Adalo, "Is Reno's affection for you being received back to him?"

"—Oh no," denied Flare, "You and I are going to settle down eventually."

Adalo turned and walked back inside the room, "I have more important things to do before coming to the thought of that," he spoke.

Flare watched him go, "One day, you'll see it my way," she smiled.

On the other side of the Academy, Kaesar and Kara were just about finished practicing their combination move.

Kara had her extended lollipop in her hand, "...I don't think I can do any more Kara clones," her breath was heavy.

Kaesar stood in front of her, "That's fine," he assured, "I think we know what we're doing."

Kara smiled as she dropped the lollipop pole and stopped Sinning. The Orange aura around her was gone. Kaesar stopped Sinning as his blue aura faded.

After a moment, Kara took out another lollipop, "I'm so happy you were my partner!" she beamed as she put it in her mouth.

"Hm?" heard Kaesar.

"—This attack is the best and it looks super pretty too!" smiled Kara, "I want to do the second stage right now!"

Kaesar took a moment, "But you can't create anymore clones," he remarked, "And those are the most important part of this attack."

"—Attack Shmack! We'll still beat Adalo!" Kara brushed it off, "If anything, you'll take care of Adalo for both us, right?"

Kaesar put his right hand in his pocket, "...I'll try too," she spoke, "But I need you at your full Power as well."

Kara chuckled, "—We'll get the job done!" she smiled, "Nobody can stop Gray and Orange!" she referred to the colours of their hair.

"Yeah," snickered Kaesar, "So let's just rest for now. The second stage begins later this evening anyways."

But then Kara's face tensed as she stared.

"...What?" asked Kaesar.

Kara squinted her eyes, "...Did you forget?" she recalled.

"Forget what?"

Kara reached into her pocket, "Now since I kept my end of the deal..." she went on, "You have to return the favour!" she took out the lollipop with Kaesar's hair stuck onto it, "—You did promise me that you'd finish it if we practiced a move!"

Kaesar saw the dirty lollipop and remembered: *"...How about if we practice one attack,"* he recalled his words to Kara, *"I'll finish it."*

"—What are you waiting for?!" smiled Kara.

Kaesar paused, "...I prefer not to have that," he spoke.

"—But you have too," reminded Kara, "You said you will finish it if we created a combo!"

"Yeah but—just look at it," pointed Kaesar, "It looks terrible."

There was pause, "B-But..." saddened Kara, "S-So you lied to me?" she wept.

Kaesar saw a change in her expression, "...It's nothing to be worried about," he brushed it off.

But then tears filled in Kara's eyes, "—Yes it is!" she screeched, "Please finish it!

"—Uh," Kaesar was stunned as he saw how emotional Kara was.

"—-Y-You lied to me!" cried Kara.

There was a pause as Kaesar took a moment, "...Alright hand it over," he put out his hand.

Kara's eyes widened, "—Great!" she beamed as she took a step closer, "—Don't choke on the gray hair though!" she put the lollipop in front of his eyes.

Kaesar heard her, *"...I have white hair,"* he corrected in his mind.

"—Well now what's keeping you waiting?" Kara kept it up, "It's here!"

Kaesar looked to the lollipop and slowly held onto the white stick attached to the candy.

"—There you go!" smiled Kara as she watched on.

Kaesar opened his mouth, he slowly geared the lollipop closer.

Kara cheered, "Thank—"

But then Ice quickly spiked out of Kaesar's finger and froze the lollipop.

"—Hey?!" uttered Kara, "That wasn't supposed to happen!"

"What was that?" uttered Kaesar.

Kara's eyes filled with tears again, she took out the lollipop that was in her mouth, "My pop..." she sobbed.

"Sorry about that Kara," apologized Kaesar, "I didn't mean too."

"—Yes you did!" sniffed Kara.

"I'm—"

"—You're mean don't talk to me!" Kara turned around and closed her eyes.

"Hey calm—"

"—Nope!" Kara shook her head, "You're a bully!"

Kaesar saw her back, "But..."

Kara quickly put her hands over her ears, "—I can't hear you!" she denied.

Kaesar opened his mouth, but then quieted.

183

There was a moment of silence.
After a pause, Kaesar looked to the right, "...I'll—I'll get you another lollipop if you want," he muttered.

Kara opened her eyes, "—Really?!" she beamed.
"...Yeah whatever," murmured Kaesar as he put his hand in his pocket.
Kara quickly turned to him, "—Thank you!" she smiled, "And its good see that your eyes are normal now too!" she compared Kaesar's eyes against Rajaul and now.
Kaesar heard her, "What do you mean by that?" he asked.

But then Kara quickly leaned into his face, "Your eyes looked mean before," she moved her eyes looking into his, "But now they're nice."
"—R-Relax," Kaesar quickly backed off.

"Huh?" saw Kara, "What happened?"

"...Don't get so close to me," spoke Kaesar.

Kara chuckled, "Aw, okay," she took out a lollipop and put it in her mouth.
Kaesar saw her smiling, *"...She's a funny one,"* he thought, *"I'm just glad that we have at least one move planned out,"* he recalled, *"And I can't forget those images that played in my mind back in the first stage...this battle against Adalo might reveal something I want to know..."*

By now, at back of the Academy, Zayden slowly took steps towards his partner.
He took a deep breath as he saw Soro, *"...He instantly took down the instructor in a flash,"* he recalled the first stage and worried, *"He even handled Veny without any effort,"* he remembered, *"Does that kind of Power root from a Full-Fledged Sinner?"*
Zayden then thought about himself, *"I have no intention of fighting him,"* he knew, *"We share the exact same goals...we can help each other instead,"* he continued walking.

On the left side of the Academy, there was Team D; Aviva and Marubee. They were going up against Lavivo Kallent

184

instead of Adalo, due to the agreement of battling a Farmake Sinner instead of a Combat Sinner was made.

The two stared at each other from a distance.

"Look at her..." thought Aviva as she glared, *"She must be just as annoyed as I am."*

"Look at her..." thought Marubee, *"Just seeing her annoys me."*

After a moment, Aviva began Sinning as a pink aura formed and her hair slightly rose.

"—Oh," uttered Marubee, she quickly Sinned as a green aura formed with her hair rising.

"Hm?" saw Aviva. She then stopped Sinning.

After a pause, Marubee stopped Sinning.

"—Why are you copying me?" spoke up Aviva.

"—I'm not copying you," denied Marubee.

"—Yeah you are," remarked Aviva, "When I Sinned, you did as well. When I stopped Sinning, you stopped as well."

"—That's not copying," opposed Marubee, "I'm a far better Farmake Sinner than you and your family," she stated, "So when I Sin, there's a clear difference between our Powers."

"That doesn't—"

"—Therefore, I am not copying you," went on Marubee, "I am better than you."

Aviva irritated, "Why are you so obsessed with me?" she asked, "I did nothing to you."

Marubee took a moment, "It's because you're so lucky to be born in the Kallent—"

"Say a different—"

"Don't interrupt—"

"You say the same—"

"Stop talking when—"

"You have—"

"You can't—"

"Stop—"

"I—"

"You're so—"

"You're so—"

"Annoying," both of them ended at the same time.

They stared at each other as they began Sinning again.

————————————

On the terrace above, Flare leaned on the railing as she viewed the two from up top.

Lavivo walked onto the terrace behind her.

Flare turned back, "Looks like you were wrong about them," she spoke.

"How so?" asked Lavivo.

Flare turned back to the field, "Just look at them," she pointed.

Lavivo looked down and saw Aviva and Marubee arguing, "Oh I wish they would get along," she sighed, "I have faith in them to be a remarkable team."

"Yeah," agreed Flare, "But when you pay closer attention to them," she went on, "It seems like Marubee sparks up all of their arguments."

Lavivo listened, "Yes it certainly does," she agreed.

"She just doesn't let up," remarked Flare, "Aviva is simply defending herself."

"I do agree with you to some extent there," spoke Lavivo, "But Aviva can still make up with her," she hoped, "Though she chooses to bring forth this passion of hers to be recognized as her own person, instead of our family."

Flare snickered, "And this makes Marubee even more hostile," she half smiled.

Lavivo quietly laughed, but then looked back to Aviva, *"...She was never this resentful,"* she thought, *"Now she seems like she doesn't even want to be a part of the family anymore."*

"—Wait it just hit me!" shrieked Flare.

"—What happened?!" worried Lavivo, "Are you okay?" she raised her hand on Flare's forehead.

"Yeah I'm fine," snickered Flare, she slowly put Lavivo's hand down, "—It's just that I realized something!"

"Oh, what can it be?" asked Lavivo.

"—In one hand, we have Marubee," went on Flare, "Who claims that Aviva is only great at Sinning because she was born into the Kallent Family," she recalled, "And

186

on the other, you have Aviva, who wards off these remarks and wants be known as her own person."

There was a pause.

"...I cannot seem to follow," spoke Lavivo, "Care to explain further?"

"—Don't you see?!" urged Flare, "This is just like you and Katana!"

Lavivo was surprised to see the comparison.

Katana Luutzki was a Farmake Sinner. She and Lavivo met each other at the time when Adalo's Sinara Academy went head to head against Juro's Sinetity Academy, to determine whose Academy was better.

Katana would argue that Lavivo is only great because she's from the Kallent family, and Lavivo defended herself by saying she earned every skill through her own hard work.

A turning point in their relationship was when Lavivo had healed Katana's little sister, following a minor incident that occurred in one of the battles between the Academies. After that, Katana and Lavivo spoke with each other more, and eventually became great friends.

"—Aren't I right?" recalled Flare, "The talks coming from the two down there are just like yours with Katana," she compared, "Or at least used to be similar when you two couldn't stand each other."

Lavivo took a moment, "I see," she understood, "Does that mean Aviva and Marubee could become just as close?"

Flare looked down to the field, "Only time can answer that question," she remarked.

Lavivo heard and paused, "Katana..." she muttered to herself then spoke up, "I haven't seen her in so long, it's kind of sad."

Flare snickered, "I'm sure she's doing fine," she assured, "She was always feisty, so I don't think anybody would mess with her."

"You are right about that," half smiled Lavivo, "I miss her a lot though, and her adorable little sister."

"Oh yeah, I forgot about her younger sister," recalled Flare, "She loved her more than anything."

Lavivo quietly laughed, "It did appear that way," she spoke, "Hopefully we get word from her soon."

Flare smiled and nodded as the two looked back to the field.

On the grass, Aviva looked to Marubee, "I find it funny that you based your answer in the first stage around me," she recalled.

"What's there to laugh about?" spoke Marubee, "Everything I said was true."

Aviva shook her head, but then remembered more of the question portion of the first stage. She recalled when Zayden answered with his goal: *"—My ultimate goal is to become a Full-Fledged Sinner!"* she thought about his words.

Marubee saw a change in her expression, "What happened to you?" she called out, "Does my Sinning make you nervous?"

Aviva was in deep thought, *"...And I sense this Power from the back of the Academy slowly rising,"* she felt, *"And if it's not Zayden...it's—"*

"—What are you so worked up on?" remarked Marubee.

Aviva took a moment, "Hey..." she murmured then spoke up, "What are your thoughts about a Full-Fledged Sinner?"

Marubee's eyes widened, *"Why is she bringing this up now?"* she was surprised.

There was a pause.

"...I'm not entitled to tell you anything," stated Marubee, "But in short, it boggles my mind that someone with that much Power is sending this world to the ground. I don't like it."

Aviva heard her, "...Looks like you do have a heart," she half smiled.

"—Shut it," opposed Marubee, "Just because I'm not fond of a Full-Fledged Sinner doesn't mean I like everything else," she remarked, "I, for sure, do not like you."

Aviva listened.

"—I don't like your abilities, your face, your clothes, your home, your reputation, your powers, your butlers, and let's not forget your false determination in trying to be your own person," Marubee took a breath and went on, "Everything about you goes against everything I stand for."

There was a moment of silence.

"Then let's agree to battle in the second stage on our own," tensed Aviva, "Obviously we can't work as a team."

"Hm, took you this long to figure that out," recalled Marubee, "Poor little princess."

Lastly, present in the back of the Academy, Zayden stood behind Soro who had his back turned. This was Team E.

There was a moment of silence.

"...S-Soro," called out Zayden.

There was a pause.

"H-He doesn't appear to be Sinning..." thought Zayden, *"So why do I feel like there's something else to him..."*

Soro remained facing the other way.

"Soro," Zayden called out again, "I want to...no, I need to ask you something."

Soro stayed quiet.

"—Soro!" yelled Zayden as he put his hand on Soro's shoulder.

But then a Blue light sparked on Zayden's hand, "—Uh," groaned Zayden as he touched Soro's shoulder.

Soro quickly turned around and stared into Zayden's eyes.

"W-What—" Zayden stumbled back as he saw him.

Never before seen, Soro had a Dark Black Marking that spread across the left half of his body, it scarred up across his face and streaked across the eye.

Zayden's eyes widened, "—W-What you happened to you?!" he was stunned.

Soro slowly put his hand over his face, "It doesn't concern you," he groaned.

Zayden took a moment, "But just like you..." he clenched his fists, "—I need to become a Full-Fledged Sinner," he remarked, "And nobody will stop me!"

Soro heard him as he had a light smirk, "Who said there are people in your way?"

Zayden paused, "Many..." he muttered then raised his voice, "There are so many people that told me not to become Full-Fledged...I've been laughed at, yelled, and even threatened for wanting to be a Full-Fledged Sinner."

Soro looked to him, "You'll fall into a void you won't be able to get back from," he stated.

"Is that where you are?" recalled Zayden.

Soro's attention was caught. He had a stern look, "My void was created by others," he spoke, "And I've accepted it."

But then Zayden tensed, "This void you're talking about means nothing to me," he remarked, "—I just need you to tell me the path on becoming a Full-Fledged Sinner!"

"There's no need for me to tell you anything," spoke Soro, "Nothing you and I speak of concerns me."

"—Nothing?" repeated Zayden, "You want to become Full-Fledged just as bad as I do," he recalled, "And that's something I want to talk about."

Soro heard him.

"We should help each other," swayed Zayden, "I know it sounds crazy...and I don't know what will happen and how we'll do it...but we should work together!"

There was a moment of silence

"...You're oblivious to everything," remarked Soro.

Zayden eyed to the ground, "T-That's the point..." he muttered, "I may not know a lot of things..."

There was a pause.

"—But the most important thing I do know is that this whole thing of becoming Full-Fledged is what I wake up to!" yelled Zayden, "My promise to my Mother drives me everyday! I don't care what anybody says, I'd be miserable without this dream! It's my only goal and purpose of doing anything! So I need your help!"

Soro listened.

"Because if your path leads to your Power and beyond," remarked Zayden, "I'm more than ready to walk the same way," he ended as a red aura formed around his body.

Soro tensed, "I mean it when I say this," he spoke, "Don't ever look at us as the same, we can't be anymore different."

Zayden took a moment, he saw the Black Markings on Soro darken, "...Tell me, what's with that scar across you."

Soro slowly put his hand over the Markings on his face. He stayed quiet as he rubbed his left and pointer and thumb together.

"Did you learn it from—"

"—Yes," answered Soro, "It's a Power belonging to him, remember it."

Zayden was stunned.

"Even so," went on Soro, "Just like you, my Father and I can't be anymore different."

"—Your Father, Damon! Let's talk to him!" tensed Zayden, "He'll help us get stronger, he's a Full-Fledged Sinner!"

"—He'll kill you," stated Soro.

Zayden shook his head, "—I can't die before my Mother sees me become Full-Fledged," he recalled, "I won't let it."

There was a moment of silence.

"If that's true and he doesn't kill you," tensed Soro, "Then I—" Lightning quickly streaked across his body as he begun Sinning.

Zayden's eyes widened, "—I'm not looking to fight you!" he yelled.

"...I'm never looking to fight," spoke Soro, "People always go after me," he then looked Zayden, "As for now, I'm only showing what a real Full-Fledged Sinner should look like."

Soro's hair waved back as the Black Markings grew down from his face and onto his right arm.

Zayden was stunned.

Soro opened his hand in front of him, "...This Power," he awed as he had a light smirk, heavy Lightning surrounded his body.

Zayden was forced a few steps back, "—Is this how far I have to go?!" he was shocked, "How much of a gap is there between us?!"

191

Soro's Lightning sharpened as the ground broke underneath.

Soro's Power sent shockwaves throughout the field. On both sides of the Academy, the teams felt a Sinning Power rise.

Marubee turned her head to the back, *"It's got to him!"* she thought.

Aviva looked to her, "You feel it, don't you," she spoke.

Marubee was shocked.

"This is what I was concerned about…" thought Aviva, *"Zayden and Soro together…both wanting to be Full-Fledged Sinners…what can they be doing?!"*

Reno laid on the grass as he was barely conscious, *"It's hard to hear and sense the ground right now…"* he thought, *"But whatever's happening doesn't sound good…"* he got jealous, *"I'm sure Zayden will take care of it anyways…"*

Dedrian angered as he had a red aura, *"This is like when Father tried to become Full-Fledged…"* he recalled, *"H-He didn't have to go like that…"*

On the other side, Kara worried about the Sinning Power, "K-Kaesar…" she muttered.

Kaesar was turned to the back of the Academy, *"…That's right,"* he heard Kara, *"Farmake Sinners have an improved Ability to sense Sinning Powers…"*

Kara looked to him, "You'll protect me right…" she asked.

"Hm?" Kaesar turned.

Kara stared at him, "We're a team," she spoke up, "So we have to protect each other."

Kaesar paused, "Why are you—" but then he stopped, as he carefully saw her.

Kara eyed to the ground, *"…I really don't like this Sinning Power,"* she worried.

Kaesar saw a change in her expression, "Y-Yeah, whatever," he assured, "We can protect one another..." he murmured.

After a moment, Kara had a light smile.

Javarus and Veny were in a middle of their spar, but then stopped.

"—It's him," remarked Javarus.

Veny stood a distance in front, "—Of course it is," he groaned, "Who else would it be?"

There was a pause, "...You think Zayden's okay?" asked Javarus.

"—He's probably on his knees seeing the true nature of Soro..." remarked Veny, "If I were him, I'd look to end Soro while he has the chance."

"—What are you saying?" tensed Javarus, "You said you've moved on from that."

But Veny stayed quiet as he glared to the back of the Academy.

"—Turn around!" yelled Javarus.

Veny slowly turned his head.

"...Veny?" murmured Javarus, "You're not going to—"

"—Sorry," opposed Veny as he lifted his arm.

"—What?!"

Blocks of Rocks Sinned out of the ground and rushed towards Javarus.

Javarus quickly looked around, "Veny don't think about—" but then the Rocks crushed and restricted him inside.

"—Just let me do what I need to do!" yelled Veny, "Soro's Father destroyed my hometown and took my Family's Sin!" he put his arm down, "—His death means a lot more than this competition!" he turned and ran off the to the back field.

Javarus saw him go, but couldn't move, *"—Veny's going to get himself killed if he goes after Soro!"* he worried, *"I can't stop him at this state—But maybe someone else can!"*

At the back of the Academy, Lightning streaked across all sides of Soro.

Zayden's eyes widened *"I-I can't matchup…"* he was stunned.

Soro gave a stern look, "Now you see why I'll become a Full-Fledged Sinner," he spoke.

Zayden took a moment, *"He has his reasons to become Full-Fledged…and I have mine!"* he thought, *"Him being the son of Damon doesn't make any difference!"*

Adalo, Flare, and Lavivo watched on from terrace.

"—If anybody's going to become Full-Fledged!" shouted Zayden, "It has to be me!" he began Sinning as Fire surrounded his body.

Lavivo saw him from above, *"I knew I sensed a lot more Sin from that boy,"* she thought.

Adalo began tapping on the railing.

Zayden looked to Soro, "What do you think of me?!" he smirked, "What were to happen if I turned Full-Fledged before you."

There was a moment of silence.

Zayden irritated, "You Sinned trying to prove me wrong!" he yelled, "Now tell me what you think of my Sin!" But Soro remained quiet as Lightning streaked across him.

Zayden angered, "—Soro!"

"—Soro!" another voice yelled.

"—Who said that?" Zayden turned his head.

Flare looked to the side, "…Participant Veny," she saw.

Zayden looked to him, "—What are you doing here?!" he called out, "I already told you that me and Javarus—"

"—Shut it Zayden!" yelled Veny, "What you and Javarus said was wrong! I have to end Soro now!"

Soro eyed to him.

Veny Sinned the rock underneath as it flew up in the air with him on top, "—And I'll do it myself!" he was as high as the Academy.

Zayden raised his head, "—I made it clear that I'll tackle you if you did anything stupid!"

194

Soro rubbed his left thumb and pointer together.

Veny looked down at Zayden from the top, "—It's about time that I finally be free from my anger!" he yelled then looked to Soro, "—You'll die embracing your Sinning Ability!"

Flare watched from the terrace, "—What should we do?" she turned to Adalo.

"His actions are reasonable," remarked Adalo, "We have no place to interfere."

Lavivo looked to him, "—Pain resulting in things that can be avoided isn't ideal," she spoke.

Adalo eyed her, "Living a life with regrets doesn't sound pleasant either," he remarked.

"—Regrets?" heard Flare, *"Does this have to do with participant—"*

But then in the sky, Veny raised his arms up, "—I won't need Javarus for this!" he yelled, he Sinned Boulders of Rock out of the ground as they were sent up the air. They were all big and sharp as they formed a circle around Veny and his Rock platform in the sky.

Zayden saw him, then looked to Soro, *"I-I can't let this go on!"* he realized, *"Soro's important for my path to become Full-Fledged!"*

Veny swung his arm in the air as a Boulder of Rock rushed to him.

Soro slowly looked up.

Veny punched through the Boulder as the Rocks fell apart, "—Here it is," he smirked as a shape of a sword dropped, "This is Rockora," he grabbed the Rock sword from the platform and picked it up.

Most of the other participants made it to the back of the Academy, "What the hell's going on?!" yelled Dedrian.

Veny looked down to Soro as he felt the sword, *"Javarus is usually here for this part of the attack!"* he recalled, *"—But now nothing matters as long as Soro doesn't breathe!"*

But then Soro quickly turned and Sinned a Blue Lightning Bolt in his hand.

"—Soro?!" saw Zayden.

Soro whipped the Lightning Bolt towards the platform in the sky.

"—Come on!" yelled Veny.

Soro vanished as he reappeared out of the Bolt in mid air, "You wanted me," he spoke as he was above the platform.

Veny's eyes widened as he looked up, "Y-You will—"

Soro landed on the Rock platform, he stated Veny down.

Veny gripped onto the Rockora sword, "—It's finally over!" he shouted as he charged forward, "You deserve all of this!" he swung his sword across.

But then Fire surrounded the platform, "—What is this?!" stopped Veny, ashes appeared in the middle of him and Soro.

After a moment, Zayden reappeared with his arms out, "—I can't let you do this!" he faced Veny, "—I have a reason and it's not only for your good!"

Soro saw Zayden's back from behind.

"—Get out of the way!" yelled Veny.

"—No!" denied Zayden, "Your fight Soro will also hurt my chance against Adalo!"

There was a pause.

Veny took a few steps back, "—You're with Soro aren't you," he angered, "You both want to be Full-Fledged!" he burst forward.

Zayden saw him coming.

"—You both want to see this world go to hell!" Veny slashed down with the sword.

Zayden quickly stepped to the side, "—That isn't it!" he yelled.

But then Soro appeared in front of Veny.

"—You!" saw Veny as he pierced his sword forward.

But then Soro evaded and appeared behind Veny, "When will you realize to stop," he elbowed him in the back.

"—Uh," groaned Veny as he fell onto his knees.

Zayden was in front as he looked down, "Veny," he remarked, "There's no use."

196

Veny looked up and saw the Fire surrounding Zayden, he turned behind and saw the Lightning streaking across Soro, "—What happened here?!" he stood up and yelled, "Are you two together?!"

"He and I can't be anymore different," stated Soro, "Don't label us together."

Veny heard him, "—That's not how it looks like!" he quickly slashed his sword to the right.

"—Not again," groaned Zayden as he disintegrated into ashes and reappeared behind.

But then Veny swung his left arm in the air. Two big Boulders rapidly came rushing in from the circle surrounding the platform.

"How can I—" uttered Zayden as he heard them. But then a Blue Spark flashed as the Boulders turned to ashes.

Zayden quickly looked back, "—Soro?!" he saw his hand out.

"—There's no mistaking it!" yelled Veny as he ran forward, "You two have the same plan!" he pierced his sword across.

Zayden stepped back but his shirt was cut, "—Veny!" he angered.

Soro saw them.

Zayden went in and swung his arm, "—No more!" he bashed his fist into Veny's stomach.

"—Uh," groaned Veny as he stumbled back.

Zayden walked towards him. Veny quickly looked up and swung his arm.

Zayden ducked and jumped his hand into Veny's stomach, "—Incinerate!" he shouted as he Sinned Explosions of Fire from his finger tips.

"Uh—" Veny knocked back towards the edge of the platform, he was forced to drop his sword.

"—I can't let you fight Soro!" yelled Zayden.

Veny held his stomach and looked up, "—You!" he shouted, "You want to be just like Damon Uzara!"

"—Me becoming Full-Fledged doesn't mean I'll end up like him!" yelled Zayden.

But then Static noises were heard.

"—What?!" Zayden quickly looked back.

Soro had his arm out with Lightning in his palm, "Oblivious to everything," he spoke as he Sinned a Lightning strike.

"Wait—" uttered Zayden as he jumped up.

But then the Lightning Strike burst towards Veny.

Veny was struck as he was knocked off the platform.

"—We're way too high!" yelled Zayden as he landed back on his feet, "He's going to crash hard!"

Veny fell through the air, "—Forget about everything else!" he shouted.

"—He's going to hurt hard!" screeched Kara from the ground.

Veny looked around the 10 boulders surrounding Zayden and Soro, "—I'll have to do Javarus' part of the attack!" he yelled as he put his arms in an 'X' in mid air, "This the final part of Rockora!"

"—Veny!" shouted Zayden as he saw from above.

But then all 10 boulders surrounding Zayden and Soro rapidly burst towards them.

Veny's eyes widened, *"—This has to be the end of Soro!"* he saw, *"—It's over! I avenged my family for losing their Sin against Damon!"*

Zayden quickly looked around at the Boulders coming, "I-I don't know what to do!" he panicked.

"—Adalo!" called out Flare on the terrace, "—This is too much!"

Zayden's eyes widened, *"—I-If this goes through!"* he thought, *"I'll—"*

But then Soro put his arm up as the Black Markings scarred across it.

Adalo looked to the sky, *"What I expected,"* he saw.

10 sharp rapid Lightning Strikes thundered down from the sky and struck the Boulders into ashes.

Veny's eyes widened, "There's no way—"

But then Soro turned and whipped a Lightning Bolt towards him in mid air.

"—Soro?!" saw Zayden.

198

Soro reappeared out of the Bolt in front of Veny, "—Don't forget," he swung his arm, "I'm Damon's son," he bashed Veny in the face.

"—Uh," groaned Veny as he crashed to the ground. A Lightning Strike Sinned out of Soro's fist shoving Veny through the broken surface.

"—Participant Veny?!" worried Flare.

Soro landed in front of the rest of the participants.

All of them on the ground watched Soro as they cautious.

There was a moment of silence.

Zayden looked down to him from the platform above, *"—Why can't you see that both of us can become Full-Fledged,"* he thought, *"You're the only one that creates this void between us."*

After a moment, Smoke flowed around Adalo. He levitated off the terrace and landed on the ground.

Soro turned to him, then looked up to Zayden, *"...You and I can't be anymore different,"* he recalled as a Spark of Lighting appeared and he vanished from the field. There was a pause as everyone was stunned, they looked to the crash with Veny through the ground.

Adalo walked over to the collision and put his arm out, "He must know now," he spoke as he Sinned slight Wind.

Veny's body slowly came out of the deep crash, "—Uh," he grimaced in pain as he laid on the surface.

Adalo walked beside him and looked down, "This is final," he stated.

Veny slowly opened one of his eyes, his aura was gone.

"It's in your best interest to not fight anyone unless you are forced to," remarked Adalo, "Or it is required during a competition stage, understood?"

There was moment of silence as Veny listened, *"A-Adalo..."* he thought, *"Y-You saying must mean something..."*

The participants watched Adalo closely.

"He's masking his Ability so well," thought Marubee."

199

Aviva was surprised, *"I've never seen Adalo this serious before…"* she saw.

"Oh—" uttered Flare from the terrace of the Academy, "—Attention all participants!"

"—Hm?" All the participants looked up to her. "—Thank you for taking part in the partner training session this morning!" she addressed, "—The second stage begins this evening in Wavern city! Whether you come there following me, or arrive on your own, you must be there or else you're disqualified!"

All of them listened, but were still stunned from Soro's Power.

Zayden relaxed as he stopped Sinning, *"…I think Veny realized that he can't beat Soro,"* he thought as he looked down to him, *"…But I realized that I need Soro more than ever."*

Adalo turned into Smoke and reappeared back inside the Academy.

Zayden looked down from the high platform, "—Can someone help me down from here?!" he called out, "Kaesar, Aviva, anyone?!"

"—He's going to be stuck their forever!" chuckled Kara.

Kaesar looked to her, then turned to the platform, "…Here," he spoke as he Sinned a path of Ice from the ground up.

Zayden saw the Ice attach to the platform, but then he turned back and grabbed Veny's Rockora sword. After a moment, he slid down the Ice Path on his back and landed on the ground.

Veny slowly stood on his feet a distance away.

"—Veny," called out Zayden, he walked towards him, "It's yours," he handed him his Rockora sword.

Veny took a moment as he glared at the sword. He then looked to Zayden's eyes as he grabbed the sword with both hands.

"—I would've seriously been hurt if it hit me," remarked Zayden with a stern look.

Veny's hands shined in dark green, "...It's no use now," he muttered as he crunched the sword apart, and in his thoughts, *"Zayden actually tried to stop me..."*
There was a moment of silence as the sword broke into Small Rock pieces.

Kara looked to the Ice Path Kaesar created, "That Ice is super—"
But then Marubee pulled her from the collar.

"Hey—" struggled Kara, "W-Why'd you—"
"—It's time to go," spoke Marubee as she dragged Kara away.

"—But Marubee!" screeched Kara, "I didn't even say bye to my partner!"
Marubee shook her head, "He's not going anywhere," she assured.

Kaesar turned his head and snickered as he Kara pulled away.
Aviva saw Marubee go.

"Kaesar, Aviva," called out Zayden behind them.
"Hm?" the two turned around.

"Everyone watched the whole thing," recalled Zayden, "But where's Reno?"
"—Your pal Reno wanted to tackle me," smirked Dedrian from the side, "I put him in his place."

The three turned to him.
Aviva recalled what Reno told her and Kaesar: *"—I'm going to fight Dedrian tomorrow!"* she remembered Reno's words, *"In our partner training session, I have to challenge him!"*

"—Why would Reno want to fight you?!" asked Zayden.
"—He wanted to prove himself to everyone and he lost!" groaned Dedrian, "He simply asked for it and I delivered the tackle!"
Zayden angered, "You—" he burst to the other side of the Academy to find Reno.

Aviva ran and followed behind, *"—Reno's Sinning Power is low,"* she sensed, *"His fight with Dedrian didn't go well."*

201

Kaesar didn't move. He looked to Zayden as him and Aviva went by, *"Zayden's got himself into tough situations these past couple days,"* he recalled, *"Him and Dedrian want at each other, and his obsession of becoming Full-Fledged has everyone on the watch...especially him being with Soro..."*

On the other side of the Academy, Javarus had broken free from Veny's Rocks and walked to Reno, "Il told you," he spoke, "I haven't taught everything you need to know, but you carelessly fought Dedrian...now look at yourself."

Reno slowly sat up, "I'll get him next time..." he muttered, "I don't need anyone..."

"—Hey Reno!" Zayden ran to them and stopped, "—What did Dedrian do to you!?!" he looked to the bruises on Reno and his torn clothes.

But Reno stayed quiet.

"—Don't play dumb," came in Aviva beside him, "Please don't say fought Dedrian just so you can get back at him for me."

Reno looked to her.

Aviva exhaled, "I knew it..." she went on her knees next to him, "I told you I don't need your protection..."

Aviva put out her hands as she healed Reno's shoulders.

Reno looked away, *"...Just stop,"* he thought in his head.

Zayden clenched his fist, "Don't worry Reno," he tensed, "I'll make Dedrian—"

"—I can take care of myself!" shouted Reno as he stood up.

Zayden and Reno looked to each other.

"—I don't need your guys' help!" yelled Reno, "Stop telling me not to worry all the time!"

Aviva looked up to him from the ground.

"...Reno," Zayden was stunned.

After a moment, Reno eyed away, "...I-I'm not coming to Wavern to explore with you Zayden," he muttered.

Zayden saw a change in his expression, "...And why not?" he asked.

"I'm just not in the mood," answered Reno, but in his thoughts, *"I don't want be with Zayden anymore..."* he felt, *"He's like Dedrian, an obstacle I have to overcome..."* But then Javarus turned to Zayden, "—On Veny's behalf," he spoke, "Thank you."

"Hm?" Zayden heard, "For what?"

"For trying to stop Veny," clarified Javarus, "I know you did the best you can."

Zayden paused, "I tried..." he recalled, "But how'd you know about it? I didn't see you at the back of the Academy."

"I sensed it," remarked Javarus, "But when Veny was knocked off the platform, he set off the second part of Rockora..."

Zayden remembered, "Yeah he did," he recalled.

"There were several big boulders that headed straight to you and Soro," went on Javarus, "So what happened to them?"

Zayden took a moment, "It was Soro..." he remarked, "He raised his arm and Lightning came out from the sky," he recalled, "And just like that, the boulders were completely wiped out..."

Javarus nodded, *"I knew Rockora wouldn't be enough to end Soro..."* he thought, *"Now Veny knows too."*

Reno was upset as he turned his back, "I-I'm going to my room..." he muttered and walked away.

Zayden saw him go, *"Words won't help when he's this down,"* he thought.

After a moment, Aviva looked to Javarus, "Were you able to sense the ground when Reno fought Dedrian?" she asked.

Javarus nodded.

"...How badly was he beaten?"

"It wasn't even close," answered Javarus, "It's Reno's fault for being so stubborn."

Aviva listened, then looked back to Reno walking away.

"Reno will eventually feel better," assured Zayden, he then smirked, "—But am I able to take on Dedrian?" he asked, "It's his promise to his Mother vs mine!"

203

Javarus turned, "It's hard to tell," he spoke, "You two are very similar to each other."
Zayden shook his head.

Inside the Academy, Reno slowly walked up the stairs and through the hallway, *"Soro, Dedrian, Zayden..."* he thought, *"They're all so strong...I can't match with any of them..."* he quietly went inside his room.

By now, the partner training session was officially over.

A few hours passed by with the morning coming into late afternoon. The second stage was set to begin in two hours at Wavern City.

Inside the Academy, Zayden and Kaesar went to the Sinara Service Desk, "Hey Attendant Flare," saw Zayden.
"Hm?" Flare was inside the glass, "What is it participants Zayden and Kaesar?" she turned and looked to them.

"Do we have to tell you or something before we leave the Academy?" asked Zayden.
"Hm..." heard Flare, "Where are you going?"

"We're going deep inside Wavern City to check it out," answered Zayden, "But don't worry, we'll find our way to the second stage in time."
Flare listened, "Okay that's fine," she accepted, "Though if you decide not to follow my guide to the second stage building, it your responsibility to show up."

Zayden nodded.
"Let's hurry it up," spoke Kaesar, "I have to buy something..."
Zayden turned, "We are," he assured, "What do you have to get anyways?" asked.

But Kaesar stayed quiet, he turned and walked towards the stairs.
Zayden rushed beside him, "Kaesar?" he called out, "What do you have to get?" he asked again as the two made their way down.

After a moment, Reno walked by the Service Desk. His clothes were wrecked clothes because of his fight with Dedrian.

Flare noticed him walking, "—Participant Reno," she called out.

"—Who?!" uttered Reno as he quickly burst to the glass, "Was that you Flare?!"

Flare saw him, "First of all, calm down," she advised, "Second, come inside this room, let me fix up your shirt."

There was a pause as Reno eyed down, "Sorry to disappoint you though..." he muttered, "But I may not be as charming as usual..." he walked inside.

Flare exhaled, *I was never charmed to begin with..."* she thought.

By now, Zayden and Kaesar walked outside onto the Academy's field. The sun was shining on the grass and on the City, as they can see a few tall buildings from a far distance.

Aviva was on the field too, *"This whole competition has been so stressful..."* she thought.

Zayden and Kaesar walked to her from behind, "Hey Aviva," called out Zayden, "You should come to Wavern with us."

Aviva turned around, "To do what?" she asked.

Zayden shrugged his shoulders, "I don't know exactly, we can do whatever we want I guess," he spoke, "It's a popular city and me and Kaesar were going to check it out."

Aviva listened, "I see..." she murmured.

"We need a third person," swayed Zayden, "We can get lost before the second stage if it's just the two of us."

But then Kaesar looked to him, "I thought we had three," he recalled, "Wasn't Reno coming along?"

Zayden turned, "...He was," he spoke, "But then he changed his mind..."

Back inside the Service Desk Room in the Academy, Reno sat on a chair.

205

Flare was in front of him as she stitched some of the ripped cloth on his collar, "I saw a few of your friends just now," she spoke Flare as she went onto the shoulder, "They said they were going to Wavern."

Reno's cheeks were red as Flare was so close to him, "Uh—Yeah," he snapped, "U-Uh…"

"I assumed you would be going with them," she went on.

"—I was!" Reno raised his voice, "But, I don't want to anymore…"

"Hm, how come?" asked Flare as she went on to sewing the back collar, *"These are some rough burns…"* she saw.

"It's because—" uttered Reno, "—I don't like Zayden anymore!"

"You can't be serious," snickered Flare.

"—I mean it!" went on Reno, "Well—kind of—I mean, the way Zayden battles others thinking he's always going to come out on top is so…"

Flare completed his words, "…Is so annoying to watch?"

"No that's not it," denied Reno, "Zayden's my best friend, seeing him win gets me excited too, he told me the same thing when we were younger."

Flare listened, "Then what was it?" she asked. There was a moment of silence.

"…I'm not too sure," muttered Reno, "But lately, I've been wanting to be just like him…"

"That's crazy talk," chuckled Flare, "Just stick to who you are and think better, your opinion of yourself is more valuable than anyone else's."

Reno was seated as he heard her.

After a moment, Flare stood up straight, "…And I'm finished with your shirt," she yawned and stretched her arms, "Just go to Wavern with Zayden and Kaesar," she suggested, "You're only beating yourself up when you're alone."

But Reno had his head down, "…I'm no good," he muttered.

"Who said that?" heard Flare, "To me, you're pretty funny," she half smiled.

Reno's eyes widened, "Uh—What'd you say?!" he looked up.

"I said you're funny..." repeated Flare.

"—I am?!" Reno quickly stood up.

Flare slowly nodded.

"—Yes!" cheered Reno as he put his fist up, "I am good at something!"

Flare snickered.

"—Thanks for helping me out Flare!" waved Reno, "This was a good husband wife kind of talk!" he burst out of the room.

Flare saw him go, *"Did he really just say husband and wife?"* she sighed.

Back on the fields, "...I've been there before," went on Aviva, "I know the way around, so I'll come."

"That's good to hear," half smiled Zayden, "Now we can't get lost."

"—Hey wait for me!" a voice was heard from the front door of the Academy.

"Who's that?" asked Kaesar as the three of them turned.

"—It's Reno!" saw Zayden.

Reno quickly ran to the group, he put his hands on his knees, "I'm coming with you guys," his breath was heavy.

There was a pause, "I knew you wouldn't stay away," spoke Kaesar as he put his hand in his pocket.

"—You're right, I couldn't," Reno stood up, "Because I want to see Wavern with my friends!" he then looked to Zayden, "It's going to be the first for us," he recalled. "We've never been anywhere else except for Ayshan."

"Yeah, that's why I wanted to go so bad," remarked Zayden, "And with the second stage coming up, who knows which one of us will remain here."

There was a pause.

"Can we just get going now?" broke in Kaesar.

"Yep!" smiled Zayden and Reno.

The four of them walked together out of the Academy's field and through a passageway.

About 15 minutes later, they arrived at Wavern City.

Aviva was in awe, "I have to admit," she spoke, "Wavern City looks better every time I see it."

Wavern City resides in a vast valley surrounded by Rocky Mountains, there's a small river not far from it. It is the most popular city in the district with many buildings in a circular formation, and some parts of the town were placed on the edge of a small cliff. The town filled with countless number of flowers decorated on the streets; in front of the many stores, houses, and more.

"—There are so many things going on at once!" Zayden looked around, "This is nothing like Ayshan!"

"—Look over there!" Reno pointed at a stand with antiques, "Let's get a souvenir!"

"—I'm right with you!" Zayden nodded at him.

But then there was a tour bus slowly driving by with tourists on top taking pictures.

The tour guide went on, "And if you look to your right, you'll see—"

"—Is that Aviva?!" one of the tourists shrieked.

"—A Kallent?!" another one stood up.

"—You can't be serious?!"

"—She's so beautiful in person!"

"—It's Aviva from the Kallent family!"

Aviva saw them, "—Oh I forgot to disguise myself!" she realized as she quickly grabbed Reno's arm and ran away with him.

"—Where are you taking me?!" freaked out Reno.

"We need to get away fast!" yelled Aviva.

Zayden and Kaesar saw them go.

But then a gold card fell out of Aviva's back pocket as she ran away.

"Hm?" saw Zayden, he walked up to the card and picked it up, "What's this?"

There was a pause, "Looks like a card to transfer money," spoke Kaesar from behind, "We should give it back when we see her."
But then all the tourists jumped off the bus, "—A Kallent is actually here!" they charged after Aviva and Reno.

Zayden watched the tourists run. He looked back to the card, "Aviva come's from a rich family," he recalled then smiled, "So I don't think she'd mind if I borrowed her card for a bit!" he snickered.
Aviva and Reno ran by one of the shops.

"L-Look Mommy, I-I see Aviva!" a little girl pointed at Aviva and Reno passing by.
The Mom was taking care of a flower in front of her shop, "Oh what do you know," she spoke.

"Who was that boy with her?" the little girl asked.
"Hmm," the Mom paused, "I'm not sure, but from the looks of it, little Aviva is now all grown up," she chuckled.

The little girl gave a blank stare and scratched her head.
Zayden took a moment, "I guess it'll be this card with just you and me Kaesar," he turned around, "—Kaesar?"

He was no longer there.

———————————————————

Kaesar had walked into a candy store called 'Sweet for Sweeties.' He was feeling out of place with all the pink decorations inside, "Where am I…" he murmured as he walked to the front desk.
"—Hello young man!" the store Cashier popped up with a smile, "What are you looking for?!"

"I was just—"
"We have bonbons, bubble gum, caramel, coconut, fudge, taffy," the Cashier went on, "White chocolate, dark chocolate, mint chocolate, milk chocolate."
The Cashier took a long deep breath.

"I was just looking for a lollipop…" muttered Kaesar.
"—Oh!" uttered the Cashier, "Simple yet tasteful!" she opened the cabinet behind her, "Which one would you like?"

Kaesar was surprised at the sight of all the flavours.

"—There's raspberry, blueberry, grape, vanilla, peach," the Cashier went on, "Strawberry…"

Kaesar took a moment, "Any flavour is—"

"Just finish this lollipop, it's cherry too!" Kara's words got played in Kaesar's mind, *"It's the best one around!"*

The Cashier continued, "There's kiwi, sour, cotton—"

"Hey…" Kaesar spoke up, "…Do you have cherry by any chance?" he asked.

"—Yes I do!" beamed the Cashier. She took out the cherry lollipop jar and walked over to the counter.

Kaesar followed her on the other side.

"—That'll be $5.00!" smiled the Cashier.

"$5.00 just for one?" Kaesar was surprised. Still, he took out the money and paid for it.

The Cashier put the lollipop in a small bag and handed it to Kaesar.

Kaesar took a hold of the bag as he eyed away.

"—Thanks for shopping with Sweet for Sweeties!" smiled the Cashier.

Kaesar looked to her, but stayed quiet. After a moment, he walked out of the store with the bag in hand.

Reno and Aviva hid behind a small shed behind a takeout bar.

"—Why'd you take me here?!" opposed Reno, "This place looks boring!"

Aviva had her head out to see if the tourists lost sight of her. After a moment, she relaxed, "Looks like their gone," she relieved as she sat down leaning on the shed.

Reno stood beside her, "Who's gone?" he asked.

"The tourists," answered Aviva, "Didn't you see them?"

"Uh yeah, but aren't they your fans?"

Aviva paused, "It gets tiring," she spoke, "Sooner or later they were going mention Lavivo, and I'm really not trying to think about her right now…"

But then Reno quickly turned the other way, "Well, I don't know why I'm here so—"

"—Wait!" called Aviva.

Reno looked back.

"I need you to buy me a jacket of some sort," Aviva told him, "Just something big so I can cover myself."

"Do I really have to?!"

"—Yes you have too!" went on Aviva, "I came here with you guys to relax before the second stage, I shouldn't have to worry about people screaming Kallent in my face."

There was a pause, "...Okay, I'll get you a disguise," agreed Reno, "But I don't have money on me."

"That's," assured Aviva as she reached into her back pocket, "You can just—" but then she felt nothing.

"...Yeah?" waited Reno.

"—My card must've fell out when I ran away!" worried Aviva.

Reno quickly stepped away, "Then I'll just—"

"—We can pay with coins!" called back Aviva, "Here," she tossed the coins at Reno.

"—Oh, oh, oh," Reno caught the coins.

"Now please can you go into a store and pick out a jacket for me?" Aviva asked again, "Just pay with the coins and everything will be settled then."

Reno forcefully nodded, "Okay..." he murmured, "Only because you're a fan of mine."

"Okay there," Aviva rolled her eyes, "Think however you'd like, I just need my jacket."

Reno looked to the right, "—I'll do this faster than anyone can!" he yelled as he burst away from the shed and out in the open.

In the middle of all the stores and people, Zayden rushed through everyone with the Aviva's golden card in hand, "Where's all the expensive items?!" he was eager.

"Hm?" Kaesar saw him run by.

"—Oh Kaesar," Zayden stopped and turned around.

There was a pause, "...What?" asked Kaesar. Zayden slowly pointed forward, "What's in the bag?" he saw the small bag dangling from Kaesar's arm.

"Oh it's—" Kaesar quickly put the bag in his pocket, "—A souvenir," he blurted.

"—Oh good idea," realized Zayden, "I should get a souvenir along with the other gifts!" he turned and ran again.

Kaesar saw him go as he patted down the lollipop bag in his pocket.

Zayden burst down the pathways of Wavern, he looked side to side at all the stories, *"—With Aviva's card!"* he thought, *"—I can really get anything I want!"*
He ran into several stores in and out and bought many items. He said his thoughts out loud, "—Mom loves cake!" he bought cake, "—Mom loves the colour blue!" he bought a blue shirt and hat, "—Mom loves bright lamps!" he bought a lamp, "—Mom always said I should get new shoes," he snickered and bought many pairs of shoes. "And when Mom finally comes back home," he hoped, "She'll love new furniture!" he bought a dressing table.

Zayden smiled as he dragged the luxurious items in a big bag across the pathway.
Civilians walking by were shocked at how big the bag Zayden dragging was.

"M-Mommy look!" the little girl from before saw Zayden, "That boy has the good card!"
The Mom was fixing the front door of the shop, "Oh you're right," she looked over to Zayden, "He must be wealthy, those are the type of cards the Kallents carry around."

But then Reno quickly rushed to the shop.
"—Reno?" saw Zayden from a distance.

"—Hey do you guys sell jackets here?!" Reno asked the Mom in front of the shop.
"Yes we—"

"Thanks!" blurted Reno as he ran inside the shop.
He quickly grabbed onto several jackets and ran back out, "Here's the coins!" he handed the money to the Mom.
The Mom made the payment, "Thank you for shopping with us," she smiled.

"No problem!" Reno smiled back with the jackets in his arms.

"Reno!" Zayden came up from behind, "Look what I got as a souvenir."

"Zayden?" Reno turned around, "What'd you get?" Zayden put his hand in his bag, "Look at this!" he pulled out an item.

Reno's mouth dropped, "Is that the Sinara Academy?!" he was surprised.

"Yep!" smiled Zayden, he tossed the key chain of the Academy to Reno, "We had a lot of fun here, hopefully our memories continue after the second stage, right?" Reno dropped the jackets, "Yeah of course!" he awed as he caught the key chain.

A distance behind the two, Kaesar saw them as he walked closer.

But then Aviva saw him from behind the shed, "Kaesar!" she whispered for him.

"Hm?" Kaesar looked to the right, "Is that you, Aviva?"

"Did you see Reno with a jacket?" Aviva raised her voice.

"—Hey is someone at my storage cabin?" the chef running the takeout bar in front of the shed heard her.

"…What were you saying?" Kaesar asked from a distance.

"Just tell Reno to come here," Aviva quietly whispered.

"—Hey Kaesar!" Reno waved him from a distance, "Look at this keychain!"

Kaesar turned and walked to him, "Hey," he nodded to the right, "I think Aviva is looking for you behind that bar."

"—Oh yeah, I better give her the jacket!" remembered Reno. He picked up the several jackers on the ground and ran over to the shed.

"—What took you so long?!" yelled Aviva as Reno came by.

"—I'm sorry," Reno shook his head, "Wait—Why should I be sorry? I didn't have to do this for you!"

"Just hand me one jacket," urged Aviva.

"—Take all of them!" Reno dumped the jackets on top of her, "Now you got choices," he snickered.

Aviva pretended to smile. She stood up and tried on the different jackets.

Reno turned his back as Aviva took her time. Moments passed by as he became impatient, "You're covering all of yourself anyways," he murmured with his back turned, "It's not like it matters how you look now."

"It still matters," spoke Aviva as she felt the jacket she wore, "How do I look?"

Reno turned around and saw Aviva. She wore a fluffy pink jacket which had fur on the hood and on the outer hands. She wore red gloves and had a white scarf around her mouth.

"...So how do I look?" Aviva asked again.

Reno looked into the only part showing which were Aviva's blue eyes, "—Y-You look normal!" he blurted.

Aviva chuckled, "What's with the dramatic pause?" she recalled, "Did you forget what you were going to say?"

"—Nothing!" uttered Reno as he turned around, "I said you look normal okay!" he walked down the hill.

Aviva was confused, "Oh well, that's good to hear," she spoke out loud, "Now I won't be recognized as a Kallent."

The two made their way out of the back of the takeout bar.

Zayden saw them coming, "...Is that Aviva with Reno?" he asked.

"That's what it looks like," spoke Kaesar, "She's probably hiding herself from the rest."

"—Hey guys!" went on Reno as they all stood together, "The person wearing this jacket is—"

"—Reno!" broke in Aviva inside the jacket.

"—What?!".

"There wouldn't be a point to the jacket if anyone overhears who I am," she remarked.

"—But Zayden and Kaesar don't recognize you," spoke Reno.

"We know who it is," remarked Zayden, "Good call though, having her covered would be better."

"I know right," agreed Reno, "I'm a pretty sharp thinker sometimes."

"—This wasn't your idea," murmured Aviva.
But then a loud ding-dong was heard from Wavern's gigantic clock tower.

The group looked up to it, "—It's 6!" shrieked Reno, "We should go find where the second stage is!"

"I'm sure the girl in the pink jacket knows," spoke Kaesar.
The boys looked to her.

"...If I remember right," went on Aviva, "When I was younger, I watched my sister participate in the second stage at Wavern," she recalled, "So our second stage must be held in the same exact location, or at least I hope so."
"And do you know remember where that place is?" asked Zayden.

"Yeah, it's down this whole city section and past a small forest," answered Aviva, "We should start walking now, it's kind of a long distance."
"—Yes!" urged Reno, "And I'll be the first one there!" he burst away.

"—You don't even know which direction it is!" called out Zayden.
The group followed Reno and made their way out of the inner city, but Zayden forgot his big bag filled with the gifts he bought.

The little girl aw the big bag in front of her shop, "M-Mommy, look over here!" she walked over to it, "What is this?"

The Mom walked over to her, "It's the bag that boy was carrying," she saw, "He seems to have forgotten it."
"—Wow!" the little girl peeked inside, "So many cool things!"

"We shouldn't pry into his belongings," snickered the Mom as she stopped the girl. She then tried to lift up the bag, "T-There's a lot of things here," she struggled.
The little girl laughed.
After a moment, the Mom turned the big bag over and read the label: *"Welcome Back Gifts for my Mom!"*

There was a pause as she took a moment.

215

The Mom stood up as the little girl went inside the bag again.

"*I don't know what's going on exactly,*" thought the Mom, "*But that boy must really love his Mother.*"

The little girl got out of the bag as she wore a blue hat, her and her Mom giggled.

The group of 4 walked through a clear passageway with forests on their left and right.

"…This is taking forever," complained Reno, "I swear it has to be 7 by now!"

"Then we're late," spoke Kaesar, "Oh well."

"—Huh?" Reno was shocked, "You don't care?!"

"He's joking around," snickered Zayden. He then looked around at the trees nearby, "Still, we've been walking down this path for a while now."

Aviva repeatedly patted down the jacket to keep herself covered.

Zayden looked to her, "Nobody's here now," he remarked, "I don't think you need the disguise anymore."

Aviva looked up, "You don't know what I've been through," she recalled, "I've seen people crawl up from anywhere just to scream Kallent."

"Don't you think you're over exaggerating a bit?" spoke Kaesar.

"Nope," denied Aviva, "You don't know about my family."

Kaesar heard her as he stayed quiet.

But then Reno stopped walking, "…Zayden," he called out from behind.

"Hm?" Zayden, Kaesar, and Aviva turned back.

"…Just a little reminder," spoke Reno then raised his voice, "When me and Dedrian go against Adalo, if Dedrian attacks me for whatever reason, I really don't want you to help me."

"Why would he go after you?" asked Zayden, "You're a team."

"Y-You know how he is," recalled Reno, "He might want to get even with me…"

216

Reno thought about when he slapped Dedrian across the face with the Rock at the end of their fight, *"I can't believe he didn't snap right there and then..."* he worried, *"He's going to explode when he sees me..."*
"Be quiet Reno," Kaesar brushed it off, "You need Zayden for everything."

"—I mean it!" snapped Reno, "I don't need his help anymore!" he tensed.
There was a moment as they saw his change in expression.

"...Zayden," continued Reno, "Say you won't help me."
"What are you talking about?" opposed Zayden, "I can't say that, we're friends."

There was a pause as creaks and footsteps were heard from the forest, but the attention was focused on Reno.

"...If you can't say that," remarked Reno, "Then I'm not going to the second stage."
Kaesar exhaled, "This is so pointless," he murmured and walked away.

Zayden and Reno looked to each other.
"Zayden, Reno, let's go," insisted Aviva, "We don't want to be late," she began walking alongside Kaesar.

There was a moment of silence.
"...Come on Reno," urged Zayden, "You can't be serious about this."
More noises were heard from the side of the forest, "Hm?" Kaesar looked over.

Zayden paused, "Reno, you're going to follow us," he murmured, "You always go through these phases every now and then..." he began walking away.

Reno watched him from behind, "I'm done following people..." he muttered to himself, "I can be just as strong as you, or anyone else."

Kaesar saw Zayden coming, "I'm surprised you left him behind," he spoke, "I didn't think you would."
"Don't worry," assured Zayden, "He's coming back."

Reno was in deep thought, *"I don't want be looked down at anymore..."* he closed his eyes.

Suddenly three Sinning Powers began rising from the side in the forest.

"—You feel that?!" noticed Aviva.

"—Yeah someone's there," spoke Kaesar.

"I'm always looking at people's back..." thought Reno as he saw the backs Zayden, Kaesar, and Aviva from a distance away.

There was a moment as Zayden looked to the forest, "—Show yourself!" he yelled.

Reno still didn't move, *"...Zayden's always so up front,"* he angered as he clenched his fists. He had a light green aura.

Zayden raised his voice, "Get out of the—"

But then someone jumped from the forest to the air, "He's the one!" shouted the person.

"—Watch out he Sins Light!" yelled Aviva as she looked up.

"Light?!" uttered Zayden, he jumped in the air towards the person as his Fire surrounded his body.

Both Sinners neared clashing with each other. The Light Sinner went down with a punch as his body shined in yellow.

But then a Sinner with a green aura burst in the middle of the two and blocked his attack.

"—R-Reno?!" Zayden was shocked.

"—Now you're seeing my back!" shouted Reno as he smashed his Rock formed hand on top of person's head.

"—Uh," the Light Sinner was knocked down as he landed a distance away in front Zayden and Reno.

But then a rapid Ice beam struck from the side heading to Aviva.

Kaesar quickly Sinned his own Ice streak out of his hands as both Streaks crashed and shattered.

"—Give us the man in the jacket!" ordered the Light Sinner.

"—Man?!" uttered Aviva.

"—No way," denied Zayden, "You're going to have to get through—"

"Me!" broke in Reno, "Fight me if you want anything from us!"

The Light Sinner saw him, "I didn't want to get my hands dirty!" he smirked as he ran towards Zayden and Reno.

Zayden took a step forward, but then Reno ran first. He came face to face with the Light Sinner, "—I'm your opponent!" he yelled as he went in with a punch.

The Light Sinner blocked it with his right arm, then went in with a kick to Reno's stomach.

Reno caught his leg and pushed him away. He put his arm out as he Sinned a chunk of Rock forward.

But then the Rock quickly got launched up the air by another person from the forest.

The Light Sinner looked up, "—That's funny," he murmured.

Zayden rushed in as he went in with a punch with his Fist inflamed.

But then the opponent caught his fist, "You got to be faster than that," he smirked.

"—Zayden duck!" yelled Reno from behind.

Zayden lowered.

"—Ariyo!" shouted someone from the side.

The Light Sinner looked over.

"—Here's my chance!" shouted Reno as he jumped over Zayden and put his fists together, "I'll smash you with my Rock!"

The Light Sinner eyes widened as he saw him, "No I—"

But then Reno's attack was caught by an Ice Sinner.

"—Kaesar?!" uttered Reno, "—Wait no, who are you?!"

The Ice Sinner had an emotionless look on his face.

"—Nice one Caiyaan," smirked the Light Sinner. He appeared beside Reno and kicked him in the side.

Reno rolled on the ground, but then got up and burst towards the Ice Sinner named Caiyaan. He went in with multiple punches.

But Caiyaan pedaled back evading each one.

"—Ariyo you fool!" someone came out from the forest, "This isn't the right person!"

"Huh?!" the Light Sinner named Ariyo uttered, "Are you positive?"

"—Just one!" Reno went down with his fists together.

Caiyaan quickly grabbed his wrists and froze them.

"—I can't feel my hands!' worried Reno as he backed up.

But then Kaesar's eyes turned Blue as the Ice on Reno's fists turned into Water.

Caiyaan looked to Kaesar on the right.

There was a pause, "Alrighty," spoke Ariyo, "We should stop now."

After a moment, Caiyaan stopped Sinning as his Blue aura faded away.

"…Sorry about that," chuckled Ariyo, "Even though it was kind of fun."

"Fun?" heard Zayden, "You guys attacked us, what do you want?"

"Hold your horses," the person near forest walked forward, "Allow me to introduce ourselves," she went on, "I'm Miya."

Miya Tutu was a small sized girl with long blonde hair and emerald green eyes. She had a voice that made her sound like a matured woman. She wore a black dress full of white add-ons, along with a black headband over her hair.

"And as you may already know by now," continued Miya, "That preposterous human is Ariyo."

"—What?" blurted Ariyo, "What does that even mean?"

Ariyo Suzuki was a Light Sinner who had short spiky orange hair and brown eyes. He wore a light brown shirt and dark pants with a black and white belt that kept it up.

Zayden looked to Ariyo, then turned to Reno. He remembered when Reno defended Ariyo's attack.

"And lastly," went on Miya, "There's Caiyaan," she referred to the Ice Sinner, "The one who blocked your attack with ease."

Caiyaan had neutral lengthy white hair and his nails were blackened. He had almost lifeless gray eyes. He wore an all black coat that had it's collars up to his chin.

Reno gave him a stern look, *"If he hadn't interfered,"* he thought, *"I-I could've finally protected someone for once!"* .

Miya then walked towards Zayden, "We were given a task to obtain the person that wore the same jacket as the lady back there," she referred to Aviva.

Miya gave Zayden a picture.
Zayden took his time looking over it. He stood beside Kaesar as they faced Ariyo, Caiyaan, and Miya.

"However, as you can see," remarked Miya, "Ariyo was clearly mistaken, as the person you see in the picture is quite evidently a man."
Zayden looked up, "I guess it's all just a misunderstanding," he realized and looked to Ariyo, "And it was kind of fun actually," he snickered.

Aviva was behind everyone as she began walking, "Now we should be on our—"
"—I know you're under there," called out Miya, "Miss. Aviva Kallent, from the prestigious Kallent family residing on the wealthy Island of Korona."

"She didn't have to say my whole life story..." irritated Aviva.
Ariyo put his hands behind his head, "It looks like I was wrong," he sighed, "Juro's going to be let me know about this one for sure."

Kaesar heard him, "Is this Juro person the one who gave you the task?" he asked.
"Yeah," nodded Ariyo, "Pretty cool, right?"
"How so?"
"—Huh?" reacted Ariyo, "You don't know who Juro is?!"
Kaesar stayed quiet.
"Well I don't mean to brag or anything," went on Ariyo, "But us three are from the Sinetity Academy! We were given this task from the man himself, Juro Shuesi!"

"—Juro Shuesi?" heard Aviva as she stood near them, "Adalo's older brother?"

221

"And one great of a Sinegious to learn from," added Ariyo.

There was a pause, "Adalo Shuesi..." repeated Miya, "Is it possible that the four of you are competing in a competition as well?" she asked, "It's uncommon to come across Sinners in this area."

"Yeah, we are," answered Zayden, "We're in the competition of the Sinara Academy."

"Ha!" bragged Ariyo, "That's nowhere near the level of the Sinetity—"

"—Keep quiet Ariyo," hushed Miya.

"I don't have to take orders for you," he murmured.

Miya ignored her, "So, I assume you're having your second stage tomorrow, just like us?" she asked.

"Nope," Aviva spoke up, "Ours is any minute now," she then looked to her group, "Which means we really need to—"

"—What is your name?" Caiyaan finally spoke in a slow tone.

Everyone looked to him.

Reno yelled from the side, "I'm—"

"I mean the Ice Sinner," said Caiyaan, "Who are you?"

Kaesar looked to him. There was a moment of silence.

"...Kaesar Kinnuan," he answered.

The two looked to each other.

But then Aviva took off her jacket, "I won't be needing this anymore," she remarked, "Nice talking with you other participants, but we're going to have to make a run for it if we want to make it on time."

"Okay then," spoke Miya, "You be on your way now," she went on, "And from Ariyo, he apologizes for this."

Ariyo irritated.

Aviva began running down the pathway.

Kaesar eyed Caiyaan as he walked by.

Caiyaan looked back with an emotionless expression.

After a moment, Kaesar ran down the path.

"—Fight me and Reno another time," smirked Zayden to Ariyo, "We'll be glad to prove the worth of our Academy against yours."

Ariyo turned to him, "Nothing can touch The Sinetity Academy," he opposed.

Zayden shook his head. He then looked to Reno beside him, "Let's go," he urged as he ran down the path.

Reno took a moment as he turned to Ariyo, "I almost had you!" he recalled, "If he didn't get in the way!" he pointed to Caiyaan, "You would've seen me protect my friends!" he yelled and ran off.

"...Okay then," heard Ariyo, he looked to the four running, "They're pretty weird people," he murmured.

"Their weird?" mocked Miya, "That's coming from someone who's pants are unzipped."

Ariyo looked down, "Uh—Why are you looking there?" his face went red as he zipped his pants.

"Silly boy," Miya shook her head as her and Ariyo walked the other way.

Caiyaan stayed for a moment, he had his eyes on Kaesar, but then turned and followed his group.

Zayden was running ahead of Reno, but then slowed down.

"...I know you can go faster," murmured Reno, "You don't have to run with me..."

"I just wanted to say you looked cool when you blocked Ariyo's attack," recalled Zayden, "Thanks for having my back!"

Reno remembered: *"Now you're seeing my back!"* he recalled his words.

There was a pause, "Can you please stop this whole thing about you not wanting my help?" asked Zayden, "It doesn't fit you at all."

There was a pause as Reno looked down as they kept running, he then spoke up, "...When I see how you go against anyone," he went on, "Whether you're in a heated moment with someone from Ayshan, or when it's Dedrian,

223

or even in front of Soro…" he continued, "I-I kind of want to be like you."

"—Forget about becoming me," denied Zayden, "Someone like me can't get someone like Flare!"

"What do you mean?!"

"I know something happened in the Academy which made you come along," snickered Zayden, "You were in such a bad mood, Flare had to do something that got you up again."

Reno blushed and scratched his head, "Uh—she was—fixing my shirt," he recalled.

"Really?" Zayden was surprised.

"—A-And," went on Reno, "She called me funny!"

"Exactly! What did I say," recalled Zayden, "Forget about me, you're already good at being yourself."

Reno looked to Zayden, then turned forward with a light smile.

"Plus," spoke Zayden with a serious tone, "The way you are is important, you're like a brother to me Reno."

Reno was stunned after hearing those words. The two continued to run, "…You know what Zayden," spoke Reno, "You might be right."

Zayden nodded, "If I'm right about anything," he tensed, "It's that I'll always need you as a friend."

"—Okay stop now!" yelled Reno, "This is getting weird!"

Him and Zayden chuckled as they passed by Aviva and Kaesar at a fast pace.

Aviva looked to Kaesar, "…That Ice Sinner," she recalled, "Odd that he only asked for your name."

"Yeah…" muttered Kaesar, and in his thoughts, *"If Kara thinks my eyes aren't normal sometimes…"* he compared himself to Caiyaan, *"I wonder what she thinks about his…"*

In front of him, Zayden and Reno ran side by side. Zayden's laughter lowered, "Reno, I don't mean to bring you down," he smirked, "But the fact remains intact, you still haven't beaten me to this day!" he picked up his speed as he burst down the path.

"Hey well—I said one day and that can even be tomorrow!" yelled Reno as he ran behind.

Zayden continued down the path in front of everyone. After a moment, he tensed, *"Second stage of the competition,"* he recalled, *"Soro, I can close the gap between us, and you'll come out of your void and we'll talk to Damon, together."*

He continued running, *"We'll both make our dreams come true,"* he thought.

The 4-person group sprinted with Zayden at the front.

"—It should be just on this right!" directed Aviva.

"—About time!" relieved Zayden as he turned and stopped.

He saw a building like the Sinara Academy.

"Hurry inside," spoke Flare as she stood in front of the door.

"—Flare!" dove in Reno as he knocked Zayden to the side, "We made it, right?!" he burst to her.

"Yes you have, participant Reno," answered Flare, "Please go inside."

Reno giggled, "Whatever you say," he blushed and went in.

"Reno..." groaned Zayden on the ground.

"—Don't play dumb," urged Aviva as she ran by, "Get up!" she went inside the building.

"—How is this playing dumb?!" yelled Zayden.

Kaesar walked towards the building, the little bag he bought earlier dangled from his pocket.

"Participant Kaesar," saw Flare, "Would you like me to hold that bag for you?"

"—Uh no," Kaesar looked down, "I'll take care of it," he quickly tucked the bag into his pocket.

"...Okay," understood Flare, "But that must be taken out and put to the side, or I'll consider it a violation."

Kaesar made his way inside the building, "You got it," he spoke.

225

"Participant Zayden," called out Flare, "You're the last one, come in."

"—Yeah!" Zayden quickly stood up and ran inside the building.

Flare closed the door behind.

Zayden walked through a small hallway leading to the main zone, he saw the entire arena.

There were stairs that lead down to the huge battleground, while the participants who were spectating had to watch from one of the two side platforms behind the railing.

Zayden looked to his right and left and saw the rest of the participants, *"Not a surprise..."* he thought, *"Soro isn't going to show up until he has too..."*

Kaesar took a step to his right.

"—Kaesar Kaesar!" yelled Kara from the left platform, "Come stand over here! I have a new attack planned!"

Kaesar stopped walking as there was a pause.

"Super please!" screeched Kara.

Kaesar hesitated, but then turned and walked to the left platform. There stood Kara, Marubee, and Dedrian, whom was on the far end.

"Dedrian..." Zayden looked his way. He then walked over to the right platform. There stood Javarus, Aviva, Reno, and Veny, whom stood away from a distance.

"You guys were cutting it close," remarked Javarus, "Just made it in time."

"Yeah, I had things holding me back," recalled Zayden, "But I'm glad we went to Wavern, it was fun."

"...But Zayden," spoke up Aviva, "Where did the bag you were carrying go?"

Zayden remembered the huge gift bag he bought for his Mom, "—I forgot it back in Wavern!" he panicked.

"—Guys be quiet!" hushed Reno, "Flare's about to speak..." he leaned on the railing with his hands on his cheeks.

"Thank you to all of the participants that showed up!" addressed Flare, she walked down the middle stairs.

Lavivo came through the front door and walked down with her.

Kara was in awe, "Oh my it's—"

"—Not now Kara," Marubee closed her mouth.

Lavivo smiled at her, "Don't mind me," she spoke, "You should be listening to Flare."

Aviva and Marubee glared at Lavivo, then looked to each other from across the platform, "Hm," they eyed away.

Flare went on, "—I will now repeat the rules for the second stage!" she announced, "Each team will battle against Adalo in a two on one scenario until either one side loses their conscious, or until the time of 20 minutes are finished!"

The participants listened.

"Also, winning or losing does not determine you passing or failing!" she clarified, "And both members of each team do not have to pass together or be eliminated together, it is quite possible that one member passes while the other does not, is that clear?"

The participants nodded.

"You will be assessed upon overall individual skills and teamwork capabilities," Flare concluded as her and Lavivo reached the battleground, "Good luck!"

"—Thank you Flare!" Reno waved down at her.

But then a quick large tornado formed on the battleground, a strong forceful Wind circulated throughout the arena.

"—What's this?!" uttered Reno as he was forced back against the wall.

"—Uh," the other participants their arms up to cover themselves from the powerful wind.

The little bag in Kaesar's pocket flew away, "—Oh," Kaesar quickly caught it back.

"—And here's your opponent!" announced Flare.

The large tornado began decreasing with a man standing at the bottom of it.

"—Adalo Shuesi!"

Adalo stood with a new attire. He wore dark pants with a silver buckle and a gray shirt underneath. He had a black trench-coat over along with black boots and a pair of black fingerless gloves.

Everyone had their eyes on him.

With the time striking 7:00 P.M. the second stage of the Sinara Academy competition had officially begun. All participants were eager to compete; Team A, Javarus and Veny; Team B, Kaesar and Kara; Team C, Dedrian and Reno; Team D, Aviva and Marubee; and Team E, Zayden and Soro.

"May Team A please come down to take part in the second stage!" addressed Flare.

"...Come on Veny," Javarus spoke to him on the left and walked towards the stairs.

Veny had his head down. After a moment, he followed Javarus as the two walked across the platform and down the stairs.

"Let's go to the back," spoke Flare.

Lavivo nodded. The two made their way behind a wall to view the battles behind a large window.

Javarus and Veny stood a distance away from Adalo.

"I need to pass this stage so I can learn and teach how to use Sinning in a positive manner," thought Javarus, *"Me and Veny need to cooperate if we want to make an impression."*

But Veny thought about his battle with Soro, *"What's the reason now..."* he wondered.

"Are we ready to start?" Flare sat down at a table with Lavivo, they both wore a small headset.

Only Javarus nodded.

"The 20-minute timer..." went on Flare, "—Has started!" Adalo quickly put his right arm forward, "—Now!" he shouted as heavy Winds shook the whole arena. All the participants watching from above were forced up the air as some hit the ceiling.

"—Adalo isn't playing around!" saw Lavivo as she had her arm over her head.

Javarus and Veny were lifted in the air.

Adalo quickly jumped forward and punched Javarus sending flying against the wall to the right.

In mid air, Veny regained his balance and went in after Adalo.

But then Adalo quickly grabbed his wrist and kicked him sending flying against the wall to the right.

"—Veny start Sinning!" yelled Javarus on the wall. His body overflowed in light green.

"I don't need you to tell me anything," murmured Veny as he begun Sinning.

Javarus put his arm out as he Sinned a Boulder from the ground towards Adalo.

Adalo landed on the surface and saw it coming.

"—I know what he's planning!" saw Flare.

As the Rock came closer, Adalo put out of his hand as the Boulder turned into Smoke.

"What the—" uttered Veny as the Boulders reappeared in front and crashed into him.

"Hm," Adalo turned to his right.

Javarus appeared as he went in with a punch.

But then Adalo quickly Sinned a tornado on the ground.

The tornado spun rapidly as it caught Javarus and hoisted him up.

Veny kicked off the wall and Sinned a Rock underneath to catch him, "—This is no joke," he groaned, "This is serious!" he quickly glided his Rock towards Adalo as he went in with rapid punches.

But Adalo moved side to side in mid air as he evaded each fist.

Veny went in for a kick.

Adalo quickly caught his leg and threw him towards the tornado.

Javarus struggled at the top of the tornado, "I can't get—" he tried to break free.

Adalo put his arm forward as he blew a strong wind.

"—Uh," Veny was sucked into the same tornado, he was hoisted up and saw Javarus, "—Get out of the way!" he shouted.

229

Javarus finally broke free and moved to the side. But then Adalo appeared at the top of the tornado as he faced both of his arms down, "—You need to be more prepared than that!" he shouted as he Sinned heavy winds from his palms.

The Wind bashed Javarus into Veny straight through the tornado and into the ground.

On the platforms above, Reno gulped as he watched, "I knew Adalo was good..." he recalled, "But it seems like it's impossible to even touch him."

"Yeah, I know," spoke Zayden beside him, "But that's why we want to learn under him."

Back on the ground, Javarus got up to one knee, "We're going to have to work as a team," he told Veny.

"—You weren't there when I needed you for Rockora," recalled Veny, "Don't talk about teaming with me!" he Sinned a Rock underneath him and soared towards Adalo in the air.

"—Veny!" uttered Javarus as he did the same.

The two went in to attack Adalo together.

But Adalo caught and blocked each of their attacks.

"—Why can't I hit you!" shouted Veny as he went in for another punch.

Adalo's body turned into Smoke.

Veny's arm went through him and knocked Javarus to the wall.

Adalo reappeared and held onto Veny's fist.

"—How?!" uttered Veny.

Adalo threw him away and blew a strong Wind from his palm.

Veny crashed into Javarus on the floor.

The ground cracked as the impact created dust.

Adalo continued to levitate in the air with his Sinning Ability.

After a moment, Javarus slowly stood up, "We can't make it seem that we're in pain," he advised, "—Uh," he grimaced as he felt his shoulder.

Veny coughed as the dust went into his throat.

"—Let's change up the arena!" yelled Javarus. He roared as his Sinning Power began to rise.

"Hm," saw Adalo, *"He finally decides to take things serious."*

"—Veny!" called out Javarus, "I need time! Go after Adalo!"

"I really dislike it when you order me around," groaned Veny, but he Sinned a Rock underneath him and rushed towards Adalo.

Adalo put his arm out as heavy Winds circulated around him.

Veny struggled to get through the Wind, "—Your ability is getting on my nerves!" he angered. He Sinned a boulder rapidly towards Adalo.

But the Winds around Adalo blew the boulder back. Veny quickly ducked, "—Look out Javarus!" he turned back.

The arena vibrated as Javarus' Sin shook the surface.

Javarus jumped over the boulder, "—Now Veny!" he shouted as he moved his arms side to side, "Get out of there!"

Javarus Sinned 4 huge blocks of Rock out of the ground as it grew up the air.

Adalo's eyes widened, "What do we have here," he saw.

"—Those are huge!" awed Reno.

Javarus put his hands together as the 4 Blocks quickly began closing in Adalo.

Adalo eyed the Blocks, *"This attack isn't meant for striking,"* he thought as he stood still.

"—You took us lightly!" yelled Veny as he levitated on a Rock above.

The Blocks closed in on Adalo and trapped him inside.

Adalo looked up, *"...My only sight is the ceiling,"* he saw.

Javarus Sinned a Rock underneath and glided up above the Blocks. Him and Veny came into Adalo's sight with their hands forward, there were several Boulders of Rock floating behind them.

"I see now," realized Adalo then yelled, "—Not so fast!"

But Javarus and Veny roared as they Sinned multiple Boulders of Rocks into the hole.

Adalo went up the air, but then a Boulder caught and knocked him down.

"—Keep going Javarus!" urged Veny.

Adalo went up the air again as he evaded one Boulder and turned another into Smoke, "—They keep coming," he groaned.

Javarus' aura slowly faded as his breath was heavy, "I-I'm trying—"

Veny looked to him, "Don't stop—"

But then Adalo appeared at the top of the hole, "—Too late," he quickly closed his hands a the two of them.

Dark Smoke surrounded both Javarus and Veny, "What is this—" they struggled to move. The Rocks they stood on broke as they fell down the air.

"—That happened to me!" Zayden and Dedrian both remembered the same attack.

Javarus and Veny crashed onto the ground.

Above in the air, Adalo saw the two, "I should applaud you," he spoke, "If you guys had more Sinning Power within, a lot more could have been done."

Aviva was surprised, *"It looks like the trapping of Smoke weakens the opponents Abilities for a moment,"* she recalled, *"And everything the Sinner creates breaks down too,"* she saw as the 4 huge Blocks collapsed.

After a moment, Veny slowly got up on his feet, "—R-Rockora is the only way!" he declared.

Javarus looked to him, "You know how I feel about that!" he denied as he stood up, "I'm never going to be involved with it!"

There was a pause, *"Why is Adalo waiting?"* wondered Aviva, *"The more time that passes by, the more time they have to regain their Sin."*

"—Come on!" Veny shook his head, he burst to the right running on the side walls.

"Hm?" Adalo turned his head.

232

Javarus put out his arm as he Sinned a Boulder from the other side of the wall behind Adalo.

Adalo quickly turned back to Javarus, but then the Boulder hit him from behind, "—Uh," he was headed towards the wall, "I won't let it," he groaned as he Sinned a Wind out of his palm stopping the motion.

Veny had already Sinned three Big boulders out of the ground.

Javarus ran to Adalo, "—Have your eyes here!" he yelled as he jumped and went in with a heavy attack.

But then Adalo dashed to the side.

"—Uh," Javarus punched into wall.

Veny quickly swung his arm as one of the big boulders rushed towards Adalo.

"—Oh," the Boulder collided with Adalo at full speed as he his arms were around it.

But then there was a pause, "—No way!" Kara was shocked.

Adalo held off the Boulder as Smoke appeared around his arms.

Dedrian smirked, *"Brute strength,"* he saw.

Javarus came from behind with a heavy punch.

But then Adalo turned into Smoke as Javarus fell onto the Boulder.

Adalo reappeared behind with his arm forward, "Smart idea at first," he spoke as he Sinned a heavy wind from his palm.

Javarus was pushed by the Wind as he was bashed into the wall with the Boulder.

Veny swung his arm again as he Sinned another boulder.

Adalo put his arm out and closed his hand.

The Boulder went through the air towards Adalo, but slowly turned into Smoke and became smaller.

Adalo blew the small Rock away with his mouth as it appeared in front him.

Veny was stunned, "...Nothing works!" he yelled, "Javarus, we're going with Rockora now!"

Javarus slowly pushed the Boulder off of him on the wall, "...No!" he opposed, "We can't control it!"

"—You're wrong!" denied Veny, "It's our only way to get him!"

Javarus came out of the wall and dropped onto his knees.

"...That settles it," spoke Veny, he Sinned a large platform of ground and jumped on top, he was carried high above the arena.

Adalo looked to Javarus on the ground, *"If you know Rockora won't work,"* he recalled, *"It's your duty to stop your partner from going through with it."*

Veny stood on the platform, "Javarus!" he yelled from above, "You have to do this with me!" he raised both of his arms up as he Sinned large chunks of Rock out of the ground. The rough big Boulders formed a circle surrounding the platform.

Javarus got up on his feet as he looked up.

"...Aren't you going to work with your partner?" asked Adalo a distance in front.

"There's no point of talking to him now," spoke Javarus, "Once he starts Rockora, I know he won't go back on it."

Adalo paused, "His own attack is going to backfire," he remarked, "As partners, I suggest you act to stop this move."

But Javarus stayed quiet. After a moment, he burst charged towards Adalo.

Adalo put his arm forward as he Sinned a strong wind.

Javarus jumped as he avoided the force.

But then Adalo jumped backwards and his body vanished into Smoke.

"Where—" Javarus' eyes widened in mid air.

Adalo reappeared behind Javarus with a kick. Javarus was sent flying through the air.

Adalo moved back as he vanished into Smoke again.

"—I can't follow this!" yelled Reno from the platform.

Adalo reappeared on the ground as he kicked up Javarus' chin, "You're going up," he spoke as put his arm up and Sinned a heavy Wind.

Javarus was bashed high up in the air as he landed on Veny's Rock platform on his back.

Veny turned, "—Get up!" he ordered, "Thanks to Adalo, you can help finish the attack!"

But Javarus' breath was heavy as he was on one knee, "Y-You know why I don't do Rockora..." he spoke.

"—Who cares what happened before with him!" yelled Veny.

"—I don't want anyone watching to get hurt!" stood up Javarus, he Sinned with his arm forward as one of the Boulders surrounding the platform broke down.

"—What are you doing?!" saw Veny.

Javarus moved his arm towards another Rock.

"What's going on..." murmured Kaesar from the arena platform.

"I'll tell you what's going on!" screeched Kara, "The Rock boys are arguing and it doesn't look good for them!"

Javarus Sinned as he broke down another Boulder.

Veny angered, "—You're ruining it!" he shouted as he ran towards Javarus.

Javarus yelled back, "Rockora won't—"

"—Looks like we met our end!" declared Adalo as he vanished into Smoke on the ground, he quickly reappeared on the platform.

"—Watch out!" saw Javarus, he rapidly Sinned the falling pieces of Rocks from the Boulders.

"—Uh," the Rocks rushed in and constricted Adalo.

"—You actually did it!" Veny's eyes widened, he pushed Javarus off the platform as he jumped off himself.

"—Wait Veny!" uttered Javarus in mid air, "Don't!"

Veny put his arms out in mid air as they shined in Dark green, "—Now the second part of Rockora!" he shouted as closed his arms in an 'X'.

High in the air, all the huge Boulders remaining rapidly rushed towards Adalo from all sides.

"—Adalo could be out after this one!" yelled Reno.

Zayden saw the attack, *"—Those boulders!"* he remembered, *"They could—"*

"—It's never that easy!" shouted Adalo as the Rocks holding him broke off.

"—How?!" uttered Javarus.

Adalo's body overflowed in Smoke as his hair waved back, he put his arm down, "—You're coming back!" he yelled as a large tornado broke loose on the ground.

The Wind forced the other participants up to the ceiling.

The Rockora Boulders were near crashing into Adalo.

But then the tornado caught Javarus and Veny and hoisted them back up on the Rock platform.

"—Your own move will be the end," spoke Adalo as he jumped high in the air and the two took his place.

"—Not them!" worried Flare.

The Boulders rapidly closed in and collided with Javarus and Veny. All 8 large and rough pieces of Rock.

A loud crashing noise was heard throughout the arena. Nobody could see Javarus and Veny in between the Boulders.

But then after a moment, the Boulders broke apart as the two fell through the air, their aura was gone.

Adalo opened both of his palms, "Could've thought it through better," he stated as he Sinned three heavy winds.

Javarus and Veny was bashed into and through the floor.

There was a moment of silence.

Zayden looked down at the carnage, "How deep are they into the ground?!" he uttered his thoughts out loud.

Adalo remained in the air as Smoke surrounding his body..

Marubee looked to him, *"What a fast turn around,"* she thought, *"It appeared that Adalo was caught in Veny's Rockora, but quick thinking caused the same move to be the downfall of the two…"*

Dust began to clear away as everyone had their eyes on the battleground.

Flare and Lavivo walked out of the small room, "Do you think their okay?!" worried Flare.

"They should be fine for the future," spoke Lavivo, "But as for now..."

The dust cleared away as Veny laid unconscious on the ground.

Javarus was barely standing, "T-That's why I don't risk Rockora..." he muttered and dropped to the floor.

Adalo gently landed himself onto the ground in front of Flare and Lavivo.

"...Thank you for competing Team A, Javarus and Veny!" addressed Flare, "We will take everything in your battle into account to determine if one or both of you pass the second stage!"

The other participants spoke amongst themselves.

Flare looked to Adalo, "You didn't have to force them through the ground you know," she recalled.

"It's a message to everyone," stated Adalo, "Plus, their own move ultimately took them out, that's concerning."

Flare exhaled as she shook her head.

"Lavivo," went on Adalo, "Go on ahead and heal the two, ensure they are well enough to stand back up on the platforms to view the rest of the battles."

Lavivo nodded and walked over to the middle of the arena.

Dedrian smirked, "—Now that's a tackle!" he yelled out loud.

Zayden looked to him, "Your partner seems more than ready," he murmured to Reno.

"Y-Yeah," saw Reno, "Maybe a bit too much..."

After a moment, Lavivo was finished healing, "You two should be fine now," she stood up and smiled.

There was a pause as Javarus and Veny felt the bruises on their body.

"...Adalo is just as good as we heard about," murmured Javarus as he slowly stood up.

"If you listened to me..." muttered Veny then yelled, "—If you just listened to me we could've won!" he stood up and faced Javarus, "Rockora is our move!"

237

Javarus gave him a stern look, then turned his back and walked towards the stairs.

"—Javarus?!" called Veny.

"—We did the best we could," remarked Javarus as he made his way up the stairs, "Now we watch and wait for the results."

Veny saw him go as he irritated. After a moment, he went up the stairs to the left platform.

Javarus walked back to the right platform behind the railing.

"That wasn't bad at all Javarus," recalled Zayden, "I'm sure you did fine."

"Yeah," added Reno, "That was fun to watch."

"Thanks, but all I can do now is wait," spoke Javarus, "You guys should watch Adalo closely, you could pick out some of his moves."

Zayden and Reno nodded.

Lavivo went onto fixing up the arena back to its original state with her Sinning Ability. Her hands shined in Pink as she went over to Adalo to heal his minor pain.

"Next one up," spoke Adalo.

Flare nodded, "—May Team B please make their way down the stairs and into the battleground!"

"—Okay Kaesar do you get it?!" beamed Kara about her plan beside him.

"I get it, but I don't agree with it," opposed Kaesar as he walked away, "It's silly."

Kara burst around Kaesar and leaned into his face, "—But with your silly eyes," she moved her eyes looking into his eyes, "I'm sure we can—"

"—Kara!" Kaesar quickly backed off, "I told you before not to get to so close…"

"Aw, okay," heard Kara, "But my plan is super good!"

Kaesar began walking down the stairs.

"—Wish me luck Marubee!" smiled Kara as she walked down with him.

"Yeah yeah…" she murmured.

"—You said you like to walk around and clear your mind!" Zayden recalled to Kaesar, "But now's not the time for that mindset!"

"Yeah!" yelled Reno, "Freeze something else aside from my water!"

Kaesar half smiled as he heard them.

"Are you nervous?" Flare asked Adalo on the battleground.

"Hm, just feels different, that's all," answered Adalo as he saw Team B approaching, "I've been looking forward to this one..." he walked towards them.

Flare walked back inside the room with Lavivo.

"—Let's do this!" beamed Kara as she put a lollipop in her mouth, "Nobody can beat gray and orange!"

"My hair is white..." thought Kaesar.

"Are we ready to begin?" addressed Flare through the headset.

"—Yes ma'am!" screeched Kara.

Kaesar looked to Adalo, *"I've been looking forward to this one..."* he thought.

"The 20-minute timer..." went on Flare, "—Has started!"

But there was a moment of silence. Kaesar and Adalo stared at each other.

Kara moved her head side to side looking to the two, "Uh..." she muttered.

The participants watched from above.

But then Kaesar burst to Adalo as he went in with a punch.

Adalo's body quickly turned into Smoke.

"—Huh?!" uttered Kara.

Adalo reappeared behind Kara and lightly jabbed her neck with two fingers.

"—Oh," Kara's body shook for a second. There was a pause, "—What did he to me?!" she freaked out.

"I don't know," spoke up Kaesar from a distance, "But don't lose focus, we're not losing this."

"—Right!" nodded Kara, "Bring out the Kara clones!" she yelled as she Sinned.

But there was no aura around her.

"…Kara?" saw Kaesar.

"—I said Kara clones!" screeched Kara again, but only bits of Smoke came out of her mouth, "…What's going on?!" she worried.

"Hm, she can't Sin," remarked Dedrian from above, "She's as good as being useless now."

It must be the jab Adalo gave," recalled Aviva.

Kaesar paused, "Not much we can do now," he spoke, "Adalo must have closed your Abilities, oh well…" he burst towards Adalo again.

Adalo vanished into Smoke and reappeared behind.

But then Kaesar quickly spun with a kick.

Adalo blocked his leg and went down to sweep him underneath.

But then Kaesar jumped up and Sinned in mid air as a blue aura formed, "It's just you and I now," he Sinned a hard ball of Ice in his hand and whipped it down.

Adalo put his arm forward as the Ice turned into Smoke, "—What?" he was shocked as the Ball picked up speed.

"—He wasn't quick enough," saw Lavivo.

Adalo dashed to the right as the Ice ball passed him.

"—Kara!" called out Kaesar.

The Ice ball was headed Kara's way.

But then Kaesar's eyes turned Blue as the Ice quickly melted into Water.

Kara was shaking her body, "—That's not fair!" she screeched, "My Sinning won't work!"

Kaesar looked to her as he was coming down the air.

Adalo went up towards him as he swung his arm.

But then Kaesar smoothly moved back and kicked into Adalo's stomach.

"—Uh," groaned Adalo as he was pushed back.

Everyone in the building were shocked, "…That's the first clean attack on Adalo," spoke Zayden.

But then Adalo burst through the air and kneed into Kaesar's stomach.

"—Uh," groaned Kaesar.

"It was only one," spoke Adalo as he put out his hand and Sinned a heavy Wind.

Kaesar was pushed back, but he caught his balance as he put his hand on the ground. He Sinned a path of Ice on the floor towards Adalo.

Adalo quickly jumped over the Ice.

Kaesar looked up as he ran and went in with a punch.

"—No so easy," Adalo's body turned into Smoke.

Adalo reappeared behind Kaesar and kicked him into the wall.

"—Uh," crashed Kaesar.

Adalo landed on the ground and stared him down. But then Kara came up from behind and wrapped her arms around Adalo.

"—What?" he looked back.

"—Go Kaesar!" beamed Kara.

Kaesar got up from the wall as he burst towards Adalo, "I won't let this go to waste," his fist was covered in Ice as he went in with a heavy punch.

But then Adalo broke free of Kara's hold.

"—Uh," shrieked Kara.

Adalo jumped over Kaesar, "—Enough playing around!" he groaned as strong Winds burst out of his body.

The entire arena shook as everything was blown away.

"—Hold on a second!" yelled Reno as he was pushed back into the wall on the platform.

Kaesar and Kara were blown away and crashed their back on the wall, "—T-The wind won't stop!" worried Kara.

Marubee saw her as she had her arms over her head, *"Come on Kara,"* she saw, *"Think of something."*

Adalo put his arm forward towards Kaesar, "Hm," he Sinned heavy Winds.

"Uh," Kaesar was bashed into the wall.

Kara looked to her right and saw him.

Adalo Sinned multiple heavy Winds,

Kaesar was bashed into the wall several times, the wall cracked.

Kara tensed, "—Kaesar you can't do everything yourself!" she screeched, "You need me if you want to take on Adalo!"

Kaesar was hit into the wall again as went down onto his knees.

"—I can't Sin but my plan doesn't need me to!" recalled Kara.

Kaesar took a moment as he caught his breath, he looked up to her, "I just don't want to hold—"

"—But that's not a problem!" beamed Kara, "Remember, we're partners!" she smiled.

There was a pause as Kaesar eyed away, "…Okay," he gave in and put his head down, "Go to the other side."

"—Yes!" rejoiced Kara, she burst away and ran on the side walls of the arena.

Adalo turned as he aimed his arm towards her.

"—Adalo!" shouted Kaesar a distance in front, "You've been acting strange around me! I've noticed!" Adalo turned to him.

"—Hm?!" Flare closely listened from the back room. The Blue aura around Kaesar thickened as Ice covered his arms and hands.

"—I'm ready to go!" beamed Kara from the other side behind Adalo.

Kaesar nodded, "—Icesarus!" he yelled as he pushed his right arm forward and held it with his left.

A flash appeared as Kaesar Sinned a huge path of Ice down the entire battleground. There were sharp spikes of Ice coming out from the sides, and many slim Mirror pieces of Ice standing up.

Adalo levitated in the air, "…Now what," he looked around.

Kaesar burst down the Ice and jumped towards Adalo, he went in with rapid punches.

Adalo moved side to side evading each fist, "Hm," he went in with a punch.

242

But then Kaesar quickly caught the attack and froze his fist.

Adalo flexed his arm as Smoke came out of his palm and shattered the Ice.

"—What?" Kaesar was stunned.

Adalo kicked into Kaesar's stomach, "That's for before," he recalled.

Kaesar bent forward.

Adalo swung him arm and bashed Kaesar in the face sending him to the side.

Kaesar crashed through one of the many Mirrors of Ice standing up.

"—Oh no!" screeched a voice.

"Huh?" everyone looked around, "Where is that voice coming from?" asked Javarus out loud.

Adalo looked up, then looked to the side.

Kara began to appear in all the Mirrors of Ice scattered on the battleground.

"—This move is crazy!" awed Reno, "How is she doing that?!"

Kaesar wiped his mouth as he got up on his feet.

But then Adalo rushed towards him through the air.

Kaesar quickly put out his arm and Sinned another Ice Mirror as his own body turned into Ice.

Adalo punched through the Mirror and the Ice figure of Kaesar.

"You missed," spoke a voice.

Now, Kaesar appeared in all the Mirrors of Ice with Kara,

"—It really worked!" cheered Kara jumping up and down.

On the reflections, Kaesar looked to her and snickered.

Adalo eyed around at all the Ice Mirrors, the other participants above did the same.

Flare quietly laughed inside the back room.

Adalo heard her and irritated, "...I'll break down this Ice now," he spoke. His body slowly turned into Smoke.

But then two Globes of Ice were whipped towards him.

"—Uh," Adalo quickly dodged them, "Where did that come from?" he uttered.

A rapid Ice figure of Kaesar shattered through a Mirror with and punched into Adalo's stomach.

Adalo's eyes widened, "How are they doing this..." he groaned as his stomach went in.

The Ice figure shattered.

"—Let's keep at it!" beamed Kara as a ball of Ice was whipped.

Adalo quickly dashed to the right.

But then another Ice Ball struck him on the back of his head, "—This is embarrassing," irritated Adalo.

Kaesar saw him from the Mirror.

"—No more!" groaned Adalo, he burst through the air towards one of the Mirrors that showed Kaesar and Kara.

"—We have to move!" uttered Kaesar, the images on the Ice Mirror showed him turned to the right.

"—Take me with you!" Kara held her hand out, "You know I can't move around the Ice without you taking me along!"

There was a pause as Kaesar looked to her hand. Adalo was nearing closer.

"This is why I didn't want to do this move..." exhaled Kaesar. He hesitated, but then took hold of Kara's hand. The images on the Mirrors of Ice showed rapid movement of the two.

Adalo stopped in mid air and looked around, "—They're everywhere," he saw. He put out his hands and Sinned heavy Winds shattering several of the Ice Mirrors.

But Kaesar and Kara were still shown on the remaining ones.

"—This is super pretty!" chuckled Kara as she continued to dash around with Kaesar.

"...They're good," spoke Javarus from the platform.

Zayden, Reno, and Aviva looked to him.

"As a team, they know what to do," remarked Javarus, "And even Kaesar alone, he's naturally quick and durable."

Tons of Ice globes were whipped towards Adalo. Adalo quickly put out his hand as he vanished a few into Smoke, "—Uh," he was struck by the other one, *"—I still can't figure out how this move works,"* he thought.

A hard ball of Ice was whipped from behind and nailed Adalo's back, *"—That actually hurt,"* he grimaced in pain.

But then the images on the Ice slowly began to show an orange aura around Kara.

"Her Sin is coming back," saw Aviva.

Kara felt her Sinning Power rise, *"I guess we don't need this move anymore…"* she thought, she then looked to her hand being held by Kaesar as they ran, *"…But this is super fun!"* she smiled and stayed quiet.

Another load of Ice globes erupted towards Adalo. Adalo saw it coming, *"…I didn't want to do this,"* he muttered as he quickly levitated up the air.

More Ice Globes were whipped towards him. But then Adalo's eyes widened, *"—Samaria!"* he yelled as his body spun in the mid air.

Powerful circles of Wind broke loose throughout the arena. The Mirrors of Ice shattered as Kaesar and Kara were blown and bashed into the wall.

Adalo's body turned into Smoke as he rapidly continued spinning. The Winds became faster and stronger.

Kaesar and Kaesar broke through and inside the wall.

Flare and Lavivo were forced to the back of their room, *"Adalo!"* groaned Flare as her hair was blown back, she looked to her watch, *"Only 5 minutes left!"*

The participants on each platform were pushed back against the wall, *"—How can he Sin so much Power?!"* Zayden was stunned.

After a moment, Adalo slowly stopped Spinning as the Smoke around him faded away, *"I didn't think I would have to use that…"* his breath was heavy, *"But of course, you were the one that brought it out of me,"* he looked to Kaesar.

The battleground was broken as the floor and walls were wrecked.

Kaesar was stuck inside a wall.

Adalo quickly burst through the air and grabbed Kaesar by the shirt, "We're almost finished," he spoke as he threw him in the air.

"—Uh," struggled Kaesar.

Adalo Sinned a tornado from the ground.

The tornado caught Kaesar and hoisted him up. Adalo vanished into Smoke and reappeared at the top of the tornado with his hands out, "—Enough is enough!" he shouted as he Sinned down heavy winds.

Kaesar was pushed straight through the tornado and into the ground.

"—There's no way Kaesar can get up now!" saw Reno.

Kaesar's body was scratched up as his clothes were torn.

"We don't know that yet," spoke Zayden.

Adalo then turned to Kara who was stuck in the wall, he levitated towards her.

Kara's eyes were closed as her aura was gone. Adalo saw her up close, *"...Looks like you're done for the day,"* he turned his back.

But then Kara grabbed his arm and flashed into a red flood.

"—What's this?!" Adalo was forcefully brought down to his feet.

"—That's my Kara clone!" beamed the real Kara, she pointed from across the arena as she stood behind Kaesar.

Adalo tried to lift his feet, *"T-This liquid is too—"* he struggled to move from the ground. Smoke appeared around the red flood, but nothing happened.

Lavivo looked to the real Kara from the back room, *"That lady is quite deceptive,"* she observed, *"Just what you want from a Farmake Sinner."*

Kaesar slowly sat up and looked to Kara, "...When did you get your Power back?" he half smiled.

"Oh—I got it a while ago!" smiled Kara, "But I was having so much fun with my move that I just couldn't tell you!"

Kaesar listened, then stood up.

"Are you okay?" asked Kara.

"...Not really," he spoke, "But I wish you told me that your Power was back, I wasn't into that whole running together part..."

"Aw why?" wondered Kara, "Is there something wrong with my hand?" she put her hand in front of Kaesar's face.

"There's nothing wrong," snickered Kaesar as he put her hand down, he then tensed, "Let's just finish this now," he spoke, "With my plan."

"—You got it!" nodded Kara, she put her hands together and Sinned two Kara clones. All three of them took out a lollipop and put in their mouths.

The red liquid on Adalo's feet slowly faded, he finally broke free, "You two work well off each other," he spoke as he turned to them, "Working together on the same move is effective instead of opposing one another," he eyed Javarus and Veny on the platform.

There was a pause, "...Good to hear," murmured Kaesar, "—Now Kara!" he yelled.

Two of the Kara clones burst on the side walls around Adalo.

Adalo quickly put out his arms and Sinned heavy Winds.

But then Kaesar's eyes turned Dark Blue as he froze the two Kara clones.

The Wind blew past them as they remained standing.

Kaesar then closed his eyes as the Ice melted

"—I didn't expect that," saw Adalo.

The two Kara clones continued sprinting around the wall.

"—Look at me!" screeched the real Kara as she burst towards Adalo in front.

Kaesar followed running behind.

Kara took the lollipop out of her mouth as it extended into a long pole, "—This is going to hurt!" she yelled as she stopped running and whipped the Pole.

Adalo saw the Pole coming, "—Way too slow," he put out his hand and blew it away.

But then Kaesar was above Adalo coming down, "—Right here!" he yelled as went in.

Adalo looked up as Smoke covered his fist, "—Why would you tell me where you were!" he went up with a punch.

Kaesar was knocked in the head, but he quickly touched Adalo's arms.

"When did—" uttered Adalo as his arms began to freeze over.

Kaesar was sent flying towards the wall.

Adalo's body slowly turned into Smoke, "This Ice should—" But then one of the Kara clones appeared in front of him and turned into a red flood.

"—Not again!" groaned Adalo as his feet were stuck to the ground.

The other clone picked up the real Kara's extended lollipop from the ground, "—You can't move now!" she threw the Pole in the air as she melted and created more of the red flood.

"—Uh," Adalo struggled.

The participants on the platform were in awe of the battle.

Kaesar landed on the side wall and kicked off of it, "—There it is!" he caught the thrown lollipop in mid air, "Kara you too!" he yelled as he went down towards Adalo with the Pole, he Sinned an Ice ramp with his other hand.

Kara ran and jumped as she slid down the Ice Ramp, "—This is so pretty!" she beamed as she went up just as high as Kaesar, "—I'm with you!" she took out the lollipop in her mouth as it extended into a Pole.

Adalo looked up to the two in the air.

Kaesar and Kara both went down with the Poles in their hands, "—It worked!" they yelled together with a Blue and Orange Aura.

"—Can Adalo do anything?!" uttered Marubee. Everyone in the arena were stunned, *"—Adalo can't move!"* they thought, *"Adalo's going to—"*

"—Samaria!" a voice yelled. Winds stronger than ever burst throughout the whole arena. The door leading

248

into the Academy broke out as all the participants above were sent flying in all corners.

The floor of the arena cracked as the door of the room keeping Lavivo and Flare inside broke in.
The ceiling above crumbled and shook as the lollipop Poles vanished in thin air.

Kaesar and Kara were bashed into the wall, Kara's aura was gone and Kaesar's aura was light.
After a moment, Adalo slowly stopped spinning as his body surrounded in Smoke.

"—Uh!" The other participants in the air fell and crashed onto the platform.
Adalo remained standing as everyone else were on the ground. His hair waved and his breath was heavy.

The Winds slowly lessened as two blocks of the ceiling broke down and crashed in the middle of the arena.

Kaesar's back dragged down on the wall as he sat up against it.
Kara dropped down from the wall as she went unconscious.

Flare crawled out of the battleground room, "...T-The timer is up!" she announced as she stood up, "T-Thank you for competing Team B, Kaesar and Kara!" she went on, "W-We will take everything in your battle into account to determine if one or both of you pass the second stage!"
There was a moment of silence as the other participants watched from above.

Kaesar slowly stood up as he used the wall for assistance, "...H-How was that?" he spoke as he looked to Adalo holding his arm.

Adalo walked forward, "It was a very good effort," he answered and looked to Kara on the ground, "She did well too," he then turned and walked to Flare.
"A-Adalo," called out Kaesar, "I know you've seen me before..." he dropped down and sat up against the wall, his breath was heavy.

Adalo looked back at him as he stayed quiet. After a moment, he continued walking as he passed by Flare,

"Don't call for the next Team yet," he spoke, "I need a breather."

Flare heard him, *"It's hard to believe..."* she thought, *"They made Adalo use Samaria twice..."*

Lavivo came out of the room, she began fixing up the arena, "—Aviva!" she called for her, "May you please heal the two behind me? This may take a while."

Aviva irritated, *"—I hate taking orders from her,"* but she still made her way down the platform and went over to heal Kaesar and Kara.

After a moment, the arena was fixed.

Kara regained her conscious, "—Oh that hurt," she chuckled as she sat up holding her elbow, "Wait—" she saw someone from a distance, "Is that—"

Beside her, Aviva had her hands on Kaesar's shoulder.

"...That's good for now," spoke Kaesar, "Thanks."

"Yeah yeah," murmured Aviva as she stopped Sinning, "—Oh, and I think you dropped something..."

"Hm?" heard Kaesar as he sat against the wall.

Aviva stood up and took out a little bag from her pocket, "Is this yours?" she held out the bag in front of him, "During the strong winds, I saw it come out of your—"

"—Uh yeah," Kaesar quickly stood up and snatched it.

"Oh, okay," murmured Aviva.

Kaesar turned and walked towards the middle stairs.

A distance away, Kara slowly walked over to Lavivo, "...I finally met you," she hugged her from behind.

"Oh," Lavivo felt her, "Hello young lady," she turned around and smiled.

Kara's eyes were tired, "You're the best Farmake Sinner ever..." she smiled, "How do you..." her voice softened.

"Oh, I'm not the best," Lavivo smiled back, "I just do what I feel is right."

"Oh I..." Kara lost her balance.

But Lavivo caught her, "You're a remarkable Farmake Sinner yourself," she commended, "You and your partner did very well."

Kara's eyes opened, "That means so much," she chuckled, "...He's super strong, and I guess I'm really—" but then she saw Kaesar walking up the stairs.

Kara burst away from Lavivo and walked up the stairs with him, "We did really well I think," she recalled, "And take that Marubee!" she stuck out her tongue at her.

"Uh—" uttered Marubee.

"We did okay," spoke Kaesar, "I wish that last attack hit though," he recalled.

"—Not to worry!" Kara put her pointer up, "Gray and orange will comeback better than ever!" she smiled.

Kaesar looked to her and half smiled, they reached the top of the stairs.

On the left platform, Dedrian smirked as his aura was red, *"Now it's my tackle..."* his turn was upcoming.

But then loud chatter was heard from the opening entry of the building.

Everyone looked to there.

"—I heard Samaria!" a voice spoke.

"—Is Adalo here?!"

"—It's the Sinara Academy, isn't it?!"

"I see," heard Adalo, "My attack must have broken the door."

A storm of people began rushing inside the building. Loud and fast footsteps were heard in the hall leading into the arena.

"—People are coming!" remarked Flare, "We can't put a hold on the competition!"

Adalo Sinned and levitated himself in front of the opening entry.

"—It is Adalo!" saw someone.

"—I heard Lavivo is here too!"

"—Wait, isn't Adalo's full name Adalowala?!"

"...Just how many people know about that," irritated Adalo.

251

"Hold on a second," noticed Lavivo, *"There's a familiar Sinning Power there..."*

"I'm terribly sorry," spoke Adalo as the people from the outside made it in, "But my Academy is busy as of this moment."

"—Oh no let them come!" urged Reno, "I can become famous!"

But then Adalo Sinned a light Wind from is palm towards the group of people.

The Wind safely blew out the unwanted guests, "—But I wanted to see the future of Sinning!" yelled someone as they were all blown out of the building.

Lavivo sighed, "I guess I'm going to have to fix the door..." she began walking up the middle stairs.

"—You've gotten soft Adalo," smirked someone who remained standing from Adalo's Winds.

"Hm?" Adalo turned in mid air as he faced the person.

Lavivo recognized the voice, *"Wait that's—"* she ran up the stairs, "...Katana?!" she saw.

Katana Luutzki was a close friend of Lavivo. She had green eyes with bandages over her long messy black hair that went down on half of her back. She wore a white and red robe. She also had bandages around her shoulders and ankles, along with a small tattoo of her little sister on the left side of her back.

"W-What are you doing here?!" asked Lavivo as she approached her.

"I just happened to walk by and hear Adalo losing his voice," smirked Katana, "I'd sure as hell would love to see what's happening here."

"Katana?" heard Flare, she looked up and saw her.

"Oh—well," went on Lavivo, "It's the Sinara Academy competition, in fact, it's the second stage as of now," she smiled, "So yeah come inside and watch with us."

"I would come without your acceptance anyways," exhaled Katana, she walked down the middle stairs with Lavivo.

"What are you doing here?" asked Adalo from above.

"—Didn't you hear?" provoked Katana, "Hm, you're Smoke must be too much for you at this age."

"Oh can't you just go on without saying such things," insisted Lavivo.

Adalo tried to ignore her.

Katana and Lavivo reached down at the battleground.

Katana looked up to the participants and pointed at all of them, "—Listen you kids!" she raised her voice, "—You only got one life so don't waste any opportunity! I better see you sweat, cry, and bleed against that Adalo or I'll force you myself!"

The participants listened as they were shocked. "—I better be falling off my chair in awe of these battles," she yelled, "Otherwise everyone here is an insult!"

"...Okay I think they get it," sighed Lavivo.

"—Who are you calling an insult?!" two voices from each side of the platforms shouted at the same time.

"—You two got something to say?!" yelled Katana. She rapidly took out two bandages from her shoulders and whipped it towards the two who shouted.

"—Watch out!" yelled Reno.

Katana's bandage wrapped the two participants as she held the stick from the other end, "—Say it on my level!" she smirked as she pulled them down from the platform.

In mid air, both of the wrapped bandages lit up on Fire as the two shouters landed on opposite sides of the ground.

"State yourself!" ordered Katana.

"—Zayden Fareno!"

"—Dedrian Bellard!"

"What's your relationship with each other?!" she demanded.

"—I-I owe a fist to his jaw!"

"—I'm itching to tackle him down!"

"Good!" grinned Katana, "—Now go at it!"

Zayden and Dedrian looked to Katana for a moment, then eyed to each other and smirked. They both surrounded in Fire and burst towards each other.

"—No this is not happening!" shouted Adalo.
But Zayden and Dedrian didn't listen. They both went in and punched into each other's face, they were pushed back but went in again.

"—Zayden!" shrieked Reno.

"—Don't butt in!" shouted Zayden.
The two Fire Sinners jumped in the air.

Dedrian went in with a punch, "—I've been waiting for this!" he yelled.
But then Zayden grabbed his arm and swung him to the wall.

Zayden sprinted and jumped as his fist was inflamed in Fire, "—I've been waiting just as bad!" he bashed Dedrian inside the wall.

The wall broke in as there were explosions of Fire. Dedrian had his arms up and jumped away.
But then Zayden jumped off the wall as he swung his arm and nailed Dedrian in the jaw.

Dedrian was sent flying to the other side of the wall. Zayden landed on the ground and burst towards him, "Now you're tasting your own blood!" explosions of Fire sparked from his hands.

"—Come on!" Dedrian felt his jaw as he was stuck in the wall.
Zayden quickly ran and jumped towards him with his hand out, "—Now I'm the one above!" he shouted as explosions of Fire ignited from his fingers.

The wall exploded again, "—Uh," groaned Dedrian.
"—Do they have to do this now?!" saw Aviva.

Adalo moved closer to the battle, but then stopped as felt his back, *Kaesar gave a good shot back there...* he recalled.
Dedrian came down on his feet, "—Don't get cocky!" he shouted, "You're still underneath me!"

"—That doesn't matter!" yelled Zayden. His Sinning Power began to rise, the Fire around him grew bigger,

"...You said my dream was stupid," the Fire became slightly darker.

"—You said my word meant nothing!" shouted Dedrian.

The two burst towards each other again.

They clashed with their fists at the same time. They kicked up at the same time, and were forced away from each other.

Dedrian put his arms forward and Sinned a wave of Fire.

But then Zayden jumped over the Fire and spun into a kick coming down.

Dedrian put his arms up as he blocked and pushed Zayden away.

"—I'll tackle you down!" Zayden and Dedrian went in with again as they clashed fists and were forced away.

The two looked to each for a moment.

Dedrian wiped away the blood from his jaw. He then held onto his right arm and roared as his arm completely turned into a Dark Red form. The sleeves ripped open as he stared down Zayden, "I've been itching for this battle for far too long."

"—Yes yes!" urged Katana, "Let's keep this going!"

"—Your obsession with me will bring you down!" smirked Zayden.

Dedrian smirked back, "—One strike in the skull," he burst forward and jumped in the air, "And you won't be standing anymore!" he went down for a strike with his Red Arm.

"—Oh," Zayden quickly moved and evaded the attack.

Dedrian's arm went through and collapsed the ground. He charged over to Zayden with rapid punches.

Zayden dashed side to side evading each fist, "This arm's tough looking!" he yelled, "But it's useless if it can't touch me!"

"—Alright then!" yelled Dedrian as he put his left hand through the ground, "—Try this!" he shouted.

Thick lines of Fire burst up from the ground.

Zayden quickly looked around as the Fire erupted around him, "—Oh," he jumped forward dodging the Flame behind, "—That's still too slow!" he smirked looking back.

But then Dedrian jumped towards him, "—You talk too much!" he yelled and bashed him with his Red Arm. Zayden was sent flying as he crashed hard into the wall above.

Dedrian charged to Zayden and jumped towards him, "—I'll end this now!" he shouted as he swung his Arm again.

"—No!" Zayden's eyes widened as he rolled to the side.

Dedrian's Red Arm broke through the wall. Zayden turned and put his palm on Dedrian's back, "Incinerate!" he yelled as large ignitions of Fire exploded from his finger tips.

The wall burst open as the two were forced outside the building.

"What do they think they're doing?!" yelled Veny.

"Maybe I waited too long…" murmured Adalo, he levitated himself outside the building.

All the other participants followed outside the building, some jumped through the hole in the wall and others through the front opening.

Outside, Zayden and Dedrian were in mid air as they traded blows. Dedrian nailed him in face, Zayden came back bashing him in the stomach.

Katana ran out of the building, "—Sweat, Cry, Bleed!" she smirked as she saw the two, "—That's what truly makes a Sinner!"

Dedrian put out his arms as he Sinned a wave of Fire, "Just stay down!"

Zayden put out his hands as he ignited explosions of Fire, "—Don't think about getting up!"

Both attacks collided as thunderous noises were heard. Both Sinners were sent crashing onto opposite sides of the ground outside.

Zayden and Dedrian got up and stared each other down.

Everyone else made their way around them.

"I've never seen a Fire Sinner like this..." saw Aviva, *"They feel so..."*

"What's with these two..." saw Marubee, *"Their aura is..."*

Aviva and Marubee thought the same thing, *"Fire Sinners are so...dark."*

"—Any other tricks you want to pull out?!" groaned Dedrian.

Zayden's fist was inflamed, "—I'd rather beat you down with my own hands!"

The two burst towards each other as they angered, they roared as they scorched the ground beneath.

"—It's over!" shouted Zayden and Dedrian as they both went in and bashed each other's faces as their fists were caught in their jaws. Explosions of Fire were created as the ground broke underneath.

The strong impact sent both of them flying to opposite sides crashing into a large tree. They both sat up as their breath was heavy, the Fire began hurting themselves.

There was a pause as everyone looked to them, "—Is that it?!" urged Katana.

Zayden and Dedrian didn't move, they looked to each other from a distance.

"You two aren't half bad," grinned Katana.

But then Adalo landed on the middle of the field outside, "Zayden," he looked to the far left, "Dedrian," he looked to the far right, "I'm sure this was enough to—"

"—Not ever!" Zayden stood up and began marching towards Dedrian.

"—To hell with him!" Dedrian stood up and marched towards Zayden.

Adalo stood in the middle, "Then I'm stating it's over," he remarked, "We're moving onto Team C for the second stage."

Zayden and Dedrian stopped walking as they were a distance away from each other, Adalo stood in the middle.

Reno was nervous from behind.

257

Zayden looked to the other participants, then saw Reno, *"You protected me before, so this is your moment..."* he thought, *"I shouldn't go further."*

After a moment, Zayden stopped Sinning, the Fire around him was gone, *"Go on Reno,"* he thought, *"You're teaming up with him,"* Zayden turned and walked away.

Dedrian saw him go, "—No!" he opposed.

But then Zayden looked back and stared into Dedrian's eyes, "—You can't tackle with the likes of me," he smirked.

"—What?!" angered Dedrian, he ran and pushed Adalo away as he went in for a punch, "Don't mock me!" he shouted.

But Zayden quickly caught his fish as Fire surrounded him again, "Don't mock me and my Mother," he gave a stern look, "I'm keeping my promise till I die."

Everyone was shocked.

Zayden let go of his fist and walked away. He stopped Sinning again as he approached Reno.

"Uh—" Dedrian was stunned, "You're not—"

"—Over here!" shouted Adalo as he Sinned heavy Winds pushing Dedrian a distance away, "Your Team is set to compete," he remarked, "Prepare."

Dedrian's Red Arm was gone, but Fire surrounded him again, "—Cheap shot," he groaned as he stood up.

"Uh-Uh," Reno hesitated to go on the field, "I don't know if I—"

"—Reno!" yelled Zayden, "Stop acting like this all the time! Just go!"

"—Z-Zayden?!" uttered Reno.

There was a pause. Zayden calmed himself down, "It's your turn," he tensed, "Show everyone you can fight for yourself."

But Reno didn't move.

"Reno," Javarus pushed his shoulder, "You can defend for yourself," he encouraged, "I saw it with my own eyes, now show everyone else."

There was a moment of silence.

"—Participant Reno!" called out Flare, "Please stand with participant Dedrian so we can continue!"

"—Flare!" shrieked Reno, he finally went towards the battle. But on his way, he looked back at Zayden and recalled his change in expression: *"Stop acting like this all the time! Just go!"* he remembered Zayden's words, *"...Just what was that?"* he was surprised.

Dedrian was inflamed in Fire.

Reno slowly stood beside him.

"—Are we ready?" addressed Flare.

"Y-Yeah!" only Reno spoke.

"The 20-minute timer..." went on Flare, "—Has started!"

The other participants along with everyone else watched from the sideline. The second stage was set to resume outside.

To be Continued

This is the end of Volume One of the series, *Sinner.* Thank you so much for reading! Feel free to contact me if you want to talk about the story, the characters, the future of Sinner, or anything, I'd be excited talk to you about it! Make sure to also check out the Sinner Series website, and let's follow each other on Twitter!

Contact: zafeeralam99@gmail.com

Twitter: @SupaSuperrr

Website: sinnerseries.wordpress.com

Thanks again and I hope you stay connected to the story, continuing with **Volume Two!**

Preview for Volume Two of Sinner

Adalo quickly rushed up the air towards him, "—Last one!" he yelled, "Samaria!" his body spun into a rapid movement. Heavy Winds broke loose and forced Soro into the tornado.

"—This is too much for me!" yelled Reno as him and the other participants were forced off the ground. "—These!" urged Katana, "These are what Sinners are made of!"

Soro's Lightning Bolt broke inside the tornado as the tornado circulated in Wind, Fire, and Lightning. Adalo quickly burst to the top of the tornado, "—We've met our end!" he yelled with his palms facing down.

But then inside the tornado, the Black Markings scarred across Soro's right arm. Adalo looked up, "You're calling for it," he saw, "Aren't you?!" he quickly burst to the side.

A sharp loud Lightning Strike thundered through the ceiling and struck into the tornado. Zayden and Soro screamed in immense pain. The tornado grew bigger as it covered in Fire and Lightning.

"—Lavivo!" Flare was stunned, "W-What's going on?!" she yelled.

"I don't know!" worried Lavivo as she looked up, "Adalo! You must stop your—"

"—I have no control of it anymore!" yelled Adalo.

Suddenly a quick split-second flash appeared in the Lightning Strike, the tornado burst out and broke apart. The platforms crumbled down as the walls of the building broke through.

Zayden and Soro rapidly crashed to the ground. "—Is it over?!" screeched Kara.

After a moment, Soro barely went up on his feet. The Black Markings on his face thickened, "—Uh," he grimaced as he felt a beating. But then Zayden's body lit up on Fire as he stood up.

"—What the hell?!" saw Dedrian and everyone else.

Zayden's body was sent up the air as his eyes were closed and he screamed in pain.

"—What's happening to him?!" worried Reno.

Slowly, a Black Marking began scarring across his body. The same Shadowy sharp Scars that were on Soro.

Soro's eyes widened as he watched him, "Don't tell me…" he muttered.

Zayden dropped to the floor as he held his face with his hand, "I feel this—" he shouted out loud, "This—" he slowly stood up as his breath was heavy.

"Take your hand off your face," ordered Soro.

Zayden slowly took his hand off as a Black Marking was revealed across his face, "I don't know about you," spoke Zayden, "But I feel as good as ever," he grinned.

48492434R00159

Made in the USA
Middletown, DE
20 September 2017